X-MEN®
THE LEGACY QUEST TRILOGY
Book 2

STEVE LYONS was born and lives in Salford, near Manchester, in the north-west of England. He has contributed articles, short stories and comic strips to many British magazines, from *Starburst* to *Batman* to *Doctor Who*. He has also co-written a number of books about TV science-fiction shows, including the official *Red Dwarf Programme Guide*. He is the author of a dozen original Doctor Who novels and two full-cast Doctor Who audio adventures, and the author of *X-Men: The Legacy Quest Book 1* as well as writer of short stories for the Marvel-related anthologies *The Ultimate Super-Villains, Untold Tales of Spider-Man, The Ultimate Hulk,* and *X-Men Legends.*

D1211864

X-MEN®

THE LEGACY QUEST TRILOGY
Book 2

By Steve Lyons

Interior Illustrations by
Nick Choles

MARVEL®

ibooks
new york
www.ibooks.net

DISTRIBUTED BY SIMON & SCHUSTER, INC

bp books inc
New York

Special thanks to David Bogart, Bob Greenberger, Bobbie Chase, and C. B. Cebulski

X-MEN: THE LEGACY QUEST TRILOGY BOOK 2

A BP Books, Inc. Book
An ibooks, inc. Book

PRINTING HISTORY
BP Books, Inc. trade paperback edition / August 2002

The BP Books World Wide Website is
http://www.ibooks.net

ISBN 0-7434-5243-7

PRINTED IN THE UNITED STATES OF AMERICA

10 9 8 7 6 5 4 3 2 1

With thanks to the people behind the
Marvel Chronology Project at
www.chronologyproject.com
for plotting a course through X-continuity—
and to Ivor at Red Hot Comics for having the issues I needed!

Author's Note: This trilogy takes place
shortly after the events recounted in *X-Men* #87.

CHAPTER 1

MUTANTS.

The African-American woman could sense them. They were all around her. She saw their shapes behind her eyelids, could almost taste the foul creatures on the back of her tongue. She knew that, despite appearances, she was not alone on this darkened street. She knew where they lurked. They thought themselves unseen behind their corners and their grime-streaked windows, but she knew they were watching her. She knew that they had surrounded her.

She knew they were closing in.

Pearl Scott's heartbeat quickened. She tried to conceal herself in the shadows of the sidewalk, but she felt their evil eyes upon her like laser beams. They were on the rooftops too, high above her, almost touching the roiling white sky that cast this nightmare place into the perpetual, uncaring gloom of twilight. Like vultures, they were ready to swoop.

"No," she moaned to herself. "No, no, no..."

She had always known that this day would come. Each time she had been forced to venture outdoors, to look for food or to collect the precious serum that prolonged her life, she had been aware of the street gangs and the lone lunatics around her. Their footsteps echoed in her ears as their sadistic intentions echoed inside her mind. She had learned to rely upon her instincts, to let them guide her through the empty streets and alleyways. Deep down, she was aware that those instincts made her a mutant too, but she refused to accept that truth. She didn't—she *couldn't*—have anything in common with the misfits, the freaks, the cold-blooded killers who preyed upon the carcass of this once-proud city.

She dropped the three dented cans with their peeling labels—all the food she had been able to scavenge on this foray—and broke into a run. But Pearl Scott had never been an athletic woman even at the best of times. She was approaching middle age, weakened by starvation rations, and the virus was eating away at her insides.

And there was nowhere to run to anyway.

Once, maybe, not so long ago, she could have found shelter among the crowds in Grand Central Station, only a few blocks away. But there were no crowds now. This place, once her favorite in the world, had become a ghost town, a hollowed-out shell of its former self. There were no trains left to whisk her away from the madness, no way to return to her comfortable, suburban home upstate and her doting husband.

Her husband was dead. And she hadn't seen her beautiful home in almost three months.

Not since the mutants had taken over New York City.

Selene could taste their fear. She feasted on their desperation.

Her body rested against velvet cushions on an ornate throne, the literal seat of her power. Her eyes were closed and her hands formed a spire in front of her nose and mouth. Her long, white fingers protruded from black leather gloves, and their perfectly manicured red nails rested against each other. But her mind was tethered to her body only by a slender thread.

Selene's astral self flew unseen beyond the Fifth Avenue mansion house headquarters of the New York branch of the Hellfire Club. It swooped between the skyscrapers and soared along the streets of her domain. It drank in the hopelessness, the all-pervading despair, exulting in the odd sweet moment of terror and the beautiful release of death that so often followed it.

The body shifted on its comfortable throne in response to the ecstasy felt by the mind. Tight muscles beneath Selene's pale skin drew her red lips back into a thin smile.

But today of all days, she couldn't fully lose herself in pleasure. She couldn't quell the tingles of anticipation that ran through her. Nor could she ignore the deeper, more unsettling feeling of anxiety, much as she tried to deny it. And so her green eyes flicked open, and her senses began to readjust themselves to familiar surroundings.

The Black Queen's throne room had grown in accordance with her stature. The tiny office on this first basement level had never been opulent—nor indeed decadent—enough for her tastes, but it had been close to the nightmare chambers and the catacombs beneath them. In the ground floor ballroom, Selene had been the perfect host to the elite of society, charming and vivacious. Down here, hidden from the sight of all but the chosen, she had always been able to reveal her true self. But the office—if it could still be called such—had grown impossibly beyond the bounds of its external dimensions. Now, slight air currents played with the candle flames as they carried the scent of brimstone up from below, and invisible creatures scratched in the shadows beneath the dusty tapestries and the crumbling cornices.

Slowly, Selene's eyes brought a figure into focus. Her current Black King stood patiently in the entranceway beneath the great stone arch, at the top of which was inscribed the Hellfire Club's upturned trident symbol. Clearly, he hadn't wanted to disturb her trance.

Blackheart had confined himself to his humanoid shape and size, squeezing his corporeal form into a neat black suit. But his charcoal eyes still glowed red in the pits of his stony face, their hue matched by his red shirt and by the folded handkerchief protruding from his breast pocket. His petrified hair, too, detracted from the image of the dapper businessman: it was swept up away from his goblin's ears, but it grew in wild spines down his back.

"Today is the day, my Queen," he said in a voice like grinding rocks.

"I am aware of that," she told him, a little more shortly than she had intended.

"When will they arrive?" Blackheart was unfazed by her rudeness, as content as always to defer to her. The fact that Selene had such a notable demon—the exiled son of Mephisto himself—in her service never ceased to excite her. Nevertheless, she was under no illusion as to the true power of this creature. He remained with her by choice—which was, in itself, a matter of pride to her. They were kindred spirits, both interested in the corruption of innocents and the torture of the human soul. Blackheart was also confined to the underground levels of the Hellfire Club building as a result of a spell cast by a rival: the half-demon, half-human Daimon Hellstrom. It suited him to play the role of Selene's Black King, for now.

She forced herself to calm down, to ignore the anxiety that spoke in its tremulous, taunting voice into the back of her mind. She nodded past Blackheart. "They will come through that door in precisely three hours, thirty-two minutes and seventeen seconds."

"Should I summon the rest of our Inner Circle?"

"No, Blackheart. That will not be necessary."

"They will fight."

"I welcome their attempts to resist me. They have already been defeated. My sole regret this past year has been that they do not yet know it."

"They will learn," rumbled Blackheart.

"Indeed they will." Selene's voice had become lower now: she was talking more for her own benefit than for that of her partner. "And once we have dealt with them, our hold on this once-human city will be undisputed. Nobody will remain to defy my Hellfire Club. We can begin to extend our power base. We can set our sights upon the next prize..."

* * *

The apartment block had already been looted. It was just as well: Pearl Scott had neither the time nor the strength to shoulder her way through locked doors. There were tears in her eyes, and she could hardly see as she ran up a stone staircase that smelled of neglect. Each step felt like a sheer cliff face, and her heart was pounding fit to burst out of her chest.

Her special senses probed ahead of her, telling her that there was a lone squatter in one of the rooms above. A predator, perhaps, lying in wait for the lost and the doomed. Or, like her, a lonely, frightened outcast, cowering from a fate that couldn't be avoided forever.

She willed her feet to fall more softly as she passed the floor on which the mutant had concealed itself, but she didn't dare slow down. She tried to hold her breath, but her lungs wheezed like bellows, taking in short, panicky gasps of air.

To her relief, the mutant squatter didn't stir. She continued her flight upward.

Her mind screamed a warning to her as the hunters from the street arrived in the lobby below. She had prayed that, unlikely as it had seemed, they wouldn't have seen which building she had ducked into. Or that they would have considered it not worth the effort to pursue her. They could have forgotten her altogether, fighting over the dropped cans, comrade turning against comrade as they so often did.

Those forlorn hopes were dashed now, leaving only one: the hope that, if she found cover in one of the apartments, then they might not find her. They might be too impatient for fresh blood to even waste time searching. They might—and God forgive her for thinking it, but—they might even find the squatter downstairs and be satisfied with taking a single life.

She left the stairwell on the fourth floor, resisting the urge to take the first door on the landing because it was too obvious. She took the second, which hung limply from its hinges, its wooden panels scarred by mutant claws.

The apartment had been trashed. The cupboards in the kitchen

6

area hung open, and one had been wrenched from the wall. They were empty, of course. But furniture had also been overturned, and the walls spray-painted with misspelled slogans. The animals who had invaded this home had had more than food on their mind: they had delighted in destruction.

Personal papers had been shredded and scattered across the floor. Pearl only hoped that their owners had escaped, that their corpses weren't lying here somewhere. To her relief, she couldn't detect the familiar stink of decomposing flesh.

The bed in the smaller of the two bedrooms was still upright, its sheets in disarray and hanging down to the floor. She hid beneath it, taking little solace from the darkness. She couldn't hear anything over the sound of her own breathing and the rasping echoes in her burning chest. But she was aware of her pursuers drawing closer.

She wished she had never come here, to the city of the mutants. She wished she could have spared herself this hell. But she had been too weak. Too afraid to die, even though she had had no hope of survival.

She remembered that fateful day, when the mutants had come from the sky.

She had feared just such an attack for months, ever since the barrier had appeared around Manhattan Island and the mutants had come to live on her doorstep. Many of her neighbors—those with somewhere to go—had moved out, joining the busloads of refugees who had been forced to abandon New York City itself. Pearl would have left too, but property prices in her area had plummeted and she had felt trapped. Anyway, she had wanted to stay put for her husband's sake. So that he would know where to find her. If he ever came back.

She hadn't seen Clyde for over two months, even before that day. He had phoned her once, to confirm her suspicions that mutants had been responsible for his sudden disappearance. He hadn't said much: just that he was working in a secret location on a cure for a mutant disease known as the Legacy Virus. He had told her that he would be home soon. He had been wrong. Slowly, Pearl had come to accept that he was almost certainly dead.

She had spent an eternity cooped up in her home, watching television coverage of the ongoing attempts to penetrate the barrier and praying that perhaps, somehow, they might find her husband behind it. She had had her hopes raised by reports of new technology, which had proved ineffective. The barrier allowed mutants to come and go as they pleased, but nobody and nothing else was allowed through.

Pearl had found hope again on the day that the world's most respected super heroes, the Avengers, sent an all-mutant team through the barrier under the command of the Scarlet Witch. It had been a reminder of a fact that she had almost forgotten: that not all mutants were bad; that some were even prepared to fight for the very people who despised them.

The heroes had failed to return, and Pearl had soon stopped hoping.

But humanity is a resilient species, and New Yorkers more than most. It seemed incredible, but things had begun to return to normal, the barrier becoming almost a fact of life. Sure, the streets of Pearl Scott's upstate community were a little emptier than before— but while nobody could forget what was happening eighty miles to their south, there were days when it all seemed a very long way away. In time, she had been able to put her fears, and her grief for her husband, aside. She had emerged into the early days of Summer and settled back into her old routines, although she had jumped whenever a car backfired and experienced a twinge of sadness each time she had had to purchase her lonely meals for one.

She had sensed the flying mutants before they had come into her sight. If only she had known then to trust her intuition, if she had turned and fled, then they might not have caught her. Instead she had tried to deny what, in her heart, she had known. She had told herself that she was being paranoid, that they couldn't be coming for her. Hadn't she suffered enough?

The mutants had descended upon the shopping center, and

Pearl Scott had screamed and cried and tried to run like everybody else. To this day, she could not recall the monsters' faces, just their feathers and their claws and the way they had circled and picked out their targets and dived, and the death rattles of her neighbors.

It had been like a game to them: picking off the few so they could savor the reactions of the many. Raking claws across their victims' guts or lifting their bodies aloft to let them fall and be dashed against the flagstones.

They had targeted her, of course. At the time, it had seemed only natural—inevitable in a sickly sort of a way—like she was somehow destined to be plagued by their kind until she died. With the benefit of hindsight, she knew that one of their number must have had senses like her own. It must have known her for what she was, before she even knew it herself.

She remembered the sensation of the world dropping away beneath her feet as talons dug into her shoulders. She hadn't been able to hear much over the rush of the air, the louder rushing of blood to her ears and the sound of her own frantic sobbing, but she had been dimly aware of the mutants discussing her in hard, cackling voices. They had said that she was like them, but her brain had railed against the truth of that statement and, for a long time thereafter, she had believed that she must have imagined the words in her terror.

They had played with her, tossing her between them for what seemed like an eternity. Her head and her stomach had performed dizzy somersaults, and she had closed her eyes and whimpered and awaited the mercy of death. It had come—or so she had thought then—with a slash to her side, delivered as if by steel, spreading hot and cold pain across her body and stealing the light from behind her eyelids.

She had woken, to her immense surprise, in a hospital bed: the only person, she was later told, to have been picked out that day and lived. She had known then, with a creeping dread, that the mutants had chosen her deliberately, and that they had spared her for a reason.

Three months later, she found out what that reason was.

She had found it harder to recover, this time. She had shut herself inside again, relying on the favors of sympathetic friends and on Internet shopping to keep herself fed, becoming a recluse. Her husband had left her provided for, and there had come a time when she had found it hard to imagine venturing beyond her front door again. More people had moved away, and Pearl had entertained thoughts of doing the same, but never for long. It wasn't the money any more: it was the certain knowledge that she was marked. The doctors had assured her that her wounds had recovered nicely, but she had itched inside. She had felt the mutant poison coursing through her veins and known that, wherever she went, they would find her.

She had known that they would return for her one day.

She had become afraid of the sky, afraid to even look out of her windows because every distant speck, each bird that wheeled above the rooftops, was transformed by her mind into a screeching predator. So, she had stopped looking. She had closed her drapes and lived in half-light. But sometimes she had woken in the night, sweat beading her forehead, for no better reason than that she had felt one of them pass overhead.

These days, she wished she had appreciated the sky more when she had had it. She didn't know how long she had lived beneath the ever-shifting white energies of the barrier—the absence of sunlight meant that time had little meaning in the city—but she had come to long for even a glimpse of the stars.

Now, lying on her back beneath somebody else's bed as the hunters continued their inexorable approach, Pearl Scott wondered if she would ever again see anything beyond the wooden slats and the threadbare mattress a few inches above her.

She remembered the kindly old doctor with his haunted face, falling over his words as he had broken the news to her. The stomach cramps, the flu-like symptoms and the weakness inside her had finally prompted her to reach for the telephone, to break her self-imposed isolation. She had learned only what she had already suspected.

The doctor had been surprised at how calmly she had taken his diagnosis. He had advised her to seek counseling but she had refused, accepting the inevitable with numb resignation.

Pearl Scott had contracted the Legacy Virus. But she had known exactly what to do about it.

She had learned all she needed to know from the TV. The disease was spreading, slowly but surely—and it didn't only affect mutants now, as it had originally, but humans too. It was fatal. And Pearl Scott knew that, despite the best efforts of the world's foremost geneticists, her husband included, nobody really understood it, let alone could come close to curing it.

And yet a cure did exist, in the hands of one person.

One of the major TV networks had smuggled a camera through the barrier once, hidden in the clothing of a mutant volunteer. Pearl had been given a preview of the world that, somehow she had known even then, would eventually become her own. She had watched in awe and horror as the freaks in their ragged clothing had supplicated themselves to their ruler—and she had seen the gleam in the Black Queen's green eyes as her demons had handed out the elixir that they needed to stave off their symptoms. Not enough to cure them, of course: just enough to prolong their miserable lives for a little longer. Selene kept her subjects on a short leash. In a few days' time, they would need her again.

Still, mutants flocked to Manhattan Island from all over the world. Many refugees arrived from the island nation of Genosha, despite the best efforts of its ruler to keep them from leaving: Genosha was in the throes of the world's worst Legacy epidemic, and Selene offered the only hope of survival to its population of genetically engineered mutates.

An hour after the doctor had left, Pearl had walked out of her beautiful home for the final time. She had carried a plastic bag full of canned goods, and just enough money to reach the George

Washington Bridge, and she had walked to the train station with her shoulders straight, her head up and her eyes fixed directly ahead. She hadn't looked at the sky.

It was easy to get onto Manhattan Island. Easy, that was, for the right sort of person. Far harder to get off it again.

Pearl Scott felt as if Fate had been leading her here for a long time, like she had never had a say in the matter. She was always going to end up dying in this dingy room.

They came for her now, and she didn't know if they had found her with their own mutant senses or because her footsteps, her whimpers, perhaps her heartbeat, had been too loud. One of them tore away her shelter, his abnormal muscles rippling as he flung the bed aside with ease. Two more took Pearl by the arms and hauled her to her feet. She saw their feathers and their talons, heard their cruel, spiteful laughter, and wondered if they were the very creatures that had attacked her in the shopping center. Not that it mattered.

Her tears had dried. She was surprised to find that she wasn't even frightened any more. She accepted her death, as she had accepted so much in her life, with quiet resignation. She let the mutants play with her, tossing her between them, digging claws and teeth into her skin, and she knew that this had been their plan all along. This was why they had taken the risk of flying through the barrier, of attacking her community in the first place. This was why they had infected her: to bring her here, to their world, so that they could enjoy this moment.

They didn't even care that she had nothing to give them, because she had given them what they wanted already.

In the Black Queen's city, the mutants didn't only hunt for food and shelter.

They also hunted for sport.

An electric hush seemed to settle upon the world as the appointed time approached.

Selene sat upon her throne and smiled quietly to herself, her icy confidence fed by the charged atmosphere. Her Black King stood at her right hand, and attendant demons lined up behind the royal couple in their incongruous blue and red Hellfire Club uniforms. It had been a long time since they had worn formal dress, but the Black Queen had commanded it of them today. Many of the costumes ill-fitted the grotesque shapes of their wearers, and several were bloodied and torn and only hung together by threads. But on such a momentous occasion, decorum had to be observed.

She didn't need a timepiece to tell her when the moment was near. She sensed the ripples in the magical field, the delicious buildup of energy and a thrill that was almost sexual. She rose from her golden seat, her black cloak tickling the floor. She took one step forward and waited, the smile still poised upon her red lips.

Framed by the grand archway was the wood-paneled door, small and unassuming: the one part of the room that had not been enlarged and improved upon in the past year.

A demon began to snicker, breaking off as it realized how obtrusive the harsh, whispering sound of its laughter was in the silence. Selene would have it flogged later. Or rather, she would have *a* demon flogged: she had no idea which one was which.

For now, she was counting down the final seconds in her mind. Three...two...one...

The door was flung open.

A gust of stale wind blew through her long, silken hair, and a burst of black light turned the world momentarily inside-out. And suddenly, where there had been nobody before, there appeared eight figures in colorful costumes. They hurtled across the threshold of the throne room as if ready for combat, although the state of their clothing, the bruises upon their exposed skin and the tiredness that they couldn't conceal in their postures betrayed the fact that they had fought long and hard already.

They took in their new surroundings and faltered.

Selene's smile broadened. They had not expected to find themselves here. They had not expected to find their foe so prepared for them, backed up by the very demons that they had thought defeated. They had already been battle-weary; now they were confused and disoriented as well. The sight of Blackheart must have been especially dispiriting for them.

One of the new arrivals—a short, feral creature clad in yellow and blue—made to press the attack anyway. The man whom Selene knew to be the leader of the group held him back with a gesture, his expression advising caution even as his eyes flashed fire behind the red crystal lens of his golden visor.

They knew that something had gone wrong, but they didn't know what yet.

Selene knew them, of course. They were old acquaintances. Cyclops, Wolverine, Phoenix, Storm, Nightcrawler, Iceman and Rogue: collectively, one permutation of the outlaw team known as the X-Men. They were mutants. Unlike her, they dreamt of a world in which humans and mutants could live together in peace, and they were prepared to fight unselfishly for that dream. To this end, they had clashed with Selene—and set back her plans—on more than one occasion.

But standing with the self-professed heroes was a more interesting individual by far: a member of the Hellfire Club himself, no less. Perhaps its most infamous member.

She almost didn't recognize the middle-aged man at first. She was used to seeing him in the deceptive guise of a Victorian gentleman: the traditional "uniform" of the club's Inner Circle, a symbol of allegiance to times past. Indeed, he still wore his black hair in an old-fashioned style, pulled back into a ponytail and secured by an elaborate red bow, his sideburns allowed to grow thick. Right now, however, he was dressed for combat: his dark green, padded, one-piece boiler suit remained in pristine condition despite all he must have been through to get here.

He had already recovered from his surprise. He was alert, prepared for whatever might come next. His shrewd eyes probed hers, and Selene could almost see his calculating mind working on a way to turn this situation to his advantage. She half expected him to offer her an alliance. She would have relished the opportunity to laugh in his face.

The gentleman's name was Sebastian Shaw—and once, long ago, he had supported Selene's bid for Hellfire Club membership. He had been her first Black King.

But like the others, he had been gone for a long time—and a lot of things had changed.

"Good afternoon," said the Black Queen, unable to prevent her smile from widening. "As you can see, I have been expecting you."

CHAPTER 2

One year earlier:

ELENE'S DREAMS of power were still just that: dreams. But she never doubted that, one day, those dreams would be realized. She had possessed great power in the past—many centuries ago—and she would do so again. Its acquisition was a game to her, and she played it well, prepared to sacrifice short-term advantage for the sake of ultimate gain.

The game had become more difficult as humanity, despite its shortcomings, had advanced and evolved. It often seemed to her that there were too many players now, too many forces lined up to oppose her, to seek power for themselves. Even so, she had maneuvered herself into a good, strong position. She had control over the New York branch of the Hellfire Club, which meant that she also controlled its affluent members.

She recalled how the Hellfire Club had been formed in London in the eighteenth century, just another exclusive gentlemen's organization. She had paid it little heed at the time, but it had grown in both size and influence until it had become worthy of her attention. Nowadays, it had branches all over the world. It catered to society's rich elite, and it was a powerful mechanism by which they maintained their financial and political positions.

If the Hellfire Club was comprised of the elite, however, then the members of each branch's Inner Circle—the Lords Cardinal, who awarded themselves ranks based on the names of chess pieces and operated from the shadows—were the elite of the elite. Selene had wheedled herself into the Inner Circles of first New York and then Hong Kong, albeit both times playing a subordinate role to Sebastian Shaw as the Black King. Recently, however, she had seen an opportunity to take the New York branch—considered by most to be the brightest jewel in the Hellfire Club's crown—for herself. Now and forever, she was the Black Queen.

And she had pawns that weren't even aware of the power she had over them.

The Black Queen sat upon her throne in a small room beneath the Hellfire Club's Fifth Avenue headquarters. She had made a start on decorating what had once been a dull office to her tastes— an exquisite mixture of the grand and the sinister, with carved demon faces leering out from behind velvet drapes and black candle wax melting onto gold holders—but it was not yet regal enough for her. She would rectify that soon. For now, however, her attention was taken by events occurring eight thousand miles away.

Eight days ago, Selene had had an encounter with the X-Man known as the Beast. He had been on a personal journey, and she had sensed that his eventual findings were likely to be of interest to her. She had wanted to see his journey through to its conclusion.

Selene's crystal ball was glowing white, and she summoned it to her with a thought. It rose from its marble dais and hovered in front of her. The mists beneath its surface were clearing, and a face came into focus. It was a young face, topped by mousy brown hair, and it wore an expression of concern.

Selene leaned forward expectantly, her chin resting on her bony fist, and watched.

* * *

"Hank! Hank!"

Somebody was shaking him. He didn't want to wake, but he had no choice. He rose to the surface of sleep, feeling as if he were swimming up through a tar pit.

Hovering above him was the youthful face of one of his oldest friends. His name was Bobby Drake—but, thanks to the incredible powers with which he had been invested by an accident of his birth, he also went by the *nom de guerre* of Iceman.

"Come on pal, time to get up. It's time for your treatment." Bobby tried to smile, but the gesture seemed forced. His eyes betrayed the fact that something was worrying him.

Hank wondered what it could be. He wondered why he had woken in an unfamiliar bed in an unfamiliar room with dull metal walls, and he wondered why he felt so weak and sick, why his body was running hot and cold and why his blue fur was matted with sweat. He tried to stand, but the movement made him feel dizzy. Bobby took him by his arm and gently helped him into a sitting position on the edge of the bed.

Hank sat with his fragile head in his hands, staring down at his clawed feet on the gray floor as the final veil of his deep sleep lifted and his recent memories settled back into place.

His name was Doctor Henry McCoy, but to the world at large he was the Beast. And like his friend Bobby, he was hated and feared by that world. Like Bobby, he had been born with a certain anomaly in his genes; an anomaly which made him a mutant, part of the next evolution of humanity. Where Bobby had the power to create and shape ice, Hank had been gifted with supernormal strength and athletic prowess.

He had also sprouted blue fur, claws, pointed ears and fangs.

He recognized his surroundings now, and an old weight settled back upon his shoulders. He was a long way from his New York home. He had gone to sleep—passed out, more like—in a tiny dormitory in a research facility located beneath an island in the Pacific Ocean.

The island was artificial, built thousands of years ago by an alien race of master geneticists known as the Kree—and they had left some of their secrets behind. Hank had come to their abandoned base in search of those secrets. He had seen a chance to realize his most fervent desire: to find a cure for the Legacy Virus, the disease that was ravaging the world's mutant population. A week ago, he had achieved that goal at long last—or so he had believed.

Along with a group of fellow scientists, he had developed a serum. In order to test it, however, he had needed to find a newly-infected mutant. Events had conspired to make the search urgent—and in an act of desperation, Hank had volunteered himself as a test subject. He had infected himself with Legacy, and then literally taken his own medicine.

But the injection of the serum was only the first stage in a long, frustrating process—and now Hank was a lot less confident that his untested cure would work at all.

His nausea had receded—at least as much as it ever did, now that he was dying. He put an arm around Bobby's shoulders and allowed himself to be lifted to his feet. He had been given the nearest room to the laboratory—a storeroom, which had been cleared out for his use and furnished with a bed and a single chair from the residential level below—but the connecting corridor still felt like it was a mile long. He tackled the arduous trek the only way he could: with one faltering step at a time, leaning heavily on Bobby for support.

"Easy now. That's right, just take it steady. There's no hurry. Doctor MacTaggert can wait. She's only got one patient." Bobby kept up his pointless commentary, talking for the sake of talking even when he didn't know what to say. No doubt he thought he was keeping Hank's spirits up. Grateful as he was for the intention, Hank would rather have been left in silence. His eyelids were heavy, and he couldn't believe that another six hours had passed already. He had slept through most of it, which was probably a blessing.

"It'll be better news today," said Bobby, "you'll see. The treatments have got to start working soon. It stands to reason, doesn't it? You checked all the figures a hundred times, and you're the smartest guy I know. You'll be up and about before you know it."

Try as he might, Hank couldn't be so optimistic. Whenever he tried to look ahead, all he could see was a big, black cloud hanging over his future.

"This time next week, we'll be back home, you'll see. In fact... say, Hank, did you ever wonder what happened to Vera and Zelda? Maybe we could look them up when we get out of here, take them out on a double date... to celebrate, you know? It'll be like old times."

Doctor Moira MacTaggert was waiting for them in the laboratory as usual. There were four other scientists—Hank himself excluded –working in this facility at present. However, he had seen little of Scott, Alahan, Travers or even Rory Campbell in recent days. Moira was an old friend and colleague, and she had taken it upon herself to supervise every stage of his treatment herself. Despite this, she had never been one to let overt displays of emotions get in the way of her work, and her manner was businesslike to the point of brusqueness. The sleeves of her white lab coat were rolled up to the elbows, and Hank couldn't help but notice the dark rings around her eyes. He wondered when she had last slept.

"And how is the patient today?" asked Moira in her rich Scottish accent as she helped Bobby to lay Hank down on his back on a hard metal bench. The Kree had designed this base with efficiency rather than comfort in mind.

He described his symptoms in clinical detail in a painful, rasping voice as Moira drew blood from his arm into a syringe. He had had so many needles inside him recently that he was surprised she could even find a spot on his skin that hadn't already been punctured.

Set into the walls of the laboratory were an assortment of keyboards, screens and dials: user interfaces for the Kree computer which ran this base, and from the memory banks of which Hank and his fellow scientists had sifted the information that had allowed them to come this far. Moira placed a vial of his blood into a small compartment in one wall, and allowed the computer to analyze its composition. It was a familiar process by now.

A screen above Hank's head lit up, casting green light across his face. He was too tired and weak to stand up and inspect the data for himself, but Moira's dour expression told him all he needed to know. "I'm sorry, Hank," she said softly.

"Has there been no improvement at all?" he asked hopefully.

"The progress of the virus is still slowing."

"Well, there you are!" chimed in Bobby, trying to sound cheerful.

"It isn't good enough, Bobby," sighed Hank. "My immune system is manning the metaphorical barricades, but it is still being forced back. We need it to repel the invader."

On another day—a better day—Hank's own loquacious nature would have urged him to explain the process to his young friend again. He would have reminded Bobby that the serum with which he had injected himself was designed to react with his own mutant gene to create a new, temporary type of cell within his system: a super-cell as he had dubbed it, which would go to war with the Legacy Virus until each had cancelled the other out. Unfortunately, a course of radiation treatment was also needed to encourage the reaction to run its course.

"Are you sure you want to try again?" asked Moira. She had asked him the same question every six hours for the past three days. By now, Hank's affirmative response was almost automatic, as was their next exchange: "Are you ready for this, then?"

"As prepared as I will ever be."

Moira nodded curtly, flashed Hank a tight smile of encouragement and operated a series of controls on the nearest vertical surface of the Kree computer. A curved piece of metal slid smoothly out from the underside of Hank's bench and encircled him, until he was completely enclosed in the darkness of a flat-ended tube. He breathed in deeply in nervous anticipation, but his chest wheezed with the effort of even that small task.

Intellectually, he knew he shouldn't have been able to feel the radiation that bombarded him. Still, he couldn't help but imagine the invisible rays ripping through his already-weakened cells. He could almost feel his dizziness and nausea—the cruel side-effects of the treatment—worsening, and his left eye was moistened by a tear as a rattling groan of pain and dismay escaped his throat.

Now, when it was too late, he began to think about what Moira had asked him. Did he really want to keep doing this? The treatments should have borne fruit by now. By continuing with them, he was clinging to a hope that became slimmer each day. At what point, he asked himself, would he have to accept failure? More than likely, he considered, the decision would be taken for him. He could tell that Moira was worried about him: she would refuse to treat him soon, for fear that his body would be unable to stand further punishment.

But he couldn't face the thought of giving up yet. He couldn't face going back to the start again, knowing that this time he would be racing against the clock; that the virus he was seeking to eradicate was coursing through his system, killing him in turn.

He thought about Moira, and immediately felt selfish. The prospect that he was dreading so much was her reality. She had contracted the Legacy Virus months ago: the first non-mutant to catch the so-called "mutant disease" but by no means the last. The symptoms had progressed slowly in her case, but the end result would be the same. She had to be under as much strain as he was right now, but she got on with her work—and with her life—with a characteristic determination, a refusal to give in to despair and death.

It was for Doctor Moira MacTaggert—and for all the people like her, now and in the years to come—that Hank knew he had to do this. Once the super-cell had been created inside his own body, it could be isolated and injected directly into other sufferers. It would save hundreds, thousands, perhaps millions of lives. That was why he had to hold on to those last threads of hope for as long as they lasted, no matter what the cost to his own health.

His eyelids had drooped, and he had almost drifted back to

sleep. He didn't notice that the curved hood of the radiation machine had slid back until he felt the recycled air of the lab pricking at the perspiration on his forehead, and heard Moira's voice. "All done!" she said with forced levity. "Now, you get back to your rest—and get better this time, do you hear?"

"I shall certainly endeavor to do so, Doctor," said Hank with a weak grin.

"Och, Henry, you'll have to do a lot better than that, I'm afraid. Our Lord and Master was in here earlier, wanting an update. I think the poor dear's getting a wee bit impatient."

"He isn't 'our Lord and Master'," snapped Hank, sounding more irritable than he had intended. Without meaning to, his fellow scientist had hit a raw nerve.

In order to gain access to this island base and its facilities, the X-Men had had to make a deal with one of their most persistent and dangerous foes. Moira herself had argued strongly against it—but when Hank had infected himself, he had forced the issue in his favor. He had believed that the possibility of finding a cure for the Legacy Virus overrode all other concerns, but the wisdom of his decision still remained to be proven.

When Doctor Henry McCoy had stuck that syringe into his arm, he had taken a gamble with more than just his own life. He had allied his team to an influential and utterly corrupt organization known as the Hellfire Club.

And to its Black King: a powerful and ruthless mutant by the name of Sebastian Shaw.

Sebastian Shaw stood on the surface of the island, in the forest clearing that housed the entranceway to the underground Kree base. An electrical storm was raging—but he maintained an easy, untroubled pose, feet apart and hands clasped behind his back, not seeming to mind the rain that spattered around him and drenched his Victorian frock coat and breeches. His head was tilted back, his dark eyes fixed on the lightning patterns in the sky and the colors they painted on the clouds.

And on the woman who soared above the treetops.

She seemed to be one with the winds themselves, so graceful and yet so assured were her movements. Her black cloak billowed out behind her, and she stretched out her arms as she luxuriated in the raw power of Nature. From down here, Shaw couldn't tell if she was conducting the storm or simply riding it. The truth probably lay somewhere between the two extremes: it was impossible for him to say where the storm ended and the woman began.

She descended from the clouds to land a few feet in front of him. Her cloak settled slowly around her lithe body as she flicked water from her long, white hair. Above, she had seemed serene; now, white eyes stared mistrustfully out of her dark-skinned face, and Shaw could see a trace of the lightning still trapped within those eyes.

"Were you waiting to speak with me?" she asked.

"I was simply enjoying the performance, Miss Munroe."

"I was not putting on a performance, Shaw," said Ororo Munroe: the X-Man known, thanks to her command of the elements, as Storm.

Shaw inclined his head graciously. "I am aware of that," he said. "You feel claustrophobic inside our underground installation. Perhaps I can ease that discomfort."

Ororo looked suspicious, and Shaw knew what was going through her mind. The pair had been cast as bitter enemies in the past: the altruistic X-Men had often obstructed the Hellfire Club's more...extreme attempts to expand its power base. Storm didn't like having to sleep only a few rooms away from Shaw, and she avoided him when she could.

In return, he had offered her nothing but undaunted politeness. And he was beginning to feel that, slowly, her attitude towards him had thawed from cold to merely cool.

"We are a long way from civilization," he said. "Most of your teammates have returned to America, and I...I have only one assistant to distract me from the gray walls beneath us."

"This base is still staffed by more Hellfire Club mercenaries than I feel comfortable with," said Ororo. "If you are feeling lonely, then perhaps you should talk to them."

Shaw waved a dismissive hand. "I do not hire my pawns for their conversational skills."

"I have nothing to say to you, Shaw, that you would enjoy hearing."

"Come now, Miss Munroe, the X-Men have won this battle. This island is no longer mine—but I am not bitter. Is it too much to ask that you be equally gracious in your victory? One meal, that's all I beg of you. The pleasure of your company for a few short hours."

"You have made this request three times before," said Ororo.

"And I pray that, this time, your answer may be different." Shaw spread his arms wide, his palms turned upward in a gesture of appeal. "We don't have to be on opposite sides."

"That, I believe, is where you are mistaken."

"Will you not concede that, in the matter of the Legacy Virus at least, we have a common goal? We both wish to see a cure, do we not?"

"A common goal, yes—but I find your methods of achieving that goal deplorable." The X-Man's eyes flashed angrily. "You infected scientists with the virus to force them into working for you. You kidnapped our friend, Doctor MacTaggert—and somehow you coerced our teammate, Henry McCoy, into joining you as well."

Shaw shook his head firmly. "In McCoy's case, no coercion was needed. He saw the benefits that a cure would bring to the world— as did you. Why else would you be here? Why didn't you shut down our project and destroy this island? You had the opportunity."

"The damage had already been done," contested Ororo. "There was no further harm—and as you said, a great deal to be gained— in seeing your work here through to a conclusion."

"Nevertheless, I was grateful that it was you who came to the negotiating table rather than your Mr. Summers." Scott Summers, alias Cyclops, was the X-Men's field leader: however, a short-term injury had forced him to leave his deputy to thrash out the details of an uneasy partnership. "I've always thought he was a little too rigid. I doubt he would have been as quick as you were to deal with those he considers to be his enemies."

"Our alliance is a temporary one," Ororo reminded him, "forged by necessity. It will last only until Moira, Henry and the others have completed their work."

Shaw sighed. "And you, like your friend Mr. Drake, are only here to ensure that I uphold my side of the bargain: that, if and when a cure does become available, the Hellfire Club will not have sole control over its use."

"Precisely."

"So we have been forced together, you and I. Does that mean we cannot at least be civil to each other; cannot help each other to pass the time?" Shaw raised an eyebrow and his lips curled into a wicked smile. "You only remain on this island to watch me, Ororo. As long as you continue to avoid my company, you cannot claim to be doing your job very well."

She regarded him with a hostile expression for a long moment as the rain sliced down between them. Then she said: "Stand aside, Shaw. I would like to dry out inside."

He stepped out of her way, indicating the hatchway behind him with an extravagant gesture. Storm swept past him without another glance in his direction, disappearing through the aperture and down the steps beyond. As soon as she was out of the Black King's sight, the polite smile froze into a sneer on his face and his dark eyes hardened.

Sebastian Shaw was a realist. He knew that there was still a long way to go if he was ever to make Ororo Munroe his ally. But she hadn't turned down his offer this time.

The image in Selene's crystal ball faded as the Beast succumbed to unconsciousness again. She lowered it back onto its dais by force of mind alone and sat back against her velvet cushions, her pale brow furrowed in thought.

There was no love lost between her and Shaw. She had allied herself with him in the past, but only when it had proved expedient to do so. However, she knew that somebody like him might prove useful again in the future. She also knew that he would make a powerful enemy. Therefore, she had stopped short of opening outright hostilities against him.

Now, however, she had set her sights upon a prize that made the risk worth taking.

Blackheart had appeared at her side—attracted perhaps, as he often seemed to be, by her thoughts of dark ambition. She had neither heard nor sensed his approach: the demon's earthly form appeared to be sculpted from stone, but he could come and go like a shadow.

"Shaw almost has it," said Selene. "A cure to the Legacy Virus." Her Black King regarded her in confident silence, his eyes ablaze in their sockets. "I wonder what he intends to do with it..." she mused. "Oh, I've no doubt that it will figure in one of his many master plans. He will find a way of using it to further his own ambitions..."

"But you could utilize the cure more...effectively."

"Precisely!" Selene's lips twisted into a grin at the compliment. "Shaw has already allowed the X-Men to tie his hands. He was foolish to involve them in this game."

"Even had he not," rumbled Blackheart, "he does not possess your vision, my Queen."

"No," purred Selene. "Nor does he have the courage to change this world as I would."

"This prize would be better suited to your care, I think."

"I cannot help but agree."

"There are many who would give much for the smallest drop of such a serum. Their desperation, their fear of death, makes for an exquisite concoction."

"As you say, Blackheart, the possibilities for corruption are quite delicious."

"I only regret that I cannot accompany you to the island," said Blackheart. Selene listened for the merest hint of irritation in his voice, but heard none. He must have found the spell that bound him to this building irksome to say the least, but he rarely showed any sign of frustration at his predicament. She supposed that, for a demon of his power and longevity, it was easy to be patient. The binding of his corporeal form to one place for a few fleeting years was a minor inconvenience—especially if this was where he wished to be.

"Oh, I don't think either of us needs dirty our hands," she said. "A few lesser demons should be adequate for this task."

"Are you certain of that? You consider this Shaw a resourceful foe."

"Shaw's greatest talent is for making prudent alliances," said Selene. "His greatest failing is that he can rarely keep them. Not for the first time, his Inner Circle is crumbling around him."

"And the X-Men?"

"Little more than children," said Selene with contempt, "and their deal with Shaw means that only three of them stand in the way of our goal. Of those three, only the weather witch, Storm, poses any threat to us. The Beast is in no condition to fight anybody, and Iceman has never had the courage or the intellect to realize his true potential."

Blackheart nodded. "Then I shall summon our troops, my lady."

CHAPTER 3

One year later:

WHAT HAVE you done to us, Selene?" snapped Cyclops. The question sounded inadequate in his ears, so he asked another, more pertinent one. "And where's our teammate?"

Only seconds earlier, victory had been in sight. The X-Men, with an unlikely ally in the person of Sebastian Shaw, had broken into the New York mansion house headquarters of the Hellfire Club in search of a kidnapped friend. After several trials—some of which Cyclops didn't even like to think about—they had reached the Black Queen's basement throne room. But even as he had thrown open the final door between his team and their goal, the world had turned black around him.

For an instant between two footsteps—an instant that had seemed at the time like an eternity but which now felt like the blink of an eyelid in his memory—he had been moving in slow-motion, his bewildered teammates picked out in negative around him.

And then the moment had ended, and Cyclops had lurched back into the real world—to find that everything had changed.

"Your friend?" repeated Selene, furrowing her brow in mock

confusion but unable to suppress a telltale smile. "Ah, yes, you came here in search of Doctor Henry McCoy, the Beast. How easy to forget after all this time." Now she wore an equally insincere expression of sympathy. "I am sorry to inform you that the Beast is dead."

"If that's true," growled Wolverine, coiled like the spring of a loaded firearm and inching forward, "you're gonna wish you could join him." His eyes were still wild with the adrenaline high of battle: a high that threatened to make him lose control. His bearing was reminiscent of that of the creature after which he was named— and with his yellow and blue costume torn to expose his hirsute chest, he seemed somehow more animalistic than ever.

Cyclops shot him a warning look. He wanted to delay combat for as long as he could. He was well aware of the dozens of demons lined up behind Selene's throne; most of all, he was aware of Blackheart, who had already put the X-Men through so much. He was beginning to realize what must have happened, and it left his team at a big disadvantage. They needed, at least, to learn more about this new, unexpected situation before they acted.

Selene flicked back her long, black hair and chuckled to herself. "Oh, do please excuse my amusement," she said, "it has been a long time since anybody has dared speak to me in such a manner. I have to say, I find it quite refreshing."

Another of the X-Men stepped forward. Her red hair was disheveled, and one sleeve of her green and gold costume with its distinctive firebird motif on the chest had been shredded. A purple bruise stood out on her exposed forearm. Still, to Cyclops, the woman presented nothing less than an image of perfect beauty. Her name was Jean Grey Summers, but she was also known as Phoenix. She was his wife, and the love of his life.

"You're obviously itching to tell us something, Selene," said Phoenix. "Why don't you just get on with it?"

"If you insist." Selene's tongue flicked out of her mouth to moisten her red lips. She was relishing the moment, enjoying the expressions on the faces of her audience. "You believe that only a few minutes have passed since you faced Blackheart and my demons on the lower levels of this building and in the catacombs beneath them. You are wrong. My throne room, you see, was not undefended. I had the foresight to mark its door with a series of powerful magical glyphs—invisible to your eyes, of course. When you raced in here, so eager to save your friend and dispense justice to she who had taken him, you activated my spell. You were transported almost precisely one year into the future."

"No…" whispered Cyclops.

"Oh, don't worry," Selene smirked. "You will have plenty of opportunity to confirm that what I am telling you is the truth. For now, all you need to know is that the balance of power on this world has shifted somewhat in your absence."

"What happened to the Beast?" blurted out Iceman from somewhere behind Cyclops.

Selene responded with an indifferent shrug. "What does it matter? You mortals live such short lives anyway, they are hardly worth mourning. The Beast has been dead for almost as long as you have been gone. The important thing is what he left behind. He bequeathed me a useful inheritance: the cure for a disease that has ravaged our kind."

Cyclops knew what she was talking about without having to ask. What he didn't know was how he ought to feel about it. He was numbed by the news of the Beast's passing: it had all happened so suddenly, he couldn't take it in yet. But the revelation that Hank had achieved his fondest ambition, by finding a cure for the deadly Legacy Virus before his death, was a pinprick of hope in a descending veil of gloom. At the same time, the knowledge that that cure was in the hands of somebody as evil as Selene chilled him to the bone.

He felt a familiar anxiety in the pit of his stomach: the sickly realization that he had lost control of events.

For as long as he could remember, Scott Summers had known the importance of control. The red blasts of energy which emanated from his eyes could only be held in check by his own eyelids, or by a shield of ruby quartz such as that which made up the lens of his visor. His own mutant power was a potential threat to everybody around him, and he could never allow himself to forget that for a second.

Control had become even more vital to him when Professor Charles Xavier had recruited him for his original X-Men team, and appointed him its field leader. As Cyclops, Scott had to remain forever alert, plan for every contingency. There was always somebody ready to take out a grudge against the embattled mutants: a xenophobic human, a mutant whose ideals clashed with Xavier's or perhaps just a megalomaniac bent on proving something to the world. An attack could come at any moment, and from any quarter.

For Cyclops, then, there was nothing worse than this: not knowing where—or rather when—he was, not knowing what forces were stacked up against him. If Selene was telling the truth, if he really had been gone for a year, then he dreaded to think what might have happened in his absence. Given the Black Queen's confident demeanor, he could only guess that the Beast's death was just the first in a series of close-to-home tragedies about which he was already too late to do a thing.

"I assume you didn't use the cure for humanitarian purposes," said Phoenix archly.

"On the contrary, Ms. Grey," smirked Selene, "there isn't a person on Manhattan Island who doesn't owe his or her life to me. I supply the medicine that keeps New York City alive."

"The entire population is infected with Legacy?" gasped Storm.

"But of course," said Selene as if it were obvious. With a playful glint in her eye, she added: "All eight hundred of them. Give or take a few, of course. It has become so difficult to keep track of all the new arrivals...and departures."

Cyclops swallowed, fighting down a cry of disbelief.

"You see, my friends, *homo sapiens* were never going to accept *homo superior.* Mutants could never have integrated into a human world: it is, sadly, only too natural for any species to rail against the one that is destined to replace it. So, I created a haven for our kind—a haven under my rule. I erected a mystical barrier around Manhattan Island, through which only mutants may pass."

"I don't believe you," said Phoenix defiantly. "What about the humans who were already here? The Avengers...the Fantastic Four...they wouldn't have let you do that!"

"I have lived too long a life to be a fool, Ms. Grey. I waited until New York's colorful champions were out of town before I made my move. No matter how great their powers, without the mutant x-factor in their genes, they cannot penetrate my shield." Phoenix opened her mouth to protest again, but Selene waved a preemptory hand. "Oh, yes, some still opposed me. New York, it transpires, housed an impressive number of small-time vigilantes: Spider-Man, Daredevil and all the rest. And then there were the mutants, of course, whom my barrier did not repel: altruists such as X-Force and the remaining X-Men; those who came here alone to challenge me for their own purposes; the Avengers even put together an all-mutant team. I might have been defeated had all those forces deigned to work together." She curled back her top lip to display her teeth, "Instead...they died."

"What about the other humans?" asked Cyclops tersely. "The ones without powers?" His throat was dry, and he didn't want to think about how many deaths of good friends had just been dismissed by Selene in a few words.

"I am not needlessly vindictive, Mr. Summers. I allowed the human population of this island to leave in safety." Selene's white face darkened. "Unfortunately, many of them chose not to heed my warnings. I don't think I have ever encountered such a stubborn herd in all my centuries. It took many deaths to drive out the last of them." She smiled again, as if enjoying a pleasant memory. "Of course, their life energies were most welcome. It will be some time before I have to worry about prolonging my own existence further." Then the smile was gone, and the Black Queen's eyes hardened. "This is a city of mutants now. *My* city. And you, my friends, will fit in well."

Cyclops clenched his fists. "If you think we're going to allow this twisted game of yours to continue, Selene, you'd better think again."

The Black Queen threw back her head and laughed. "You talk as if you have a choice. The truth is that, once you are infected, you will be trapped like the rest of my subjects, reliant upon regular does of my serum to survive."

She made a tiny gesture with one hand, and her demon helpers moved forward. Cyclops tensed, prepared for battle although his aching muscles complained that it was too soon. He rested two fingers of his yellow-gloved right hand upon the sensor in his palm, ready to open his visor and unleash his optic blasts. He scanned the approaching creatures: they came in all shapes and sizes, but each of their ghoulish faces was twisted into an expression of eager malice. Their skin was parchment-thin and lined with cracks, and their bared fangs and raised talons dripped with a clear liquid, which glinted in the flickering candlelight.

"They've got poison on their teeth and claws," warned Wolverine, sniffing the air. His highly developed sense of smell would have confirmed the evidence of his eyes.

Cyclops nodded. "The Legacy Virus," he surmised.

The demons sprang, and their would-be victims—despite their weariness, both physical and mental—responded like the components of a well-honed machine. Cyclops let loose with a wide-angled blast, not powerful enough to cause much harm but calculated to stun as many of his foes as possible and leave them vulnerable to the others.

Storm took to the air, the raised ceiling of the throne room working in her favor. From her vantage point out of the demons' reach, she could take time to survey the battleground without fear of attack from behind, and deploy her elemental powers where they would do the most good. Her first fork of lightning sliced through the air and struck the foremost demon as it was aiming a swipe at Cyclops: it rocked on its heels, its eyes wide with surprise in its charred face, and then it crumpled.

Wolverine favored a more direct approach, barreling into the demons' front rank and bringing down four of the startled creatures like a row of dominoes. Two sets of three claws each—sheathed in adamantium, the hardest known metal—had extruded from the backs of his hands, and spots of viscous, black demon blood burst into the air as he lashed out. Wolverine didn't need much of an excuse to give in to his feral side, and the non-human nature of his opponents was enough.

Rogue too ploughed forward, her fists flailing. Her particular mutant ability was that she temporarily acquired the physical and mental characteristics of anyone she touched with her bare skin. Her control over this power had lessened with time, and she had come to think of it as more of a curse than a blessing. She wore a hooded green bodysuit which left only her face exposed, lest she inadvertently brush against somebody and be overwhelmed by alien thoughts. However, she also possessed tremendous strength and the ability to fly—she had taken both from somebody a long time ago, and thanks to a terrible accident, they had never faded—which made her one of the X-Men's most useful hand-to-hand fighters.

Between them, the pair kept many of the demons occupied, but others poured around them and tried to surround their teammates. Storm conjured a wind to blow the right hand flank off its collective feet, while Iceman converted atmospheric moisture into a frozen barrier to the left. In the process, however, he left his back open to two demons who had fought their way past Rogue. In his ice form, protected by a thick coat of frozen armor, he might have been able to deflect their claws—but Cyclops wasn't about to take that chance. He downed them with two rapid-fire optic blasts. Beside him, Phoenix's green eyes flashed red as she thinned the odds against Rogue by telekinetically levitating four demons into the air. Bewildered and disoriented, thrashing their arms and legs, they were easy prey for Storm: the wind-rider cast them into the darkest corners of the room, from which they didn't return.

This was where long hours of training paid off. The demons

were scrambling to reach their targets, pushing each other aside and trampling their fallen, but the X-Men were used to each other's abilities and fighting styles, and well practiced in their own, and they worked in harmony. They didn't even need to speak: Phoenix, a telepath as well as a telekinetic, opened a mental channel between them so that they could discuss tactics without being overheard.

We can't win this one, sent Cyclops, kicking aside a fallen demon, which had tried to sink its poisoned teeth into his ankle.

I concur, echoed the thoughts of Phoenix in his mind. Despite the situation, he allowed himself a tiny smile at the telepathic touch of his lover. *Selene and Blackheart are content to watch for now—but we're in no condition to fight them should that change.*

That was certainly true. Selene was not only a powerful sorceress and an energy vampire but also a mutant, with powers of telepathy, pyrokinesis and molecular control over inanimate objects. With the son of Mephisto at her side, she would be near impossible to beat even under ideal circumstances.

Which I suspect it soon will, sent Storm. *We are gaining the advantage over the demons.*

Then I suggest we get out of here! Wolverine's thoughts manifested themselves in an internal voice as gruff as his external one. *Much as I enjoy cutting these critters into shish kabobs, they're costing us precious time and effort—and I'm sure it'll be no great sweat for Selene to replace them.*

Agreed, returned Cyclops. *Time to fall back to the door, people. I'll take the point. Storm and Rogue, you're fighting a rearguard action. Nightcrawler, run interference.*

Nightcrawler was the X-Men's resident teleporter. In some people's eyes—generally those who hadn't experienced his kindness, his generosity and his unstinting chivalry—he also resembled a demon himself, or at best a malevolent goblin. His skin was indigo blue in color, and he tended to disappear in shadows. His eyes, in contrast, were a luminous saffron yellow—and his ears and teeth grew to fine points as did his long, thin tail. As if to complete the

effect, he left behind a fierce pop of imploding air and a dark billow of brimstone-scented smoke as he disappeared from Cyclops's
side to reappear in the demons' midst. He gave them a second to
react to his presence before bracing himself against the shoulders
of two of them, taking a prodigious leap upward and kicking out
with his white-booted, three-toed feet at the faces of the creatures
who had inadvertently supported him. Claws sliced through the
air, but Nightcrawler tucked his knees into his chest and somer-
saulted out of their reach. Kurt Wagner had been brought up in a
German circus, and the acrobatic skills he had learned there com-
plemented his mutant abilities well.

The demons jostled to escape as he unfolded himself and fell
back towards them, feet first. He vanished again as they closed in
on the space where he had been. When he reappeared a second
later, he was holding a dusty tapestry that he must have wrenched
from one of the recesses of the room. He dropped it neatly over six
demons and danced on their covered heads until their fellows
came too close for comfort, whereupon he teleported three more
times in quick succession, keeping them confused and busy.

Sprinting for the door, Cyclops emerged into a corridor that
was much as he remembered it: deep-carpeted and wood-paneled,
lined with expensive paintings, speaking of a quiet opulence that
contrasted with his infernal surroundings of a moment before. At
least his geographical position had not changed, then. He counted
out his teammates behind him, ushering them towards the stairs
that led up to street level. Iceman was first, followed by Phoenix
and then Wolverine. The latter was reluctant to disengage from the
battle, and Cyclops was relieved when he finally chose to obey
orders. Wolverine possessed an accelerated healing factor, which
allowed him to shrug off most wounds, but it was not likely to
help him against the Legacy Virus should it penetrate his bloodstream.

Next came Sebastian Shaw—and Cyclops was alarmed by the
realization that, with so much else to think about, he had lost track
of the erstwhile Black King during the melee. To judge by his

appearance alone, Shaw had been left untouched by the demon attack. He was unruffled, still holding himself with characteristic confidence, and he made his withdrawal from the throne room seem unhurried. Perhaps it was just that he had the ability to absorb the kinetic energy of any blow directed at him and turn it into power; however, even his green boiler suit displayed no cuts or even stains. Cyclops had noticed before that Shaw seemed to be able to stand aloof, blending into the background as combat raged around him. It was as if he considered it beneath his dignity to dirty his hands, although he certainly wasn't averse to using his amplified strength when he felt it was required. Scott berated himself inwardly for having taken his eye off his famously treacherous ally: Shaw had worked with Selene more than once in the past, and the X-Men's leader had been half expecting a betrayal ever since he had grudgingly agreed to accept his assistance. He wished he had seen how Shaw had reacted to the Black Queen's revelations.

Storm backed out of the throne room next, still using her winds to keep the demons at bay. Those who fought against the ferocious air currents found themselves on the receiving end of Rogue's sledgehammer fists. Her green costume took several cuts, but the skin beneath it was almost invulnerable and no claws could puncture it.

From the foot of the stairs, Cyclops heard the familiar *bamf* sound of Nightcrawler's teleportation, which told him that the German X-Man had joined the evacuation and was indeed now ahead of him. "We're all out!" he yelled, and Rogue fell back into the corridor and allowed the demons to spill out after her. She and Cyclops fled after their teammates, Scott glancing over his shoulder and delivering another wide-angled burst from his eyes to discourage pursuit.

No other obstacles stood between the X-Men and the main doors of the Hellfire Club's mansion house. But as they emerged onto New York's Fifth Avenue, all eight mutants found themselves brought to a stunned halt.

Cyclops was the first to recover his senses and to check behind him, to be sure that the demons hadn't followed their prey up the stairs. They hadn't. Perhaps they were afraid of the daylight, such as it was. More likely, he suspected, Selene had not wanted them to interfere with this moment. She was probably watching now with her crystal ball. She had allowed her foes to escape so that they could witness the full horror of what she had done.

Their surroundings were familiar, and yet at the same time eerily different. The buildings of New York City were still standing, although some had been blackened by fire or daubed with graffiti—but their dirty windows were dark and empty. Deprived of the crowds that had once pumped through them like their lifeblood, the buildings seemed forlorn and bereft of purpose.

A thin late November wind whipped through the overgrown vegetation of Central Park across the street. It blew along the empty road that had once been clogged with taxicabs and tourist buses, and sent a wave of discarded cans and papers clattering and rustling ahead of it. Wolverine wrinkled his nose in distaste, but Cyclops didn't need his teammate's enhanced senses to detect the odor of rotting garbage and backed-up sewage: the stench of decay.

The sky was white—but it was an imperfect, dirty white, across which ripples of some darker energy occasionally passed. There were no birds beneath this strange canopy, no songs or beating of wings to distract from the dreadful silence that hung over what had once been one of the noisiest and busiest cities in the world.

"Home sweet home," said Iceman dryly, but his attempt at black humor was undermined by the dismayed tone of his voice.

"Such defiant spirits," rumbled Blackheart. "I look forward to breaking them."

"You will have your chance tomorrow," Selene promised him, "when they return."

The Black Queen's business had gone well, and now it was time for a little recreation. The royal couple were enjoying a stroll around the basement levels of the Hellfire Club building, en route to the catacombs. They had reached the corridor that ran behind the nightmare chambers, and the paneled wall was lined with paintings of some of Selene's most persistent enemies trapped in a variety of soul-destroying scenarios. Every few seconds, the pictures underwent subtle changes as they updated themselves. She savored the images, knowing that they represented the tortured dreams of the captive minds behind them.

In answer to her Black King's unspoken question, she continued: "Oh yes, I know my adversaries well, Blackheart, and I have had a long time to prepare for their arrival. They will fall eagerly into the trap set by our Inner Circle: our Black Bishops, our Rook and, most importantly of all, our loyal Black Knight. They will return to this building willingly, under the pathetic delusion that they still have a prayer of defeating us."

"And they will join their vanquished mentor in eternal torment."

Selene pursed her lips as she followed Blackheart's gaze to one particular painting. As self-inflicted Hells went, she considered the one dreamed up by the X-Men's founder, Charles Xavier, quite banal. Still, the pain it caused him was both real and sweet enough. Xavier dreamt of a future in which mutants were branded with numbers. Their identities were recorded in a long row of gray filing cabinets, and any use of their abilities was subject to the conditions of a special license. Any infringement of those conditions was punishable by incarceration in a maximum security prison. Xavier himself did not have to endure the harsh regime of such an institution, but he was forced to watch as those he had once considered his charges, his fellow mutants, suffered in his stead. He had failed them.

"Some of them, perhaps," purred Selene, thinking that perhaps she would set Xavier free soon, let him see the future that *she* had made. His nightmares might become more colorful then. "Cyclops, Phoenix, Wolverine, Storm...those who provide us with good sport. Those with whom we might like to play again some day. The others, we can discard."

"And Shaw?"

"I have a special fate in store for him." Selene smiled to herself as she continued along the corridor, passing images of the Scarlet Witch, the mutant from the future known as Cable and Daimon Hellstrom, the man who had once presumed to be her White King. As the son of a powerful demon himself, Hellstrom knew exactly what dire underworlds awaited the blemished soul, and his nightmare scenario was especially edifying.

Confined beside him was one of the world's most powerful mutants and certainly one of its most arrogant and ruthless, now humbled at last. "Ah, Magneto," Selene whispered fondly as she caressed the painted face of the master of magnetism with her long fingernails. "You too were a member of our Inner Circle once. Is it foolish of me to harbor the faint hope that you might serve us again?"

"His will is yet strong," said Blackheart, "but perhaps in time, once he has been worn down by decades spent in the death camps and gas chambers of his mind..."

They walked on in silence for a moment before the demon spoke again. "It is a shame that the X-Men cannot spend a while longer in our city."

"Their own impatience will force an early showdown," said Selene. "I have merely ensured that we are aware of the time and place before it happens."

Blackheart nodded. "They are afraid, perhaps, of how this environment will affect them. The rules of their old world mean nothing here. The X-Men may come to fear for their souls, and rightly so. They have only recently wrestled with their dark sides; they do not know how far they might have to go—how far they are *prepared* to go—to preserve their lives. I will be interested to learn the answers to those questions."

"And yet," said Selene, "they will not leave, although the barrier would not obstruct them."

"It is the very purity of the hero's soul that endangers itself," said Blackheart. "Such has it always been. And I—like you, my Queen—would have it no other way."

"Selene, it seems, was being truthful with us—about one thing at least." Storm glided back to her waiting teammates on a gentle air current. She dismissed the tiny pang of reluctance she felt at having to end her communion with the elements so soon and return to a world of gray concrete. "I flew a dozen blocks in each direction, but saw only one young man. He ran from me and took refuge inside a building. The city is almost deserted."

The very nature of Manhattan made aerial reconnaissance difficult. Storm had had to climb above its highest skyscrapers, far from the streets that she was meant to be searching. When the boy in his ragged clothes had seen her swooping towards him and had taken flight, she had been too far away to stop him, to reassure him that she meant him no harm. She hadn't followed him: she had been under instructions not to walk into potential danger alone.

"Nobody else?" asked Cyclops glumly.

"There is a fire burning on the far side of Central Park, but I could see nobody through the trees."

"We should check it out," said Cyclops. His initial shock at the state of his home town had passed and, as always, he had shut away his feelings behind a mask of grim urgency, determined that they shouldn't get in the way of his handling of the situation. "OK people, we've got a missing year to fill in, which means we need to do a little fact-finding. There are approximately eight hundred mutants in this city, and some of them could be old friends. We need to know who the players are, who's on our side, and we need to find out as much as we can about Selene's habits and potential weaknesses. Now there doesn't seem to be any immediate danger, but that could change at any time. I think we should split up to cover more ground, but only into teams of four, and Jean should keep us linked telepathically."

"We should also investigate Avengers Mansion," said Phoenix. "Chances are it's been gutted already, but we might be able to salvage some of their communications equipment and make contact with them—or with one of the other mutant groups."

"Heck," said Rogue, "the length of time we've been gone, there's probably a whole new crew of X-Men out there." She was trying to sound cheerful but she probably realized, as did Storm, that that any such team was bound to have faced Selene already, and lost.

"Worth taking a look down the sewers too," said Wolverine. "It wouldn't be the first time our kind has been forced into hiding in those pipes."

"OK," said Cyclops. "Phoenix, Nightcrawler, Iceman, you're with me. We'll investigate that fire in the park, scout around the Upper West Side and then drop down into the sewers. Storm, you and the others take Avengers Mansion, then continue downtown."

The X-Men did as they were ordered, dividing into two groups without question. Still, Storm felt a flutter in her stomach as she realized that, along with Wolverine and Rogue, she had been teamed with Shaw. It seemed to her that she had hardly enjoyed a moment away from his scrutiny since she had dined with him on the Kree island.

In the clinical surroundings of his scientific base beneath an island in the North Pacific Ocean, Sebastian Shaw had made Ororo Munroe an offer. She still had no idea whether or not she would accept it. Every time she tried to think about it, her thoughts went round and round in circles until her head hurt. Without meaning to—and despite the fact that there were more important things to consider—she found herself dwelling upon the details of the offer again now. She couldn't deny that it was enticing; perhaps more so than it ought to have been. And perhaps, she thought, that was the problem.

She was aware of Shaw's intense eyes upon her, almost looking through her as if he knew what she was thinking. She felt as if she had lived with this burden, this unmade decision, for weeks, but in fact her conversation with the Black King had taken place only one day ago.

One year and one day ago, she corrected herself, and this stark reminder of the X-Men's immediate predicament served to refocus her mind.

The Avengers' former base was only a few blocks away, down Fifth Avenue. "I'll fly ahead," said Storm. "Wolverine, I want you to take the rear and watch out for an attack from behind. Under the circumstances, we have to consider this entire city hostile."

Shaw, she thought, would just have to wait a little longer for his answer.

CHAPTER 4

ORORO DIDN'T know if she was doing the right thing.

There were no mirrors in the underground Kree base, and the metal walls were too dull to hold a reflection. She couldn't see how she looked, but she felt like a princess.

She had found the dress waiting for her when she had returned to her room after her conversation with Shaw on the island's surface. It had been lying, wrapped in brown paper, on her bed. The accompanying note had simply given her a time: 1900—7:00 P.M. There had been no name attached to it, but Ororo had never doubted the identity of her benefactor.

At first, irritated by Shaw's presumptuousness, she had left the parcel unopened. But curiosity had got the better of her. Anyway, she had arrived on the island without a single change of clothes, and stayed for far longer than she had intended. She had been wearing her black X-Men costume for a week now—and although she had washed it with a localized rainstorm and dried it with warm air, it still felt dirty and uncomfortable.

The red dress, on the other hand, felt better than it had any right to. The silk slid across her skin like the hand of a lover, flattering the curves of her body without trying to restrict them. It exposed one rounded shoulder, and made her seem as if she were

50

gliding across the floor when she walked. It made her feel desirable, even sensuous. In her line of work, with her chaotic lifestyle, this was a rare treat indeed.

The dress, with its designer label, probably cost more than any inhabitant of Ororo's native Kenya could earn in a year—and yet Shaw had paid for it without a thought, and given it to an enemy, as part of a cat and mouse game he had chosen to play today. And for what purpose? Just to keep himself from becoming bored?

She shouldn't have played his game, but she didn't think she could help herself.

At precisely seven o'clock, there was a soft tap at her door. She hesitated for a second before opening it, suddenly self-conscious, realizing that she had already compromised herself by putting on the dress. She wondered how she would explain herself if her visitor turned out to be Iceman or Moira MacTaggert, even though that was unlikely.

It was just like Shaw, she thought, to have anticipated her doubts; to know that, left to herself, she might never have taken that first step out of her room.

He hadn't even come for her personally, hadn't given her the chance to slam the door in his face. He had sent one of the Hellfire Club's hired mercenaries. The man was dressed in the red and blue uniform and blank-faced, skin-colored mask of his organization. He also wore a white dinner jacket and bow tie. As he executed a formal bow, Ororo couldn't help but giggle at the incongruity of it. Her anticipation thus dispelled, if only for a second, she found herself taking his proffered arm and allowing him to lead her out into the corridor.

Somehow, without Ororo ever having taken a firm decision, a meeting with Shaw—if not an actual dinner date—had become an inevitability. She tried to prepare herself. She didn't know how to react to him, what she should say. Perhaps she ought to throw his meal back in his face, metaphorically if not literally; tell him exactly what she thought of his attempts to manipulate her, turn around and walk away. But then, she was already wearing the red dress. So, perhaps she would play him at his own game instead—only she would show him that she wasn't as suited as he might expect to the role of the mouse.

The agent led Ororo down several flights of stairs, deeper and deeper into the base, and a familiar anxiety rose within her. As Shaw well knew—as he had said to her on the surface—she suffered from a fear of enclosed spaces. She had managed to conquer that fear, but it never quite went away. She tried not to think about the weight of the island above her, of what might happen if the walls of the facility should buckle beneath it. She tried not to think about being buried under rubble, unable to move as she had once been, a lifetime ago.

She must have reached the lowest level of the base, because the stairs went no further. Down here, the walls throbbed in rhythm with the generators hidden behind them. By now she was ready for anything, suspecting every shadow, afraid that Shaw's invitation—and the red dress—had been no more than an elaborate plan to lure her into an ambush. Would he really be so brazen? Even if he could overpower her and hide her body down here, if he could feign ignorance of her disappearance, the others would still be suspicious. They would call in the rest of the X-Men.

Unless Bobby, Hank and Moira were even now walking into similar traps.

The agent pulled open a door and ushered her into the green-tinted light beyond. Ororo's hand hovered over the pocket in which she had secreted her comm-set—her direct line to her teammates—but she passed him with her head held high, determined not to betray her apprehension. She failed to hide her surprise, however, at the sight that greeted her.

She was in a huge, semicircular room, and the curved wall facing her was transparent. It was the first window she had seen in the Kree base, and she had always imagined—she hadn't been able to stop herself, especially at night—rocks pressing in behind the metal walls. Here, however, she was beneath the island itself, looking out across the crystal clear Pacific Ocean at the unspoiled works of Nature. Green fronds waved gently in the underwater currents as shrimp and cod swam by, blithely unaware of her eyes upon them. Patches of underwater algae clung to vast outcrops of rock and shingle, providing a touch of pastel color to the panorama, and she caught her breath at the beauty of it all.

"Do you like it?" asked Sebastian Shaw. He stood in front of the window, his unblinking eyes upon her, hands clasped behind his back, his face illuminated by the emerald light.

"Very much," said Ororo.

"We could dine on the surface if you'd prefer," he said, "but I thought we would be more comfortable in here. I find the view quite soothing."

"It's perfect," said Ororo, despite herself.

Shaw inclined his head graciously. Set up beside him was a rectangular dining table with a white cloth and napkins and a place setting at each end. He pulled back a chair and waited for Ororo to take it. "I'm glad you decided to wear the dress," he said. "I think it suits you."

"It's a perfect fit," she said. "How did you know my size?"

Shaw gave her a half-smile. "I have a talent for such things, one of my non-mutant gifts." More likely, thought Ororo, he had had his telepathic personal assistant, Tessa, pluck the information from her mind. She considered leveling the accusation against him, but it felt too soon to break the mood of strained formality. Let him make his move first, she thought. She still hadn't found out what he expected to gain from this assignation.

Shaw took a seat opposite her, rolled back the cuffs of his velvet smoking jacket and clapped his hands twice. Immediately, the door opened again and three of his lackeys appeared. Each was dressed in the same manner as Ororo's erstwhile escort, but their masks made it impossible to tell if any of them was the same man. The first agent brought a bottle of champagne in an ice bucket and, at Shaw's signal, poured a glass for each of the diners. The second agent bore two large plates, which he set down in front of them. They contained king prawns in their shells, in a red sauce.

The third agent placed two silver bowls in the center of the table, and lifted the lids with a flourish to reveal steaming rice and noo-dles.

"I hope this meets with your approval," said Shaw as his color-fully clad waiters departed in silence. "I had the ingredients—and the chef—flown over from Hong Kong this morning."

Ororo thought the food looked and smelled wonderful—but rather than flatter her host with another compliment, she said, "It all seems a little extravagant."

"I place little value on money," said Shaw with a shrug. Ororo raised an eyebrow pertinently, and he smiled. "It has no intrinsic worth, it is simply a means to an end."

"And your end, in this case, is...?"

"Simply to enjoy good company and intellectual discourse."

He raised his glass toward her, but she did not respond. "I know you better than that, Shaw. There is an ulterior motive behind your invitation. There always is." He smiled again, but did not contra-dict her. She stared at him with narrowed eyes for a moment. Then she sighed, lifted her glass and clinked it softly against his.

"You have never appeared short of company," said Ororo as she ladled rice onto her plate.

"I am often surrounded by people," said Shaw. "It is not the same thing."

"I believe you were close to Madelyne Pryor." She tried to make the statement sound as casual as possible: she began to eat and concentrated upon her plate, avoiding Shaw's gaze. Madelyne had once been a member of the X-Men, but she had become a bitter foe. Shaw had taken her into his Inner Circle—and if the rumors were true, into his bed too.

"I am under no illusions about Madelyne Pryor," he said stiffly. Ororo glanced up to see that his expression had darkened. "I took a succubus to my chest. Now she has gone."

"Oh?" Ororo was genuinely surprised.

Shaw met her gaze and, in a perfectly even voice, he elabo-rated: "She could not get what she wanted from me. Therefore, she left. No doubt she has returned to her pet, the Grey boy." He was talking about Nathan Grey: a mutant from an alternative dimension, the son of an alternative version of Ororo's teammate, Jean Grey. Ororo was aware from Jean's reports that Nathan and Madelyne had been spending time together, although even Jean didn't know the precise nature of their relationship. "Perhaps she will return," said Shaw. "She has done so in the past. She has also betrayed me in the past, although she thinks me unaware of it. Perhaps I will not see her again." He shrugged as if he did not care either way, but Ororo thought she detected a flicker of sadness in his eyes.

"And your Black Queen? She has defected to the Hellfire Club's New York branch, has she not?" It was an impolite question, and she wasn't sure why she had asked it. Perhaps it was because she had rarely seen anything get under Shaw's skin, and some malicious part of her had wanted to see if she could unsettle him further.

"Selene has made no move against me."

"Not this time," said Ororo, "not yet. But she has betrayed you before."

"In that, she is no different to many people."

"True. And yet you continue to strike these dangerous alliances: Madelyne, Trevor Fitzroy, Donald Pierce...are you really so bad a judge of character?"

Shaw held his expression carefully neutral, but his eyes had darkened. "As I have already said, I labor under no illusions. In my business, the stakes are invariably high. I choose my partners for what they can offer me, even if only in the short term. I deal with the great and the powerful or with those who have the potential to be both. I expect no less of such people than to seek to use me in return. And once they have taken what they want from me, or more likely found that is not for the taking, they will turn on me like snakes."

"As you would them," said Ororo, "if the situation were reversed." Shaw inclined his head as if accepting the truth of the accusation. Feeling daring, Ororo added: "As did your son."

There was silence for a moment. Then Shaw cracked open a prawn, and the sharp retort resounded around the spacious room. "I taught Shinobi well," he said quietly, grim-faced.

"And he tried to kill you. We thought he had succeeded."

"He disappointed me."

"Is that all, Shaw?"

"You misunderstand, my dear. He disappointed me because, when I returned from the dead—so to speak—he chose to flee, to go into hiding, rather than face me."

"Perhaps he had good reason." Shaw didn't answer that, and his expression was inscrutable. Ororo changed tack. "Then you have no idea where he is?"

"I should rather ask that question of you," said Shaw. "You have spoken with him far more recently than I; indeed, I understand the two of you shared a great deal."

Ororo's startled eyes flicked upward towards him—she couldn't stop them—and she felt sure that he could read the guilt therein. He smiled, probably with satisfaction at having disconcerted her, having turned the tables. "My dear Miss Munroe," he said pleasantly, "you must realize that there are some things a son simply cannot keep from his father."

"My relationship with Shinobi was extremely brief," she said coldly, "and not entered into by choice on my part." She had pushed the whole affair to the back of her mind. Had she not, then Shaw could never have taken her by surprise like this.

"I am well aware of the circumstances of your dalliance." Abandoning his meal, Shaw leaned forward with an eager glint in his eye. "But tell me, my dear, do you really believe that even the most powerful hypnotic drug can cause somebody—an X-Man, no less, one of the most strong-willed people I have ever encountered—to completely betray her nature?"

"What are you implying?"

"That on some level—oh, one buried deep within your subconscious mind, I don't doubt it—you were attracted to my son."

"No," said Ororo firmly.

"It is understandable," continued Shaw as if she hadn't spoken. "A younger man; a handsome man, I am led to believe; a man with so much power. The head of the Hellfire Club's most influential Inner Circle, no less, at that time. You have always been attracted to powerful men, haven't you, Ororo? And if those men have a touch of the darkness about them—as most powerful men have—then so much the better."

She was lost for words. Half of her wanted to jump to her feet, to slap him across the face and leave, but she refused to let him see her lose her cool. Her blood had rushed to her cheeks in shame, and she still wasn't sure how Shaw had managed to turn the conversation around so that it was now her life, not his, that was under scrutiny. He was playing her at her own game, she realized, and winning. She had to regain control, but she didn't know how—because in her heart she feared that what the Black King had said was true.

"I apologize," said Shaw, although he sounded insincere. "I did not mean to embarrass you. I myself know how seductive power can be."

"I do not agree. The old adage that it corrupts is, in my experience, well founded."

"Or perhaps it is just that the corrupt seek power."

"Either way," Ororo snapped, "you are wrong." She took a deep breath and forced herself to calm down. Bad enough that he had touched a raw nerve; she didn't have to let him know it.

"Are you sure?" asked Shaw with a hint of amusement. "Would you have accepted a dinner invitation from Fitzroy? Or Tessa? Or from one of my uniformed agents?"

Ororo set down her cutlery with an annoyed clatter. "Is that what this is about? Do you expect me to profess my undying admiration for you? A secret crush? If so, Shaw, then you overestimate your own charms. Like the people with whom you deal, you are a snake. A ruthless, selfish, amoral man. You represent everything I find loathsome in humanity."

"More so than the infamous Victor Von Doom?"

Ororo winced. Shaw seemed to know everything about her life, her every failing. Her relationship with Doom—the ruler of a small European nation, and probably one of the most evil men in the world—had never had a chance to get started, but there had certainly been a spark between them. The memory of it often haunted her.

Shaw abandoned his food too, and leaned back in his chair. He rested his hands on his chest, interlacing his fingers. "You may not like me, Ororo, but I possess everything you desire."

"No," she said bluntly.

"I beg to disagree. Why did you join the X-Men? Why do you wear that garish costume and make yourself a target for those who would render our kind extinct? I think your Professor Xavier offered you something you wanted; something for which you would do anything."

"The Professor awakened me to my responsibilities, that is all."

"I think he did more than that. You were born into a poor country, Ororo. You saw suffering all around you. You watched as people died, knowing that humanity had the ability but not the political will to prevent those deaths. Even in better times, in the rainforest where you were worshipped as a goddess, you must have felt unfulfilled."

"You presume to know a great deal about my feelings."

"We are not so dissimilar, you and I."

"Now it is I who must disagree."

"I am right though, aren't I? You had the adulation of a superstitious tribe—you had power over them—but it was not enough, because they in turn were powerless. When you were offered a chance to change the world, you took it. But that was a long time ago, Ororo, and it is time you asked yourself: did Xavier live up to his promise? Is your life with the X-Men everything you thought—and hoped—it would be?"

"We have made many things better."

"You have had some minor victories, nothing more. You have

58

failed to halt, much less reverse, the deterioration in mutant-human relations. After all your hard-won battles, all your personal sacrifices, you are further than ever from achieving Xavier's much-vaunted dream."

"We have prevented people like you from making the situation worse," said Ororo.

"You have addressed some of the symptoms of the problem," countered Shaw. "You are a long way from tackling the causes. Meanwhile, people still die in the Third World."

Ororo looked down, her lips set into a sullen scowl. "There is only so much we can do. I have learned that lesson."

Shaw shook his head. "No, no, no, no. One man, to use another old adage, can move mountains—but only with the right lever. And in this world of ours, it is financial and political power that affects real change. You can deny that if you like—you can cling to a dream that can never be realized—or you can accept the system and work it to your own advantage." Shaw leaned forward again. "Between the Hellfire Club and my own company, Shaw Industries, I control vast sums of money. I have the ear of presidents, judges and, most importantly, the captains of industry. I can change the lives of thousands of people in real, practical ways in an instant. Can you honestly tell me that you would refuse such power, Miss Munroe; that you could not find a single positive use to which to put it?"

Ororo had butterflies in her stomach and prickles down her back. Shaw was saying nothing that she hadn't thought herself a thousand times before. Not that she intended to tell him so—but then she couldn't bring herself to lie to him either. Instead, in as steady a voice as she could muster, she asked: "What are you suggesting?"

"Join me," he said.

She started, her eyes widening. "You are proposing an alliance?"

"The Inner Circle must remain strong—and of late, it has become depleted. Only two of us remain, and I would not lay odds on Fitzroy's continued loyalty. You, my dear, would make an excellent Lord Cardinal. So determined, so self-assured, so ambitious..."

"It did not work before," she reminded him. Some time ago, she had shared the rank of White King in Shaw's Inner Circle with the X-Men's long-time adversary—at that point, an uneasy friend—Magneto. It had been, so she had thought, an opportunity to broker a new peace between at least some of the various mutant factions. It had not lasted. Magneto, like so many before and after him, had turned against Shaw. In time, he had turned against the X-Men as well. Ororo had attended only one full meeting of the Lords Cardinal, and she had achieved nothing.

"This time," said Shaw, "you would be a member in your own right."

"I would not be your pawn."

"Indeed not," he agreed. "You would be my White Queen."

She didn't have to ask what that meant. Sebastian Shaw was the Black King. As the White Queen, she would be his equal, at least in theory; the head of the opposing house. She could even, subject to the approval of her opposite number, recruit new members into the Inner Circle herself: a new White tier, separate from but allied to its Black counterpart. She could apply checks and balances to the excesses of Shaw and his followers.

She could share in his power. She could use it to pursue her own dreams.

Ororo was tempted; sorely tempted. But she was well aware of the magnitude of what she was considering. If Shaw wanted her to believe that she could somehow rehabilitate him, turn the Hellfire Club into a force good, then he would be disappointed. She knew him too well for that. He had already admitted to her that he made allies only for what he could get out of them, and discarded them when he was done. But he expected the same treatment in return. He was offering Ororo a chance to play a dangerous game, and in some ways she was still naïve about the rules. The cost to herself, if she lost, was potentially huge.

But what if she didn't lose?

Her thoughts were in turmoil. There were so many things she wanted to say, so many questions, but she didn't know where to start. Shaw sat back in his seat again, and watched her with the ghost of a smile on his face. He was confident. Too confident for her liking. He knew that he had hooked her, and she hated being so transparent.

In some ways, then, it was a relief when the door crashed open and a Hellfire Club agent raced into the room.

It was one of the waiters, still dressed in his white dinner jacket, but he now carried one of the lightweight machine-guns that were standard issue for Shaw's uniformed troops. Ororo leapt to her feet, momentarily recalling her earlier suspicions—but she could see from Shaw's expression of barely controlled anger that he had certainly not planned this interruption.

"Sir, sir," panted the agent as he skidded to a halt, "we're under attack!"

With immaculate timing, there came a muffled explosion from one of the upper floors.

"By whom?" asked Shaw, tight-lipped, taking the time to dab at his mouth with a napkin.

"I don't know, sir. One of our agents on Level Four radioed in a distress message, but he was cut off before he could finish."

Shaw nodded curtly, stood and laid his napkin aside. Ororo reached for her comm-set and activated it. "Iceman, we have trouble."

"I've just heard," Bobby Drake's voice crackled in the tiny receiver.

"Any idea what we're up against?"

"Not yet—but whoever they are, they've taken out half of Shaw's agents already."

Shaw marched out of the room, and Ororo followed him as she continued her conversation. "Where are you?"

"Outside Hank's quarters. I don't want to leave him."

She nodded in approval, although her teammate couldn't see her. "Stay there."

The jacketed agent was joined by his two colleagues in the corridor outside. The bizarre trio scampered ahead of their employer protectively, guns at the ready. The Black King himself maintained an unhurried air, but his strides were deceptively long and Ororo found it an effort to keep up with him. "Level Four," he growled. "They've already penetrated deep into the base without us knowing about it. They can only have teleported in."

Ororo acknowledged the information with a nod. She reached down, took the hem of her red dress in both hands and pulled, creating a tear up the side of her right leg. It seemed a shame—but if she was to go into combat, then she would need absolute freedom of movement. And a part of her also took a childish delight in destroying Shaw's gift to her.

She reached the foot of the stairs and looked up to see that somebody was crouching in the shadows at the first corner. The figure had its back to her, but it was wearing the familiar Hellfire Club uniform. The three agents were already hurrying forward, concerned for what was apparently an injured colleague. Storm frowned as she detected something unnatural about the figure's posture. It didn't quite fit into its clothing, and its skin, exposed through tears in the blue cloth, was yellowing and flaking. The faint, musty scent of decay played with her nostrils, and she made to cry out a warning but it was already too late.

The figure whipped around, razor claws extended through the fingers of its red gloves, staring blankly out of a jagged hole in its flesh-toned mask. With one fluid movement, it gutted two of the agents. The third, his white jacket spattered with blood, pumped bullets into its chest, but the creature's lip-less mouth split into a grin as it shrugged off the attack. It lashed out with its claws again, but its would-be victim dodged its swipe and backed away from it. Storm tried to help him, but it was difficult to generate weather patterns in such a confined area. She was forming a heavy cloud above the stairwell, ready to bring down a lightning bolt, when the creature sprang for the last agent's throat. Its weight bore him down the stairs to land at Storm and Shaw's feet, his head lolling at an impossible angle.

Standing astride its third kill, the creature looked up at Storm. Its tongue tumbled out of its mouth and saliva flowed down its chin. With the speed of a striking serpent, Shaw moved in behind it and delivered a chopping blow to the side of its neck. A bone snapped, and the creature's white eyes misted over. A moment later, its legs folded beneath it.

Iceman was shouting over the comm-set, his tinny voice almost swamped by static. "Ororo, it's Selene's demons—and they're wired to explode!"

Storm and Shaw exchanged the briefest of glances before they looked down at the fallen creature in unison. A bulky black belt was tied around its waist—and on the buckle, a red light had begun to flash insistently. Storm reacted without stopping to think, her X-Men training kicking in. She gathered Shaw up in her arms and summoned air currents to propel them both out of danger. They soared upward, past the next level; they had almost reached the one beyond it when they were engulfed by a tremendous blast from below, almost overcome by a ferocious wave of light and heat and sound. Blown off-course, eyes stinging, Storm struggled to regain her bearings—but there was another explosion above her, and suddenly she was being showered by hot shrapnel. A sharp edge glanced off her forehead and left a shallow gash. Her eyes were watering, and through a veil of tears she saw the opening of a passageway to her left and veered dizzily into it. Her feet hit the ground, followed by her knees. Her passenger tumbled out of her grasp and she collapsed on top of him.

Behind Storm, the staircase crumpled: it sent a thick cloud of dust along the corridor and enveloped her in a white shroud. Her lungs heaved and her throat burned and she fought to resist an old terror, trying not to think about the fact that she was now trapped underground. The floor beneath her hands was shaken by more distant explosions, and she knew now that the demon intruders wanted no less than the total destruction of the Kree base. She could hear a rumbling sound above her head, and the terrible shriek of tortured metal. She rolled over onto her back to see that the ceiling was bulging inward.

"Goddess, no!" she screamed—but she had no time to do anything else but throw up a futile warding hand as the world fell upon her.

CHAPTER 5

WOLVERINE'S ENHANCED senses were on full alert as he followed Storm, Rogue and Shaw into the grounds of Avengers Mansion. Manhattan Island may have been quiet, but its sidewalks were stained with old blood—and every so often the scent of a decaying corpse hit him, drifting out through a broken window or up from beneath the rotting garbage stink of an overflowing dumpster.

He could smell something else too: fear. It permeated the very air of this nightmare future.

The mansion was abandoned, as Phoenix had predicted. Its gates had been wrenched from their hinges, its door hung open and vegetation had gained footholds in its masonry. The front lawn was neat and green, but Wolverine could tell that the grass was fake. Mixed in with the unpleasant, sterile aroma of plastic was the acidic tang of engine oil. He reminded the others that, despite appearances, the Avengers' defenses may yet be active.

They inched their way cautiously along the driveway, gaining confidence when nothing appeared to bar their path: a misplaced confidence, as it transpired.

They were only a dozen steps away from the inviting doorway when the attack came. Wolverine's sensitive ears picked it up first:

a deep mechanical rumbling from beneath his feet. His barked warning came just in time for Storm and Rogue to take to the air, avoiding the thick metal coils that erupted from the ground and sought to entangle the quartet. Wolverine popped his claws from the backs of his hands, experience enabling him to ignore the pain as they shredded his skin: it would heal in moments anyway. He twisted and turned, pushing his squat but athletic body to its limit to keep himself out of reach of the grasping tendrils. He tried to cut one, and was disgruntled to see that he only struck sparks from its surface. Like his claws, the coil was constructed from—or at least sheathed in—near-impervious adamantium. He was keeping one step ahead of them—just about—but their attack patterns were designed to drive him away from the building and he couldn't get past them. Out of the corner of his eye, he noticed that Shaw had already been caught.

Then a second threat presented itself: small, square sections of the artificial lawn flipped over to reveal short, stubby, platform-mounted guns on their undersides. The guns rotated upon their mountings, tracking the two airborne X-Men, and one of them spat a stream of dark energy at Rogue. She had seen the danger, but evidently it had approached faster than she had anticipated. She swerved, barely avoiding the first blast, and flew into a second. The guns had been programmed well. Rogue was winded and in pain—which meant that she had taken what, to anybody not blessed with her tough hide, would have been a fatal hit. Which, in turn, meant that somebody must have refitted the guns since the Avengers' departure from their headquarters.

Wolverine relayed that information to the others, including the team in Central Park, via Phoenix. *Looks like there could be some-one here,* he telesent. Cyclops asked if reinforcements were needed, to which he replied: *No need to send in the cavalry yet. We'll keep you posted.*

Storm disposed of two of the guns with well-targeted lightning strikes. Wolverine leapt upon a third: it was adamantium-plated, of course, but he forced his claws into its seams and pried it apart.

Its power source exploded in his face, causing minor burns to his skin, but they too would be gone in no more than a few minutes.

The guns were ignoring Shaw, presumably on the grounds that his threat had already been neutralized. Rogue must have seen this too, as she landed and took cover behind him. She was still a little unsteady on her feet, but the gambit worked: hidden from the guns' sensors, and with the nearest coils already occupied with holding the Black King in place, she was able to gain a short breather. As Storm and Wolverine rushed the coils nearest the door together, hoping that they couldn't cope with two attackers at once, Rogue laid a hand upon Shaw's shoulder, spun him around and punched him three times in the face. He was unmoved by the powerful blows, reacting only with a small nod of gratitude. Energized by Rogue's gift of kinetic force, he flexed his muscles and tore the coils that held him right out of the ground. Relaxing their steely grips, they flopped lifelessly around his feet.

A coil whipped around the hovering Storm's ankle, holding her fast and pulling her down. But her sacrifice allowed Wolverine to reach Avengers Mansion at last.

He dropped to his haunches in the cool, dark hallway of the building, detecting multiple scents in the doorways around him and the staircase above, presenting a smaller target to the unseen watchers. His keen eyes picked out their shapes through the gloom an instant before they rushed him. Their form-fitting two-tone costumes of various colors marked them out as Genoshan mutates: human beings whose latent mutant genes had been artificially stimulated by the corrupt government of their island nation. Once, they had served as a secret army of unpaid, super-powered slaves. Then Magneto had taken control of Genosha—which, to Wolverine's mind, was not much of an improvement but at least its subjects had been freed.

It made sense, he supposed, that Genoshan refugees should have found their way here, given that the Legacy Virus was rife in their own country. These particular mutates, however, still had shaved heads and bore their old numbers upon their chests. Some attempt to reassert their pride, he wondered, by co-opting and sub-verting the former symbols of their servitude? Or had they simply exchanged one despotic master for another?

He didn't have time to ponder that question. Sympathetic as he felt towards the plight of his attackers, he couldn't afford to pull any punches with them, particularly as their powers were unknown. Rather than stand his ground, he rushed to meet them, fists and claws flailing.

Within seconds, he had been buried beneath a pile of heaving bodies.

Cyclops could see the flickering light of a dying fire through the trees, and he motioned to his three teammates to slow down and approach with caution. Gray smoke curled around the tree trunks and brought with it a deeply unpleasant smell that was familiar from a hundred battles. The smell gave Cyclops an idea of what to expect even before he reached the edge of a small, untended and overgrown meadow and had his awful suspicion confirmed.

Iceman was unable to suppress a gasp of horror. Nightcrawler lowered his eyes and crossed himself, no doubt offering up a silent prayer. Phoenix remained focused upon the matter in hand, and Cyclops heard her voice in his mind: *I can't detect any thought patterns in the vicinity.* She sounded distant, no doubt because she was still concentrating on maintaining the telepathic link between the two X-Men teams. She was probably also monitoring the other team's situation, after Wolverine's warning that they had run into trouble.

They moved out into the open, but still trod softly. It felt right somehow, like a mark of respect for the dead. The stench of burnt flesh was stronger now, and Cyclops almost gagged on it. Iceman curled his lower lip into a snarl and extinguished the fire with an angry burst of watery ice, the consistency of snow. It was far too late, however, for the middle-aged African-American woman who lay suspended above the now-fizzling flames, lashed to a lattice-work of gnarled and blackened sticks like a wild boar on a spit.

Cyclops's nausea deepened as he recognized the mutilated corpse.

"Her name was Pearl Scott," he said numbly. "Storm and I met her a few days ago at her home in Poughkeepsie. Her husband Clyde was one of the scientists kidnapped by the Hellfire Club." Having made that connection for the others, he didn't need to continue. They already knew how Sebastian Shaw had captured three prominent geneticists and put them to work on finding a cure for the Legacy Virus in the research facility beneath his Kree island. Even after the X-Men had ostensibly liberated Clyde Scott and his colleagues, the trio had had little choice but to continue their work: they had been infected with Legacy themselves to ensure that it was in their best interests to cooperate.

Cyclops remembered Clyde Scott's ultimate fate, and a dark wave of sadness—tinged with a small amount of guilt—washed over him. "He was one of the people who died when Selene's demons attacked the island." He had promised to get Pearl's husband back for her. He hadn't even had the chance to tell her what had happened to him. From her point of view, Clyde had been killed a year ago and she almost certainly hadn't even been told. She must have gone to her own death with that aching void of uncertainty in her heart.

His gloomy reverie was interrupted by a sound from behind him. The snap of a twig.

It had come from somewhere beyond the tree line. The others had heard it too, and they reacted instantaneously. Nightcrawler teleported away: Cyclops felt him through the link as he materialized in a nearby tree, only to report that he could see nothing even from this new vantage point. Phoenix performed another quick scan of the area, but she shook her head as she came up blank for a second time. If there was indeed somebody there, then he or she was not only invisible to the eye but also to Jean's extra-sensory powers.

Cyclops cast a meaningful glance at Iceman, who knew what to do. He stepped forward and sent a wide-angled flurry of snow ahead of him. Five blank spaces were picked out by the blizzard; five short figures, each no taller than four feet, among the trees. They realized that they had been sighted, and their postures betrayed their alarm. Three of them turned to run, but Nightcrawler appeared behind them in a cloud of brimstone and they recoiled from his demonic form. Scanning the figures, Cyclops saw that one stood a short way apart from the others, its fingers to its temples, its head bowed in concentration. He targeted it with a low-powered optic blast, no more than enough to shock it.

His hunch was proved right. The figure recoiled, startled, and the cloaking field that it must have been maintaining around itself and its fellows was dropped. The holes in Iceman's snowstorm were abruptly filled in, and Phoenix gasped: "They're children. Just children!"

"That doesn't mean they can't be dangerous," Cyclops reminded her, aware of Pearl Scott's toasted corpse behind him.

The children—three boys and two girls—looked like the archetypal impoverished orphans from a movie adaptation of a Dickens novel. The eldest of them was about ten, the youngest about four. Their faces were grimy, their hair unkempt, and they were dressed in rags. However, as if acting upon some inaudible signal, they sprang at the X-Men in unison. Blue sparks emanated from the clenched fists of one boy; another sprouted protective spines all over his skin. One of the girls was coming right at Cyclops: her short body elongated in midair, her clothes dissolving into a coating of white fur as her forehead receded and her eyes became scarlet. Staring into the salivating jaws of a monster, Cyclops prepared to unleash his eye-beams again. Despite his warning to the others, however, compassion stayed his hand. He simply threw himself out of the way of his attacker—to find that she hadn't been aiming for him at all.

The children scattered, leaving the X-Men in disarray. "Wait!" cried Phoenix. "We don't mean you any harm." Her plea was to no avail.

"I don't think they did it," said Nightcrawler quietly. Cyclops turned to him with a quizzical expression. He was looking at Pearl, and his headlamp eyes were dimmed by sadness. "Those claw marks on her body—none of those kids could have made those. They're too deep even for the lycanthrope."

"They weren't killers," concurred Phoenix. "They were just afraid."

"But they were going to...to...if we hadn't come along...." Iceman couldn't complete the sentence. He turned away and put a hand to his stomach as if he were about to be sick.

"Perhaps they felt they had no choice," said Phoenix.

There was silence for a long moment as the X-Men considered that chilling statement. Then, finally, Cyclops said: "We should give her a dignified burial. It's the least we can do."

"And may God have mercy upon her soul," added Nightcrawler.

"And the rest of us," added Iceman under his breath. "And the rest of us."

Even bound as she was, Storm was able to bring down lightning strikes to dispose of the remaining platform-mounted guns. They pivoted this way and that, unable to discern the origins of the attacks upon them until they had been blown apart. Shaw watched the spectacle, almost dazzled by the flashes of light, his nostrils full of ozone. The display of sheer power was awesome, and his respect for its wielder deepened all the more.

He had allowed the coils to catch him again, at least partly to prevent the more deadly guns from targeting him. He could have absorbed the concussive force of such a blast, of course, but its heat energy was another matter, and he didn't relish the prospect of being burned. Now that it was safe to do so, he tore himself free once more. He saw that, likewise, Rogue was using her considerable strength to disentangle Storm. Most of the tendrils had been uprooted now: they lay on the artificial grass, sometimes convulsing and throwing off sparks.

Shaw turned his attention to Avengers Mansion itself and to the seething pile of mutates—at least twenty of them—in its hallway. As he watched, the pile erupted, bodies flying everywhere, and a furious Wolverine emerged from within. Several of the bodies didn't stand up again.

Storm and Rogue joined the battle without hesitation. Shaw followed them, but paused in the doorway of the building and scanned the chaotic scene with calculating eyes. He was beginning to weaken again, having used up much of the energy that Rogue had fed to him. He set his sights upon one particular mutate: a young man dressed in dark blue, a head taller than most of the others, with wide shoulders, a barrel chest and overdeveloped arm muscles. He was lashing out with his fists, repeatedly finding Wolverine too fast for him, and it was a fair bet that his only power was his supernormal strength. Shaw set out towards him, almost untroubled by the other mutates as they concentrated on defending themselves against the more aggressive X-Men. Only once did a spindly, aged creature leap at him with remarkable dexterity, to be repulsed by a casual but painful jab to her nose from Shaw's elbow.

Shaw reached the muscular mutate, reached up and tapped his shoulder politely. When he turned around, confusion clouding the tiny eyes beneath his low brow, Shaw slapped his face. The mutate's jaw dropped open in abject surprise. Then he frowned, drew back one meaty, gloved fist and returned the gesture with a hundred times its original force.

By the time his knuckles reached their target, they had lost all momentum: they brushed against Shaw's cheek like the merest breath of the wind, and the Black King smiled as he felt the considerable power of the punch flowing into him. He raised his right hand and crooked his fingers, inviting his foe to hit him again. The mutate—like many of the people with whom Shaw had done battle, both physically and in the boardroom—must have been of pitiful intellect, because he did as he was bade. And he kept on punching even when it became clear that his blows were ineffectual, even as Shaw's smile spread wider, because his limited imagination could come up with no better strategy.

By the time he had absorbed nine punches, there was liquid fire pumping through Sebastian Shaw's veins. The tenth, he blocked with his palm, whereupon he closed his fingers around the mutate's fist and squeezed until he could feel the crunch of breaking bones. He was still smiling, but he pulled back his lips and bared his teeth as the mutate howled and sank to his knees. The wretched boy clamped his free hand around Shaw's wrist and tried in desperation to loosen his grip, but Shaw's strength now exceeded his by far.

When at last he judged that his foe had suffered enough for his presumption in assaulting him, he brought up his knee sharply and made contact with the mutate's head, rendering him unconscious. Then he surveyed the battleground once more to see how his allies were doing.

They had had a long day, stumbling from one fight to another—and unlike Shaw, they couldn't simply recharge. They were also outnumbered, and their foes' abilities were as varied and impressive as their own. Many of the mutates possessed enhanced strength and stamina, and some were incredibly fast or agile. At least two of them could deliver explosive bursts from their fingertips, while another appeared to generate electricity and conduct it by touch. One yellow-clad young woman could blow herself up and reassemble her molecules in a matter of seconds, and another spat a glistening poison, her neck swelling up like that of a puff adder as she collected each deadly payload therein.

The X-Men, nevertheless, were not easy to defeat. Rogue shrugged off countless blows with casual ease, while her own punches in turn proved devastatingly effective. The mutates could hardly lay a hand on Wolverine as he threaded his way between them, his lightning reflexes keeping him ahead of any attack as his claws struck out with surgical precision. Shaw's gaze lingered longest on Storm: her powers were little use to her in close quarters, but she was more than holding her own. She had been trained in hand-to-hand combat by the best, of course, but she also possessed remarkable discipline, a complete self-awareness and focus that Shaw admired. He could see it in her confident but controlled actions—and he could also feel it in the back of his mind thanks to Phoenix's psychic link.

He felt something else too: a warning from Rogue, unvoiced but plain in her thoughts. Caught unawares, he reacted almost too late. He pivoted to his right and ducked as an energy beam fizzled and crackled above his head. It was black—so black that it seemed to leech the colors from the world around it—and he felt a wave of intense cold as it passed. Only now did he see that Rogue was grappling with a dark-skinned mutate. The same black energy coruscated around his eyes, but the X-Man had her arm around his throat and she had pulled back his hairless head, causing him to aim high. "Best save the daydreams for later, sugar," she called out loud to Shaw in her Southern drawl, a grim smile on her face.

Shaw narrowed his eyes, annoyed by the implied criticism—and all the more so because it had been justified. Whenever he had fought alongside others in the past, it had been a case of "every man for himself." His primary concern had been his own safety, because he had known that nobody else would think to preserve it for him. He was still getting used to the fact that, with the X-Men, things were different. He was still getting used to trusting them.

In assisting Shaw, Rogue had left herself exposed: she was still wrestling with his erstwhile attacker when three more mutates rushed her from behind. Shaw took a powerful leap and intercepted the trio, a swipe of his left arm sending the first of them soaring above the heads of the crowd. The others charged and he braced himself, although it was hardly necessary. They rebounded from him, and he picked them up from the floor and knocked their heads together. At the same time, he put an earlier observation to use, directing a telepathic message at Wolverine: *Female mutate at ten o'clock. She's about to spit venom in three...two...one...*

Wolverine didn't acknowledge the information, but he seized a particularly bulky mutate and pushed him into the adder-woman's path at the very moment that she discharged her poison. He cried out in pain, falling to his knees and clawing at his face. As the woman's neck began to swell again, Wolverine turned his attention to her and brought her down with a swift chop to the back of her knees.

Shaw had always exulted in the rush of combat, the cathartic release of his mutant energies. He often—not always, but often—denied himself that pleasure, knowing that true, lasting victories were gained by stealth, with prudent deals and secret handshakes in locked rooms. But he had rarely enjoyed a battle as much as this. He fought alongside Storm, knowing without having to ask that she would watch his back, doing the same for her in return. As the odds against them lessened, he felt a great thrill of achievement. He knew that as part of a team, he was accomplishing far more than he had ever been capable of on his own.

The tide turned against them in an instant.

Wolverine sensed the new arrival, but not in time to act. All Shaw got was a vague telepathic sensation of something big and gunmetal blue at the top of the stairs. He whirled around as twin rockets whooshed towards him, blazing trails of fire. He resisted the urge to try to dodge them, realizing that they would pass to each side of him. They embedded themselves in the floor and exploded. Shaw gritted his teeth as he was caught in the center of a maelstrom of fire and falling masonry. Bricks and beams bounced harmlessly off him to collect in a pile at his feet, but his boiler suit was shredded and dust stung his eyes and tore at the back of his throat. He weathered the onslaught, aware of Wolverine and Rogue falling and of Storm's desperate prayer that she would not be buried again. He heard the screams and dying gargles of the mutates, and knew that whoever had launched this attack had cared nothing for their safety, had desired nothing more nor less than total destruction.

He had closed his eyes to protect them, but he looked up as he heard a whine of servo-motors from above him. The lower half of the staircase had collapsed, but a huge armored figure simply jumped the gap. It passed through a newly created shaft of daylight before landing heavily and compacting a pile of debris, sending up another white dust cloud.

Standing untouched in the ruins of the Avengers' hallway, surrounded by the injured and the dying, Shaw found himself looking into the face of his opponent. He was not at all surprised to see that it was the face of a one-time ally. When last he had seen Trevor Fitzroy, the young mutant had held the rank of White Rook in the Hong Kong Inner Circle. One look at his malicious, mad-eyed expression told Shaw that he felt no loyalty toward his Black King now.

Not that this was any great loss. Fitzroy had never displayed much potential, least of all intellectually. Shaw had put up with his arrogance and occasional petulance only because his origins had made him vaguely useful. The self-styled Technomancer hailed from a distant future: he had fled to the present day using his mutant ability to open portals through time and space. His bio-armor, which increased the bulk of his wiry form tenfold, came from that future too. It was presently configured for maximum offence, bristling with weaponry. The rocket launchers on its shoulders still smoldered, and five red-tinted, multi-jointed claws protruded from its right gauntlet, each of them as long as a man's arm. Fitzroy's exposed head, with its long hair and short beard dyed green, looked faintly ridiculous, dwarfed as it was by the metal suit from which it protruded. But Shaw knew better than to underestimate the technology at his disposal.

Outwardly, he betrayed no sign of worry: he was far too skilled in the art of bluffing. In his mind, however, he formed a telepathic message to the rest of the X-Men. *I think,* he told them calmly, *we would appreciate that offer of assistance now.*

"I don't think that will be necessary," said a woman's voice.

Shaw raised an eyebrow in surprise as Fitzroy's expression went blank and his eyes rolled back into his head. He sidestepped neatly as the enormous suit of armor toppled towards him like a marionette with its strings cut: even with its kinetic force stolen, its weight would have crushed him. However, it never hit the floor. The air was rent around Fitzroy, screeching as it formed a flat circle of roiling energy into which he plummeted. As soon as he was out of sight, the gateway shut again, leaving only a dead silence in its wake.

It was broken by the slightest of sounds: the skittering of stones as Rogue shifted and began to pull herself out from beneath the rubble. It didn't occur to Shaw to help her.

He was staring at the new arrival: the woman who had spared him from a potentially unfortunate encounter. He had recognized her voice, of course, as soon as he had heard it. The fact that she had tapped into his telepathic conversation and responded to his thoughts had been another clue. But her appearance had changed so much.

She stepped into the light now, and Shaw could see her properly. Her face was older than he remembered: it hadn't just aged a year, it had become more lined and careworn. It was framed by her black hair, which she had let down. Most surprising of all, though, was her costume: she dressed in figure-hugging black leather, with one shoulder exposed. And around her waist she wore a red belt, the buckle of which displayed a familiar "X" logo.

"Hello Sebastian," said Tessa with a cool half-smile. "Welcome back."

Nightcrawler was the first of the reinforcements to reach Avengers Mansion. As Cyclops, Phoenix and Iceman hurried across Central Park back to Fifth Avenue, he simply concentrated on Sebastian Shaw's thoughts until he had formed a clear picture of his surroundings. That picture enabled him to teleport directly to the scene.

There was no disguising the noise and smell of his arrival. However, he materialized in the shadows at the top of the ruined staircase and clung to the wall with his adhesive toes, hoping to give himself time to take in the situation before his position could be pinpointed.

Rogue had already emerged from the wreckage and was giving Storm a hand to do likewise. Some of the mutates were standing too, but their appetites for violence had been quenched and most of them scampered or limped away while they could. Shaw himself seemed blind to the activity around him. He was staring suspiciously at a black-clad young woman, who looked back at him with wide, guileless eyes. It took Nightcrawler a moment to recognize the Black King's one-time personal assistant.

"You can show yourself, Mr. Wagner," said Tessa. "There is no danger."

Nightcrawler moved warily into the light. Tessa had long been an inscrutable foe of the X-Men, her telepathic ability complementing her computer-like mind. However, she had also been fiercely loyal to her master. Perhaps she was telling the truth.

He leapt forward, somersaulting to a graceful landing in the hallway between her and Shaw. "Then what happened here?"

"Fitzroy happened!" The snarled answer came from Wolverine, who was struggling to rise from beneath a heavy beam. Nightcrawler would have helped him, but his proud friend wouldn't have thanked him for it. Glowering at Shaw, Wolverine spat: "You pick some pretty lousy friends."

Tessa smiled. "He always did as I recall. But Trevor Fitzroy plays for Selene's team now."

"He has joined her Inner Circle?" asked Storm, brushing brick dust from her cloak.

"As its Black Rook," confirmed Tessa.

Shaw hadn't taken his eyes off her. "You shut down his mind," he said evenly.

"His bio-armor was in full attack configuration. He should have settled for a few less guns and kept the psi shielding up and running. Taken by surprise, he made an easy mark."

"Where is he now?" asked Nightcrawler.

"Teleported away. He's made improvements to that metal suit since you last met him. In an emergency, it taps into his own mutant power and opens a gateway for him back home to the Hellfire Club. It makes him difficult to remove from the board."

"We're beginning to realize that a lot has changed in our absence," sighed Storm.

"But you seem none too surprised to find us here," said Rogue.

"We've been expecting you," said Tessa.

"We?" repeated Shaw sharply, his gaze rooted to the "X" symbol on her belt.

"Times change," she shrugged, "and needs must. I go by the code name of Sage now."

"Indeed?" murmured Shaw.

"Where are the other three?" asked Sage. "Cyclops, Phoenix and Iceman."

"On their way," said Nightcrawler, wondering just how much she knew.

Sage acknowledged the information with a nod. "We need to leave this building before Fitzroy recovers and returns with more mutates, or with Hellfire Club demons." She was already making for the door. "Tell your friends to meet us at the corner of 49th Street and Sixth Avenue. I'll take you all to meet my group."

Do you trust her? Phoenix's telepathic message was meant for her husband only.

I don't know, responded Cyclops. *I get the feeling that even Shaw isn't sure.*

They had rendezvoused with the others as planned. Ever since then, Tessa—or Sage, as Cyclops supposed he ought to call her now—had been leading them through the near-deserted city. They were heading broadly south along Sixth Avenue, but their guide diverted them off the main road wherever possible, leading them down narrow alleyways and through neglected yards.

That's because she's wearing our colors, Phoenix pointed out.

An attempt to gain our trust at the expense of his? mused Cyclops. Shaw had stayed close to Sage throughout the journey, but the pair had exchanged no words. Looking at the Black King now, Scott couldn't help but think how vulnerable he looked, his green tunic torn at last, all but shredded so that his bare chest was exposed. *I'm not sure that would be logical.*

And if there's one thing we know about Tessa, it's that she's always logical.

I don't think we have a choice, he concluded. *We have to trust her. Look at us—we need a place to rest before we collapse from sheer exhaustion. And we need to take stock.*

Phoenix let out the mental equivalent of a sigh. *I'm not sure I even want to think about everything that's happened. To have lost all that time, Scott, to have let Selene do all this...and our friends....Hank, and who knows how many more...*

We can't afford to dwell on regrets, Jean. We can only deal with the situation as it stands.

It's just that it all happened so fast...we haven't even had time to think about what Blackheart did to us, what he showed us.

Cyclops shivered at the reminder. *Now that's something we should forget. None of that was real, Jean. If we start to believe otherwise, then Blackheart has won. If you want to take something from it, then take this: we mustn't ever compromise our ethics, no matter the temptation, no matter the cause.*

You're thinking about Hank, aren't you? You think he did the wrong thing, choosing to work with Shaw and the Hellfire Club.

I know he did it for the right reasons, thought Cyclops grimly, *I know he thought it was better to have a cure to the Legacy Virus exist in the hands of somebody like Shaw than to have no cure at all. But look around you, Jean. Look at what Selene did with that cure!*

None of this was Hank's fault, Phoenix protested. *He couldn't have foreseen Selene's involvement. That cure was meant to save the world.* A hint of bitterness had entered her internal voice. *So many people worked so hard to achieve something good, something worthwhile, and it only took one—just one—to take that work, that hope, and to twist it into something evil. It makes me wonder if we aren't pursuing an impossible dream after all.*

Impossible, maybe, returned Cyclops, *but I still think it's a dream worth fighting for.*

Two figures stood atop a Sixth Avenue skyscraper.

Up here among the rooftops of New York, the world was white, dominated by the shifting energies of the Black Queen's mystical force field. That field, however, provided no protection from an icy Winter wind, although the two figures were hardly aware of the cold. Their gazes were fixed upon the X-Men and their allies as they wended their way through the concrete canyons below them. They were a long way down; far enough that even Wolverine could not have caught scent of their secret observers. To normal eyes, they would have resembled nothing more than a procession of unusually colorful ants. These watchers, however, could make out every detail in their expressions, see every tear in their costumes and read every word on their lips.

"Seven X-Men in all," said the female observer in a voice devoid of emotion, "accompanied by Shaw and the rebel known as Sage."

"So Fitzroy defeated none of them." The man's voice was deeper, tinged with menace. It also betrayed a grim satisfaction at the failure of his colleague. "Perhaps now Selene will see the folly of inviting that young upstart into our Circle."

"Fitzroy is impatient," said the woman. "That has ever been his downfall."

"Whereas we, my dear," said the man, "have finally tracked our foes to their lair."

On the street below, Sage was ushering her comrades into an abandoned subway station. They hurried down the stone steps in single file, glancing furtively around them but failing to notice two dark specks four blocks to their north and eighty stories above them.

"The Black Rook falls," said the woman, her voice remaining as cold as ever, "but the Black Bishops move in for the kill."

CHAPTER 6

THE BEAST was only dimly aware of the sounds of destruction at first. He could hear explosions, but they seemed a long way distant. But the sounds became louder and closer until he couldn't ignore them any more. He surfaced from sleep, already throwing the covers from his bed as he swung his oversized feet to the floor. He was acting without conscious thought, his years of training kicking in and taking over his body, reacting to the first sign of danger. He had already yanked open the door of the dormitory when his brain caught up with his actions, his memories falling into place in a way that was becoming depressingly familiar.

The Hellfire Club. The Kree island. The Legacy Virus. The radiation treatments.

And now, his teammate Iceman stumbled backwards into him, hands raised as he struggled to fight off a seeming horde of demons with his ice-generating powers.

"Oh, my stars and garters!" exclaimed the Beast. Instinctively he leapt away, rolling into an alert squatting position in one corner of the room, ready to defend himself as he took stock of the situation. The demons were wearing Hellfire Club uniforms, which presumably made them agents of Selene. They crowded into the doorway after Iceman, fighting each other to be the first through but flinching from a bombardment of dart-shaped hailstones.

And that was when the side-effects of Hank's treatment crashed back in upon him. His display of athleticism had been a mistake. His stomach cramped and he was almost overcome by a dizzying rush to his head. He had been balancing on the balls of his toes, but he rocked back onto his heels and almost fell over. He closed his eyes and gritted his teeth, and heard Iceman's frantic voice: "Hank, you've got to get out of here!"

"Gladly," he responded tartly, knowing that the room had only one door. "And what manner of egress did you have in mind, pray?"

"The demons have bombs, but they aren't using them around here." Iceman tried to seal the doorway, but his attackers smashed through his ice barrier before it could harden. "They've been doing their best to get into this room. They want you, Hank." Three demons closed in upon him, their claws raised, forcing him to fall back again. He made a circular ice shield for himself and used it to fend off their blows.

A fourth demon set its eyes upon the Beast, and an expression of malicious glee lit its crack-skinned features. With an unearthly howl, it pounced upon him. He couldn't get out of its way—he didn't trust his weakened body not to betray him—so he blocked its lunge with the room's only chair, which splintered into pieces.

It took him a moment to deduce what Selene might want from him. His illness, he chided himself, must have slowed down his brain as well as his body. She wanted the blood that flowed through his veins: the blood that might yet prove to contain the precious cure to the Legacy Virus. But if he was taken from the Kree base now, if he was denied further radiation treatments, then the prognosis for his recovery was not at all hopeful.

Another explosion, much closer than the others, shook the room around him. His skin flushed cold as he realized that it had come from the direction of the laboratory.

Iceman had fallen. Without his conscious mind to regulate its temperature, his body armor was beginning to seep into the floor. The demons—about a dozen of them in all—crowded into the small room, and the Beast found himself backed up against the far wall, wielding a broken chair leg like a sword. To his surprise, the oncoming creatures hesitated as if waiting to see what he would do.

He summoned up all his remaining strength, threw the stick as a diversion and took a prodigious standing leap. He bounced off two heads, leapt over another six, handed off two more, performed a double somersault and landed behind the demons, the unguarded door in his sights. For an instant, hope soared in his heart—but then, as he had feared, he was engulfed by another wave of nausea. Stars exploded in front of his eyes and his legs almost buckled. He reeled, and suddenly the demons were upon him, clawing and biting as they bore him down to the floor.

A fresh emotion surged through him. He had been so close to curing the Legacy Virus at last, to saving countless lives, and now these monsters—and the bigger monster who had sent them—were taking that from him, from the world. The Beast was angry, and that anger lent him strength. Temporarily powered by adrenaline, he let out a primal scream, lashed out with his fists and feet and scored a series of palpable hits. For a minute or more, the demons couldn't lay a hand upon him. They were in disarray, struggling to restrain their foe but falling over each other, being tossed about like leaves in a hurricane.

It couldn't last. The Beast was overwhelmed by a combination of force of numbers and exhaustion. His arms became heavier until they felt impossible to lift, and his eyes lost focus until he couldn't see where he was aiming his blows anyway. His anger drained away until it was only a small voice inside him railing against the injustice of Fate.

And the world turned black around him, and stayed that way for a long time.

Moira MacTaggert heard the explosion as she was straining to push a lab bench—a huge block of solid metal—across the laboratory. She dropped behind it for protection as the large double doors strained inward—but thankfully, the heavy bolts held. To the naked eye, the doors appeared to be constructed from the same dull gray metal as the rest of the alien base, but it made sense that they would have been reinforced somehow.

The blast had deadened her ears, and she didn't hear Rory Campbell hobbling up behind her. She started as he spoke to her. "I've got the cover off the ventilation duct!" he shouted, obviously suffering from temporary deafness himself. He jerked his head toward the small annex in which he had been working. "I suggest we get out of here!"

Moira shook her head. "Not yet. Not while we can still slow yon beasties down at least!" She glanced across the room to where a ribbon of paper was being churned out of a narrow horizontal slit in the wall. At the first sign of the demon attack, she had instructed the Kree computer to print out the contents of its genetics database. But there was too much information and not nearly enough time. "Come on," she said, leaping back to her feet, "help me get this bench up against those doors."

"This is madness!" protested Campbell, but he did as he was told. He had lived and worked with Moira once, before his defection to the Hellfire Club, and he knew that it was rarely worth the effort of arguing with her. "You see what their bombs did downstairs. How long will this delay them—a few seconds?"

"Right now," said Moira grimly, "I'll take all the seconds we can get. We've worked too long and hard on this cure, made too many sacrifices, to let it be destroyed now."

The lab bench scraped and squealed reluctantly across the metal floor. Moira's leg muscles ached with the effort of pushing it, and her shoulder felt numb. She gasped with relief as it slid into place at last, but there was no time to relax. She had hoped that the demons would have withdrawn after placing their explosives—or that they might have collapsed the corridor outside, blocking their route to the laboratory altogether—but they were already skittering and scratching about on the other side of the doors again.

The two geneticists had barely had time to push a second bench up against the first when they heard the sound of footsteps pattering away. They were prepared, then—crouched behind the benches, fingers in their ears—when the next explosion came. This time, both doors were blown off their hinges; they buckled, but the benches held them in place. The eager demons returned within seconds, and twisted claws pried their way between doors and frame. Moira and Campbell pushed against the benches with all their might, but they were fighting a losing battle. Slowly but inexorably, they were forced to give way.

Abandoning the unequal struggle, Moira shed her white lab coat to reveal a yellow and black bodysuit. The contrast summed up the dichotomy of her life: as a physician she was trained to heal, but her public association with mutants meant that she often had to fight instead. Resigned to this fact, she had trained with the X-Men to ensure that she could at least hold her own in combat.

She looked for a weapon, and found a curved metal bar on the floor. She didn't know where it had come from—it was just part of the general clutter; for all she knew, it could have been a delicate component of an advanced Kree machine—but it would suit her purpose.

"Get out of here, Rory!" she yelled as the first demon squeezed itself through the widened gap between the doorway and the erstwhile barrier. Glancing over her shoulder, she saw that Campbell was hesitating. Turning on him, she physically propelled him into the annex. "I'm not being noble, you idiot, I'll be right behind you. But you're the slowest, so you get to go first. Go! I'll hold them off as long as I can."

Easier said than done, she thought wryly as Campbell accepted her point and left as quickly as his artificial leg would allow. Demons were pouring into the room now; she was only still alive because they were keener to destroy her work than they were to kill her. They were plucking explosive devices from the belts of their Hellfire Club uniforms, scattering them to every corner. Remembering her incomplete printout, Moira ran to it and snatched it from its slot—but even as she tried to fold it into a manageable bundle, a demon leapt at her. She dropped the paper and wielded her bar, delivering a good crack to the fiend's head. But its companions were beginning to turn their attentions to her.

Stubborn as she was, Moira MacTaggert had the sense to know when discretion was the better part of valor. She backed into the annex, swinging her weapon in front of her to discourage pursuit. Campbell had already got clear, and a ventilator duct lay open at ground level. She threw the metal bar at the nearest demon and hurled herself into the aperture.

She found herself in a cramped, square metal pipe; she could feel claws scrabbling at her feet, trying to hold her back, and she kicked out at them in desperation. Something whimpered, and suddenly she was free. She crawled as fast as she could, bumping her knees and elbows but not daring to slow down because she couldn't tell if she was being followed. Even as she reached an intersection, she had no choice but to trust to blind luck, to choose a direction at random and pray that it would lead her out of the base.

The pipe trembled and a fierce wave of heat rolled over Moira as the bombs in the laboratory behind her were detonated.

Storm's eyes were closed, as much to keep herself from seeing the horrors around her as to protect them from the dust that pried its way into her nose and mouth. Still, she couldn't help but picture the tons of debris that must have fallen upon her. She couldn't help but think about her childhood home in Cairo, of how quickly it had become a tomb, and of the hours she had spent buried therein, unseen by the over-stretched rescue teams.

As she fought to calm herself, a hopeful voice inside her pointed out that she hadn't actually *felt* anything hit her. She was held down nonetheless by something heavy pressed against her body. She was trapped. But the weight, she was surprised to real-ize, was not cold like stone or metal, it was warm and soft. It shifted in time to the sound of deep breaths that she had thought her own, and to the exhalations of hot air upon her cheek.

Her eyes snapped open, and she gasped to see Sebastian Shaw's face an inch above hers. His palms lay flat to each side of her head, his body braced by rigid forearms. His smoking jacket and his hair were almost white, and his features had lost their habitual smugness.

"I'm glad to see you're still with us," he said with a grim smile.

"You protected me?" croaked Storm hopefully, remembering his powers.

"From the force of the fall-in, yes," said Shaw, "but I am bearing a considerable weight upon my back, and my borrowed energy is draining fast." His smile had become pained and, squinting through the darkness, Storm saw beads of sweat upon his forehead.

"How long can you keep going?" she asked, dreading the answer.

"Twenty minutes, perhaps."

She slapped him across the face, but it was a feeble blow. Lying on her back like this, with debris piled up around her, she couldn't manage any better. "I'm afraid," said Shaw, "it will take a great deal more kinetic force than that to keep my cells charged."

"Every little," said Storm hoarsely, "may prolong our lives by precious seconds." She hit him again—and then a third time, using both hands but grunting with the effort.

"My dear Miss Munroe," smiled Shaw, "if I didn't know any better, I would swear you are enjoying this opportunity to assault me."

"What do you expect?" she retorted. "You have been playing games with me ever since I arrived on this island." As she spoke, Storm reached out with her inner self, finding pockets of air and drawing them towards her, teasing them through hairline cracks in the rubble. A shortage of oxygen could only make Shaw's task more difficult. She focused upon him, turning her fear into anger, giving herself no time to think about anything else. She set about his arms and shoulders with short, petulant child punches. "If you had not lured me down to the lowest level of your stolen base, we would never have found ourselves in this situation."

She had managed to whip up a slight breeze, and Shaw's expression softened appreciatively as it caressed his brow. "We have both survived far direr perils than this," he reminded her.

"You sound very confident."

"We have resourceful associates."

"Most of the X-Men are a long way away."

"I am assured that a rescue team is on its way."

"By Tessa?" deduced Storm. Only Shaw's telepathic personal assistant could have contacted him without her knowing it. "You trust her, don't you?"

"Implicitly—and that makes her uniquely special to me."

Ororo frowned. Her questing senses had found the base's stairwell, which, to judge by its air currents, was still largely open. She tried to summon some of that relatively fresh air to her, but it felt damp and heavy. A terrible fear struck her—and a moment later, her ears confirmed it as the truth. "Goddess!" she whispered.

"I wondered when you would hear it," said Shaw. The lines around his eyes had deepened and, with his dust-white hair, he suddenly looked like a much older man.

"The base is flooding!" Storm's voice was little more than a squeak. She was beginning to hyperventilate. *Don't think about it!* She gritted her teeth and pummeled Shaw with renewed zeal, as if hoping to make him strong enough to smash a tunnel out of here with his bare fists.

"You must try to relax," he said in a calm but forceful tone. "We can do nothing about the rising waters, but we don't need to exhaust our air supply faster than you can replenish it."

"A week ago," said Storm, still breathing heavily, "you had your Black Rook, Madelyne Pryor, delve into my thoughts and use my claustrophobia against me. Now you presume to advise me on how I should cope with my weakness? I don't know how to react to you, Shaw—and that is becoming a familiar dilemma."

"Believe me, Ororo," he insisted, "we are not going to die here."

His dark eyes glistened as he added: "And once we are freed, I will expect an answer to my proposal."

Bobby Drake slept soundly, his subconscious mind swathing him in protective dreams of his boyhood home back on Long Island with his parents. A small part of him was aware of a woman's voice telling him to wake up, but he refused to acknowledge it.

The voice became more insistent, almost painful, and Bobby realized that he couldn't shut it out because it was already inside his head. Jean Grey wandered into his dream in her Phoenix guise with her radiant smile, but hers was not the telepathic presence he had sensed.

He sat up with a start, crying out as he registered the sight of a woman clad in black leather standing over him and thought of Selene. He threw up his hands and reinforced his half-melted ice armor with a thought, although the effort sent a shard of pain into his skull.

"We have no time to waste," said the woman. "I have need of your powers."

Iceman finally recognized Shaw's lapdog, Tessa. She was dressed in full Hellfire Club regalia: a black leather teddy, boots up to her upper thighs and a red-trimmed cloak secured at her left shoulder by a trident-embossed clasp. The look was unusual for her, at least in public: he was used to thinking of her as a demure young woman, a silent pen pusher, but now she looked like a Black Queen in waiting. He suppressed a shiver.

"How long have I been out?" he asked, still feeling dizzy.

"Long enough," she said pointedly.

Iceman's eyes widened as he realized that the room around him was a mess, the bed upended, and he remembered the battle that had been fought here. "Hank!" he cried.

"Selene has him," said Tessa. "There's nothing you can do for him right now. Your other teammate, however, will not survive much longer without your assistance."

"Storm's in trouble? Well, why didn't you say so?" That was

just the wake-up call he had needed. Iceman shrugged off his grogginess and clambered to his feet, although he was a little unsteady and Tessa had to take his arm and guide him out into the corridor.

An embarrassing memory came to him unbidden, and he hoped that it was just a fragment of his fading dream. Or had he really mumbled "Just a few minutes more, mom," to the loyal confidante of one of the X-Men's greatest enemies?

"Yes," said Tessa without a trace of humor, "I'm afraid you did."

She led him to the stairwell, or rather to the gap where the stairwell had once been. Hellfire Club agents—human agents, he was relieved to note—were busy tying ropes to a wheel-mounted gun that looked like a cross between a cannon and a giant laser weapon from an old science-fiction B-movie. Iceman stared into a dark pit, frowning as a dim light spilled out of the corridor behind him and glinted off a rectangle of water.

"It's rising," he said, suspecting that the observation was unnecessary.

"That's why we need you," said Tessa. "You have to stop it. Freeze it."

"It won't be easy," he told her. "You can't just hold back the full force of an ocean."

"Two lives depend upon your being able to find a way, and quickly."

Iceman was already lowering the water's surface temperature. "Two?" he queried.

"Your friend is trapped on Level Nine along with Shaw."

"Uh-huh." He nodded to himself. Now that he had gleaned Tessa's true motive for helping the X-Men, life made just a little bit more sense. "And you're worried about Storm, right?"

"In fifty-four seconds," she said coldly, "it will become an academic point."

Iceman's throat went dry as he saw that the black water was lapping at the lower edge of a blocked corridor opening. "That's Level Nine?" He didn't wait for an answer. The water wouldn't stop rising until it had equalized its level with that of the ocean without. To stop it, he would have to hold back thousands of gallons, defying immense pressure. His lower lip protruded stubbornly as he concentrated, pushing himself to his limit. He was able to freeze a thin surface layer, but it cracked and shattered as the water pushed up from beneath it. It had begun to sluice down the Level Nine corridor now: the torrent found its own way through the wreckage, carrying lumps of ice in its flow. Bobby imagined the claustrophobic Storm, trapped and helpless as the frigid liquid began to pool around her.

He dropped his ice shell, diverting all his resources to his arduous task. He started to sweat as his mutant gene abandoned the unconscious chore of regulating his body temperature. He reached deeper into the water, drawing all the heat he could from its molecules. His own body was dehydrating with the effort, and his head was pounding. Soon, all he could feel—all he could sense—was the pain, and he couldn't tell if he was even having an effect any more.

He wasn't consciously aware of the moment when he was forced to surrender. As the world came back into focus, Iceman found himself doubled over, leaning on a wall for support, his lungs heaving. Bereft of his armor, he was clad only in a pair of black trunks into which was sewn a red "X" logo. Normally he didn't feel the cold, but now the beads of perspiration that rolled down his exposed skin felt like jagged ice shards.

At first he was only vaguely aware that Tessa had clicked her fingers and gestured toward the Hellfire Club agents. Then he realized that they had wheeled the laser-weapon-cum-cannon out over the edge of the precipice. They had taken the strain of the ropes that held it, and they were lowering it slowly but shakily into the pit.

"Hold on a minute!" he protested weakly. "I'm not sure if the ice is strong enough to take the weight of that thing." The truth was, he had no idea how much water he had succeeded in freezing; he was just relieved that, for the moment at least, it had apparently ceased to rise.

"It will have to be," said Tessa in a tone that brooked no objection. "My employer and your friend cannot have much time left. We must blast our way through to them."

The weapon landed clumsily, and a sharp crack echoed up the erstwhile stairwell. Iceman winced and took a deep breath, steeling himself. He could feel his frozen barrier losing its integrity, returning to liquid form. He fought to maintain it, to repair the cracks, as two Hellfire Club agents dropped the end of a rope ladder into the pit and scrambled down it.

A minute later, he winced as their weapon blasted fire at the obstructed corridor, bucking on its stand and sending fierce vibrations through his head.

Cyclops hadn't garnered much information from Iceman's hurried distress call. However, the X-Men had been on standby ever since they had left three of their own—not to mention a good friend—with Sebastian Shaw and the Hellfire Club. They had expected trouble. Their Lockheed SR-71 Blackbird stealth jet, modified with alien technology, made short work of the long journey to China and beyond, but Cyclops still fretted and wished he had stationed reinforcements closer to the Kree island.

Four of the Blackbird's occupants bailed out as the island came into view. Wolverine rode on Rogue's back, his keen eyesight locating their destination even in the dark. Phoenix used her telekinesis to lower herself and her husband. Nightcrawler stayed at the controls: he would teleport to join the others once he had put the plane down.

Cyclops and Phoenix made a gentle touchdown in the forest clearing that housed the raised entrance to the underground Kree base. Rogue and Wolverine had already landed and rushed inside. Cyclops took in the situation at a glance: smoke was drifting up the metal steps to dissipate on the night air, and Hellfire agents were coughing up bile and nursing fallen comrades. Doctors Moira MacTaggert and Rory Campbell were present: they were trying to help the injured, but they could do little more than wrap their wounds in scraps of clothing and offer words of comfort.

"Thank goodness you're here," said Moira, pale and breathless. "Half the base has collapsed. They've pulled a dozen bodies out of the wreckage—Shaw's goons, mostly—but there are still people down there. We were lucky to get out ourselves."

Cyclops nodded and opened his mouth to ask about his missing teammates. But the question was answered, at least in part, as a group of eight uniformed agents staggered out into the clearing, led by Tessa. Two of them carried a barely conscious Bobby Drake between them. Bringing up the rear of the procession, bedraggled and weary, their arms around each other's shoulders for mutual support, were Shaw and Storm.

"What happened?" asked Cyclops. "Where's Hank?"

Storm shook her head; it was clearly an effort for her to speak. "Taken," she rasped.

"By whom?"

The answer came from Shaw. "Selene," he said grimly.

Cyclops scowled. "If this is a trick..."

"Selene and I may have been allies once," said Shaw, "but evidently no longer."

Cyclops chose to accept his word for that, at least for the present. There was no more time for talking; despite the Beast's predicament, the rescue effort here had to take priority.

Under his direction, working as a team, the X-Men speeded up the process considerably. Phoenix probed the ruins for thought patterns, and Cyclops's optic blast pulverized the more difficult obstructions. This allowed Rogue and Wolverine to get in closer to the few survivors, whereupon they bent their combined strength to the delicate task of digging them free. Meanwhile, Nightcrawler's teleportation and his ability to cling to any surface enabled him to reach places that the others, for all their raw power, could not.

Some people, however, were already beyond help.

It did not seem to concern Shaw overmuch that he had lost nineteen of his men in the attack. To him, Cyclops supposed, they were nothing more than resources, a number at the end of a column, hired mercenaries who could be replaced with a telephone call. Moira, on the other hand, was wounded by the deaths of two of her fellow scientists, crushed beneath a falling ceiling as they had fled their quarters. She had only known Professor Travers and Doctor Scott for a week, but she mourned their loss all the same.

And there was something else.

"They didn't just destroy our work," said Rory Campbell dispiritedly as the tired X-Men rested in the clearing, enjoying a fine, refreshing watery mist that Storm had conjured up. Ororo herself was slumped against a tree, her eyes closed, breathing deeply. "They trashed all the equipment we'd need to ever have a hope of duplicating it."

"That's not to mention the small fact that they killed two of our colleagues," said Moira bitterly, "and took Hank, who understood what we were doing here better than any of us."

"There's no chance of salvaging anything?" asked Cyclops glumly.

"Och, you saw what it was like down there, Scott—and those demons deliberately targeted the laboratory. Selene wanted this project well and truly terminated."

"But your serum," said Phoenix, "it's still in Hank's bloodstream, isn't it?"

"Not the serum itself, not any more. But the super-cell it created: aye, that's in there right enough. And maybe—just maybe, mind—Hank's had enough radiation treatments to give it the strength it needs to have a fighting chance against this damned virus."

"Either way," sighed Campbell, "win or lose, the super-cell itself will be destroyed in the fight. If you want to rescue it as well as the Beast, you don't have much time."

"How long?" asked Cyclops.

Campbell shrugged and looked at Moira, who was equally uncertain. "It's impossible to say—but I wouldn't like to lay odds on it lasting much more than another twelve hours."

"Then our course of action is plain." Cyclops hadn't noticed

Shaw sidling up behind him; he wondered how long the Black King had been standing there, listening. "Tessa and my agents can deal with the situation here. We must retrieve the Beast from Selene's clutches."

"You make it sound like you'll be coming with us," said Rogue in an unkind tone.

"That is indeed my intention."

"Not a chance, Shaw," snarled Wolverine, his hackles rising.

"I think you will find," said Shaw, "that I know both my former Black Queen and the building she currently occupies better than any man alive."

"You mean the New York Hellfire Club?" asked Rogue. "Who's to say she's taken the Beast back there? She must know it's the first place we'd look."

"If she thinks she can hide anywhere," growled Wolverine, "then she doesn't know the X-Men very well."

"Indeed," said Shaw, "so where better to prepare for the inevitable confrontation than at the seat of her power?"

"He's right," said Phoenix. "Selene has allied herself with the demon Blackheart—and, according to our latest information, he's confined to the underground levels of the Hellfire Club building. With him by her side, she's almost invincible."

"May I also remind you," said Shaw, "that the Hellfire Club and Shaw Industries do still maintain a controlling interest in the Legacy project. What Selene has taken is as much my property as it is yours."

"What Selene has taken," said Nightcrawler, "is our friend—or are you forgetting him?"

"And we're not likely to rescue him without a fight," said Cyclops. "In that eventuality, we need to know we can rely on each other implicitly."

"Comes down to it," said Wolverine, "we don't know whose side you'll fight on."

"I believe we can trust him."

Cyclops was surprised by Storm's quiet interjection. She had opened her eyes and sat up, but she still looked weak. Her expression, however, was determined. He gave her a quizzical look, and she elaborated: "Sebastian saved my life down in the tunnels."

"Saved his own life, more like," scoffed Moira.

"No," said Storm, shaking her head firmly. "He didn't have to shield me, too."

A long silence followed, during which Cyclops tried to think of a way to refute that statement but could not. "He is also right," Storm added quietly. "His assistance could prove invaluable to us."

"OK," said Cyclops, unable to conceal his reluctance. "But this is an X-Men mission, Shaw—and as long as you're fighting with us, you'll follow my orders. Do you understand me?"

"Oh, I understand perfectly," said Shaw with an infuriating smirk.

The sun was rising, coloring the North Pacific Ocean in shades of red. But Shaw's mood was dark as he perched upon the edge of a plush leather couch in the back of a Hellfire Club jet and stared out of a tiny window at the water far below him. He had told the X-Men— much to their annoyance—that he had some business to attend to before he could meet them in New York. Still, as much of a lead as he gave them and as fast as their Blackbird was, he knew he could beat them there. He would reach the Club's headquarters on Hong Kong Island in a matter of minutes, whereupon his White Rook, Fitzroy, could open a portal between continents for him.

In the meantime, he glared at the portable computer in his lap as if it might explode. His agents had fetched it for him along with the plane. His old one had likely been flattened along with his office beneath the Kree island—although he would still have to retrieve it, whatever the cost or the danger to his people. He couldn't leave open the possibility that the files stored upon it might be salvaged by political opponents.

On the screen of the laptop, a trident icon was blinking. Shaw's partner in the Legacy project wanted to speak with him. Impossible as it seemed, Shaw had no doubt that he knew what had happened already. He had been putting off the moment when he would have to return his call. He sighed and glanced around, but the only other person in the spacious compartment was Tessa. She was lost in thought, presumably adapting to the loss of the island, running cost projections and situation analyses through her computer mind.

As Shaw's fingers flickered across the small keyboard, he set his lips into a line and his face into a studiedly neutral expression. His partner usually kept him waiting, but this time his digitally disguised image sprang onto the screen almost immediately. The man's eyes burnt in his blacked-out face. His voice, electronically filtered, was harsh with contempt, making the laptop's tiny speakers pop and crackle. "Can I trust you to do nothing, Shaw?"

Shaw bit his lip but fumed inwardly.

"First, you allow the X-Men to become involved in our project. Now, as a direct result of that folly, you have lost both the Beast and the island."

"Selene's intervention was unexpected," Shaw conceded, "but not necessarily unfortunate."

"It happened as a result of your ineptitude. It was your choice to welcome that witch back into your Inner Circle, to share your secrets with her when she had betrayed you before."

"And now," said Shaw through clenched teeth, "we have the opportunity to play off the X-Men against another force. I can turn this situation to our advantage."

"As you have promised before. You are running out of chances, Shaw."

"May I remind you," said Shaw, controlling his anger, "that we entered into this partnership on equal terms. I do not care to be spoken to as if I were a mere lackey."

"And may I remind *you*," snapped his anonymous partner, "that had I not raised the abandoned Kree island from the seabed and helped to fund your research into the Legacy Virus, then we could not have come even this far."

Shaw bowed his head as if accepting the point. The truth was that, of all the temporary alliances he had made in his life, all the dangerous deals he had struck for the sake of expediency, he had resented none more than this one. His current partner's money alone could not have bought him a stake in a project so close to the Black King's heart. His offer of alien technology, however, had proved impossible to resist.

Shaw had taken a tiger by the tail; he was under no illusions about that. He had to tread very carefully. He couldn't afford to reveal his contempt for this loathsome man just yet.

"There is still hope," he said evenly. "The cure may still exist in McCoy's blood."

"Clearly," snapped his partner. "That, I imagine, is why Selene took him in the first place." He leaned forward until his angry eyes seemed to fill the screen. "Get him back, Shaw."

"I intend to."

The communications link was abruptly broken, and Shaw allowed himself a secret scowl. He wouldn't put up with being belittled for much longer.

He sank back into the soft couch and formed his fingers into a steeple in front of his nose and mouth as he slipped into quiet contemplation. The X-Men, he knew from hard-earned experience, were formidable opponents. With him at their side, he prided himself that their chances against Selene were quite good. Whether they could defeat her in time to rescue their ailing comrade before the super-cell in his system extinguished itself was another matter. But Shaw's most challenging task would not be to dethrone the Black Queen; it would be to ensure that the Legacy cure, should it be retrieved, was kept out of the outlaw mutants' hands. Out of their hands, and out of the hands of his so-called partner.

Sebastian Shaw had been working towards this goal for a long time; since long before the X-Men, Selene or anybody else had chosen to interfere. He had invested a lot of time and money into the battle against the Legacy Virus. He had made plans and dreamt of possibilities, and all of them depended upon his being the sole benefactor of the eventual fruits of his labor.

Now, it seemed that his longed-for cure was almost within his grasp at last—albeit still tantalizingly out of reach—and he had no intention of sharing it with anybody.

CHAPTER 7

AT FIRST, Phoenix didn't know why Sage had taken the X-Men and Shaw into the subway station at 24th Street and Sixth Avenue. It appeared long deserted, its floor layered with dust and the windows of its ticket office cracked and cobwebbed. At some point, it had been the site of a fierce battle: one end of the station had collapsed, and much of the fallen brickwork and earth was fused into slag. Jean could detect no thought patterns. Still, Sage approached the blocked entrance to the PATH system—the train line that connected Manhattan to New Jersey—and spoke in a loud, clear voice: "Knight to Queen's 8, checkmate."

The obstruction fizzled out like a television picture cut off from its signal. A flight of steps was revealed, and Sage led the way down toward bright lights and the sound of low voices. She passed three teenaged boys, who stared at their colorfully clad visitors with saucer-wide eyes. "Lightshow has the power to create solid holograms," said Sage, "and with Booster here amplifying his power, he can make them all but permanent. DK will replace the dust that we disturbed on our way through." She glanced at Phoenix. "And we have four telepaths. We work on a rota system, keeping our presence masked from psi-sensitives."

"You're sure well hidden down here," said Rogue.

"We have to be."

Their arrival on the PATH platform was greeted by a sudden hush as a dozen heads turned towards them. To Phoenix's disappointment, she saw no familiar faces. If Sage's group represented the main opposition to Selene's rule, she would have expected to find at least some X-Men, past or present, among its members. Unless, she thought with a chill, there were no X-Men left. Perhaps she ought to have put the question to Sage; she was wearing the team's logo, after all, and must have had some contact with them. But she didn't think she was ready for the answer yet. She tried to console herself with the thought that so far she had seen only a small portion of the rebels' base. The platform and the tracks to each side of it had been partitioned into many smaller areas by white sheets hung from frayed ropes.

A young woman with a shaved head—another Genoshan mutate, presumably—had disappeared between two such sheets upon the X-Men's arrival. She returned now at the heels of a taller man with a confident gait and a regal bearing. His clothing was pure white, which made him look as if he had just stepped out of a detergent commercial; it also covered every inch of his skin. He wore a white jacket and breeches, white boots and gloves, a white waistcoat and a white cravat around the collar of his white shirt. He even wore a white mask, which covered his face and hair and left only his eyes exposed.

Sage went to him and slipped an affectionate arm around his waist. "Allow me to introduce the savior of mutantkind," she said.

The X-Men approached the pair more warily. "Looks like Hellfire scum to me," growled Wolverine.

"Selene only allows Black royalty into her Inner Circle," said the white-clad man, his voice muffled by his white mask. "She is too arrogant—and yet also too weak—to expose herself to contrasting opinions."

"So, let me guess," said Nightcrawler, "you must be the White King, *nicht wahr?*"

"For now, I am merely a White Knight, charged with leading my troops to victory."

"Whereupon," said Phoenix, "you will be 'crowned,' I expect."

"Indeed," said the White Knight. "But I will be a benevolent King. My first act will be to lower the barrier around this city. Then I shall ensure distribution of the Legacy cure to all who need it. I will liberate New York, and mutants worldwide."

"If your motives are so pure," said Cyclops, "why the mask?"

"I might ask the same question of you, my friend."

"The White Knight is the figurehead of our movement," said Sage. "If Selene learned his true identity, she would hunt him down and subject him to unimaginable torments. If his followers do not have that information, then they cannot be tortured for it."

"You must all be tired," said the White Knight. "I know what you have been through to reach us. We have prepared quarters for you, if you would care to follow me."

Phoenix, like the rest of the X-Men, looked to Cyclops for his lead. She knew that her husband was exhausted and would welcome nothing more than a few hours' sleep, but he concealed it well. "I think we have a few things to discuss first," he said tersely.

"On the contrary," said Sage, "everything is well in hand."

"And you must get some rest," said the White Knight, "before we make our final assault upon Selene tomorrow night."

He turned and swept through a join in the hanging sheets, as if in no doubt that he would be followed. Cyclops hesitated for a second before proving him right. His teammates took their cue from him. Shaw, who had been silent since they had left Avengers Mansion, stepped through the gap alongside Storm. Sage brought up the rear. Phoenix fell into step beside the former Tessa as they made their way down a narrow corridor formed by sheets on each side. It was like walking through a circus tent—except for the intermittent sound of hacking coughs, which served to remind her that New York was a city under self-imposed quarantine.

"How many rebels are there?" she asked.

"Thirty-seven," said Sage with typical precision, "in addition to our leader and myself."

"I didn't recognize anybody." It was a simple statement of fact, but the possible implications of it caused a sick, nervous flutter in Phoenix's stomach as she spoke.

"Twenty-four of our people are Genoshan mutates, who came here seeking Selene's cure. A further seven were made aware of their mutant genes only when they became infected."

Phoenix was about to ask about the remaining seven when one of them pushed her way into the makeshift passageway from a small compartment beside it. She was a young woman, short and slender, with blonde hair cut short at the back but falling over her face at the front. Unlike most of her colleagues, who were dressed in simple fatigues or Genoshan slave uniforms, she wore a stylish trouser suit which had no doubt been expensive. Jean recognized her, but she couldn't quite place her. Most likely, she had seen her picture in the X-Men's files. The woman looked startled, and she turned away and threw her hands up to her face as if hoping to hide it. Phoenix followed the broken line of her sight, and was interested to see that it ended at Sebastian Shaw. He didn't appear to have seen the woman.

The White Knight dropped onto the left-hand set of tracks and, brushing aside a final white sheet, led his guests into the tunnel. A train had been stranded there, its doors jammed open. The X-Men made their way in single file between the vehicle and the tunnel wall, and followed their host on board. The seats had been ripped out of the carriage, five camp beds and a pile of blankets jammed into the narrow space instead. "We have made our finest rooms available to you," said the White Knight with a trace of humor. "The five gentlemen can sleep in here; the ladies will find a further three beds in the adjoining carriage."

"Sage wasn't exaggerating then," said Nightcrawler. "You certainly were expecting us."

The White Knight cleared his throat. "We have known for some time of Selene's spell, and we have been awaiting your return."

"Unfortunately," said Sage, "we couldn't greet you when you arrived. We couldn't station agents too close to the Hellfire Club without their being sensed. We had to wait until you had escaped from the Black Queen, and then find you."

"We shall leave you now," said the White Knight, "and talk more tomorrow. I am sure you have many questions."

That was certainly true—but right now, those questions didn't seem to matter. It was still early evening, but the X-Men hadn't slept last night and Phoenix was weary. She wanted to draw a line beneath the events of this difficult day. Perhaps things would look better in the morning. Perhaps, at least, she would be able to think more clearly, to start to deal with everything that had happened. She followed Rogue into the next carriage and lowered her aching body onto a camp bed, covering herself with warm blankets.

Storm, she realized, had lingered in the doorway to conduct a muttered conversation with Wolverine. Phoenix shouldn't have been able to overhear them, but she inadvertently caught the pair's surface thoughts, which served to amplify their words for her.

"Just thought you ought to know," said Wolverine, "I caught the White Knight's scent. Didn't quite believe it at first—thought I must've been mistaken—but now I'm sure."

Storm nodded. "I don't know how it can be possible either."

"You recognized him too, right?"

"His body language, his speech patterns...yes, my friend, I recognized him."

They parted then, Wolverine returning to his own carriage as Storm took the final bed in this one. Phoenix drifted into sleep, with one more puzzle to ponder on when morning came.

Shaw lay still and listened to the sounds of breathing—and the occasional snore—until he was sure that none of his roommates were awake. He had been through as much as most of them, but his energy-absorbing powers had allowed him to refresh himself repeatedly, and he had needed no more sleep than usual. His body clock had been thrown off by his journey through time, but he guessed that midnight was some hours past, dawn yet to come. The light from the platform, some of which had found its way into the train carriage last night, had been extinguished and he could hear no voices.

He levered himself out of his camp bed, wincing as it groaned beneath his weight. He tiptoed towards the nearest door, but caught his breath as he saw that the one bed in his way appeared empty. Then he remembered that the berth was occupied by Nightcrawler, whose mutant gene allowed him to blend into the darkness. Concentrating, he was able to discern the outline of the goblin-like X-Man, fast asleep.

As he stepped out into the tunnel, however, he was assailed by the stink of cigar smoke. Wolverine was blocking his way to the platform, leaning against the side of the carriage. "And where do you think you're slipping away to, 'Your Majesty'?"

"I find myself restless," said Shaw. "I desired some fresh air." He looked pointedly at Wolverine's cigar, and the Canadian X-Man seemed to accept his explanation. He allowed the Black King to squeeze past him and continue on his way.

As he hauled himself up onto the platform, Shaw heard Wolverine's soft but threatening growl behind him. "I'm watching you, bub."

A few night-lights had been jury-rigged into the roof wiring to dispel the subterranean blackness. Shaw's eyes adjusted slowly to the desultory illumination as he made his way along the platform and peered into each partitioned cubicle in turn. His gaze was met by more than one pair of wide eyes from the camp beds therein, but nobody spoke to him nor raised an alarm. He saw no sign of Sage or the White Knight, but presumed that their quarters were housed further along the train or in a second one at the other end of the station. Either way, he had no doubt that they would be together, in adjoining rooms if not in the same bed. He was hurt by that thought. As often as he had been betrayed in the past, he had come to rely on Tessa, trusting her as he had trusted few others in his life. Bad enough that she had thrown in her lot with the X-Men in his absence; now she also had a new master, to whom she showed as much loyalty as she ever had to him.

He put such thoughts from his mind. It was not Tessa who concerned him at present.

He found the young blonde woman asleep on her back, hair splayed across her pillow, a displaced blanket revealing an elegant silk negligee. Three confident strides took him to her side. He dropped to his haunches and placed one hand across her nose and mouth, the other atop it. Her sleep became fitful as her brain slowly registered the fact that she could not breathe. A second later, her alarmed eyes snapped open.

"Good morning, Ms. Payge," said Shaw with a cruel smile. "I do apologize for my earlier rudeness. I trust you didn't think I had forgotten you?"

The world distorted around him. The white sheet walls of Reeva Payge's quarters became screeching ghosts, reaching out to entangle the unwanted intruder. Shaw had been prepared for this. Even with her mouth covered, Payge could sub-vocalize notes which, although beyond the range of human hearing, wreaked havoc with the neurochemistry of the brain. He closed his eyes, but he could still see the leering phantoms and feel the floor pitching beneath him. He ignored the illusion and the dizziness that came with it, and focussed upon his own body, determined not to move a muscle.

"Not a very bright idea, Ms. Payge," he said through gritted teeth. She was more powerful than he had thought. Not powerful enough, though. "I am well aware of your abilities, and I can assure you that they won't keep me from suffocating you, should you force me to do so."

His surroundings returned to normal, although he wasn't sure if Payge had given up because of his threat or because she had run out of breath. He had pinched her nostrils closed; she could still suck in air through her covered mouth, but not nearly enough. She tried to remove his hands, but he was pressing down too hard. She ceased her struggle at last, and her eyes pleaded with him for mercy.

"That's better," said Shaw. "Now I am going to take my hands away in a moment—and, when I do, you will have one chance and one chance only to speak to me. If you wish to survive this night, you will use that chance to answer one simple question."

Beneath his hands, Reeva Payge nodded eagerly, her eyes saying: *Anything.*

"I have been waiting a long time to find you, Ms. Payge—you or one of your colleagues. I know all about you. I know you served on the Inner Circle of the New York Hellfire Club under my son. All I want to know is this: where is he? Where is Shinobi?"

He loosened his hold, then, just a little, and Payge's chest heaved as she sucked in great lungs full of air. Shaw waited until finally, in a halting voice, she gave him his answer.

A minute later, he sank into a canvas chair in the small communal area at the front end of the platform. He hadn't expected to find one of his son's minions here, of all places. After all this time. Her presence had complicated things. Now, he had two matters to attend to; two tasks that were each as important as anything he had ever done. He burned with impatience to get started, but he was trapped in this hovel by the boy Lightshow's so-called solid holograms. He had no doubt that the tunnels would be blocked as the stairs were. His original plan had been to wake the young mutant and force him to lower his barriers—but that might cause a commotion which, with Wolverine on the alert, he could well do without.

Somebody had left a combat jacket slung over a collapsible table. Shaw took it and donned it over the shredded top half of his boiler suit. He settled back in the chair again, and fought down his own mounting frustration as the slow seconds ticked by. Whatever the situation, he had always known the importance of biding his time.

Wolverine had familiarized himself with the layout of the station, in case of an emergency. One of his concerns had been that an enemy could stumble upon the rebels simply by exploring the sub-way system; however, a hundred yards beyond the train on which the rest of the X-Men slumbered, the tunnel ended at a brick wall. He had tested it, feeling that its texture wasn't quite right. A solid hologram, then. He had given it a few experimental taps and felt it vibrate beneath his knuckles. Its function was to deflect attention rather than force; chances were, it wouldn't take much of the lat-ter to get through it.

When his worst-case scenario was realized, then, he was pre-pared.

He leapt into action before the echoes of the explosion had died down. He popped his claws and clattered them along the side of the train as he loped past it, shouting: "Heads up people, we're under attack!"

He caught the decaying stench of Selene's demons before he saw them. They rushed out of a pall of smoke towards him, at least eight of them, and he greeted them with deadly force. But the demons and the smoke overwhelmed his sensitive nostrils, and he didn't detect the less pungent scent of an old foe until it was too late.

She reared up in front of him and took him by surprise. Her claws were as sharp and unyielding as his, and he roared in animal pain as she raked them across his face. He made to strike back, his anger fuelled by the burning lines on his cheek, but she had already sprung away from him with remarkable agility and grace. Snarling, he lunged for her, but the demons held him back. They were trying to bear him down by sheer weight of numbers, and he was forced to concentrate on extricating himself from a headlock. As he was thus distracted, the woman darted in behind him and struck again, her claws biting into his back.

As Wolverine's rage grew, he abandoned his attempts to fight defensively. He lashed out as hard as he could, not caring what damage the demons did to him as long as he could hurt them in return. Three fell and didn't rise again, but a fourth got a hold on his back and wouldn't let go. He sensed the woman moving in behind him and twisted around, bracing himself against the demon and meeting her charge with a two-footed kick to the gut. He felt like he had stubbed his toes on the hull of a battleship, but he succeeded in repulsing her.

A cold smile spread across her pale face, and her dead eyes glowed. She returned his glare with a calculating gaze, waiting for her next chance. She flexed the foot-long, double-jointed fingers that Wolverine knew were artificial. They were forged from metal, laced like his own claws with adamantium, wrapped in artificial flesh and sharpened to cruel points. Much of her body was artificial too, replaced in an insane quest to make herself stronger and more durable. Her legs were armor-plated, and Wolverine doubted that there was much flesh, blood or bone left beneath them. She wore a scarlet and white Japanese-style headdress and robes as if to remind him of the Samurai training that had made her a deadly warrior even before her surgical enhancements. She had done all this to herself for one reason: to become Wolverine's nemesis. Once, she had been called Yuriko Oyama; now she answered to the name of Lady Deathstrike.

His senses gave him advance notice of the arrival of two team-mates. It took them seconds to enter striking range, but to him the delay seemed huge. Then a blast from Cyclops's eyes stunned the demon on his back and dislodged it, as Phoenix hurled a second creature away with her mind. Freed at last, Wolverine lunged at Deathstrike. Her torso, he knew, was protected, so he aimed for her eyes. She was too able, and he was too hurt already, for him to risk holding back.

She was fast. She pulled her head away from him, but he marked her face. She struck back but, unhindered now, Wolverine dropped beneath her arms, drove his shoulder into her stomach to unbalance her and delivered a double uppercut to her jaw.

The Hellfire Club demons had tried to follow him, but Cyclops and Phoenix had reached them and they were keeping each other busy for now. "Looks like it's just you and me, lady," snarled Wolverine as he and Deathstrike circled, each looking for an opening, each waiting for the other to let down his or her guard.

"I would have it no other way, gaijin," she hissed. The skin of her cheek was already being regenerated, knit back together by microscopic nanites; her artificial healing factor was at least as impressive as Wolverine's natural one.

"Yeah? Looked to me like you were quite happy to hide behind Selene's foot soldiers a few seconds ago. What's up—they change the definition of 'honor' while I was away?"

"It is not my fault if you were foolish enough to be caught alone."

"What are you doing here, Deathstrike?" sneered Wolverine. "You ain't a mutant, you're a cyborg. Selene let you through the barrier in return for doing her dirty work, did she?"

"My agreement with Selene—" Deathstrike began, but he didn't hear the rest. He saw an opportunity and seized it. He flew at her, concentrating his attack upon her face again; he cut her skin to ribbons, exposing metal beneath it, but she wasn't hurt. Mechanical modifications to Deathstrike's nervous system ensured that her brain no longer received pain signals. Wolverine should have been so lucky.

Deathstrike was an excellent hand-to-hand fighter, perhaps even too good. Her apparent savagery masked her mastery of the martial arts. Wolverine knew a few moves himself, but she kept him on the defensive, forever having to shift his body weight as she tried to throw him, denied an opportunity to take the initiative. Had he not already been wounded, had she not begun the battle with the advantage of numbers, then things might have been different. As it was, it was all he could do to keep his opponent busy.

The merest slip on his part and she would kill him.

Even as the X-Men had leapt out of the subway train, they had heard screams from the platform and realized that, whatever was happening, it was a two-pronged attack. As Cyclops and Phoenix had rushed to help Wolverine, Rogue had headed in the opposite direction, followed by Storm and Iceman. Nightcrawler had teleported ahead of her.

At first, it was difficult to tell what was going on. The dim lighting cast indistinct, undulating shadows on the hanging white sheets. Storm took to the air for a better perspective, but a blood-curdling shriek just a few meters ahead of Rogue convinced her that she had no time to wait for a report. She waded into the labyrinth, trusting to her tough skin to shield her from unexpected attacks. She found herself in an empty sleeping cubicle.

"Rogue," called Storm from above her, "an assailant is heading your way at two o'clock."

She turned, in time to watch as a partition was torn down the middle and a Hellfire Club demon sprang through the gap. It seemed pleased to have found a victim, and saliva dribbled from its mouth in anticipation. Rogue's fists soon changed its expression.

A klaxon alarm began to sound; it was tinny and swamped in static, and she guessed that it was being broadcast over the station's public address system. "This base has been compromised," reported the calm voice of Sage. "All resistance fighters will evacuate immediately and regroup at Location D." Simultaneously, she heard Phoenix's voice in her head, informing her of the identity of one of the intruders.

Rogue stumbled into the main passageway to find a melee in progress. A blinding flash—Storm's doing, no doubt—seared her eyeballs but allowed her to see that Nightcrawler was fending off another three demons. He teleported into the air above them, wrapped his prehensile tail around one of the ropes from which the sheets hung, and swung past them like a trapeze artist. One of the demons tried to follow him by climbing a sheet, but only brought it down upon its own head and those of its fellows. Nightcrawler confused them further by striking out from above, behind, beside them while they were blinded.

Rogue threw him a quick grin and a wink as she flew by. She had set her sights upon another figure, who had appeared at the end of the passageway. He was taller—or perhaps simply more upright—than the demons. She realized who it had to be a second before she saw him clearly; after all, if Deathstrike was here, then he couldn't be too far away. She was still too late to react, though, as beams of force stabbed from his eyes. The pain knocked her out of the sky, but she gritted her teeth, picked herself up and continued towards him on foot.

"Where is Shaw?" he demanded in a deep, resonant voice.

"Y'all know how to make a girl feel unwanted," complained Rogue. "Shaw's dance card is all full at the moment, so you'll just have to tango with me, Donny boy."

Donald Pierce met Rogue's charge unflinchingly. She had forgotten how strong he was—or perhaps he had made himself stronger. Like Deathstrike, he was a cyborg. When the X-Men had first encountered him, as a member of Shaw's Inner Circle, he had passed for human. Some years and many self-inflicted operations later, he looked like a tall, gaunt android. His regal red robes disguised the alterations somewhat, but the powerful arms that shot out from beneath them to return Rogue's blows were pure metal. He wore a black headdress, the inside of which was doubtless imprinted with circuitry, and long scars on his face betrayed the fact that the skin had been folded back to allow devices of various kinds to be implanted.

There was something wrong with his eyes and, as Rogue grappled with him, she realized what it was. He had three eyeballs in each; knowing Pierce, at least two of them had to be weapons. She held him in a headlock, forcing him to look away from her so that he couldn't blast her again. Her ears were full of the klaxon alarm, and of Sage's voice as it repeated its message word for word. It was recorded, she realized, playing on a loop tape.

"I'm not interested in you, girl," snarled Pierce, "only Shaw. Step away from me now and I will allow you to live."

"That's mighty big of you, sugar," said Rogue, pummeling him in the face, "but you'll forgive me if I don't take the word of a self-mutilating freak for that."

He let out a furious roar, flexed his muscles of steel and sent Rogue reeling. Suddenly, she was in danger from his eyes again;

he stunned her with her another blast and leapt on top of her, metal fingers reaching for her throat. She staggered backward into one of the cubicles and fell onto a camp bed, flattening it. Pierce landed on her like a ten-ton weight. She succeeded in rolling out from beneath him—but before she could regain her footing, he drove a fist into the back of her head. She returned the gesture in kind, but stars were exploding in front of her eyes. She blinked, and suddenly Pierce was lifting her off the floor by her neck.

She heard footsteps, and hoped for a moment that reinforcements were arriving. Two young mutates came into view, both reacting with horror when they saw what was happening. They ran for the exit, giving Rogue and her attacker a wide berth. So much for the White Knight's "resistance fighters," she thought. And her teammates were obviously still occupied with the demons and who knew what else, oblivious to her predicament.

Pierce was channeling more power into his hydraulic fingers, strengthening his grip. Rogue was used to considering herself near invulnerable, but even she had her limits. It was getting hard to breathe, and black shapes crowded her vision. She kicked against him with her dangling feet, but only hurt her toes on his armor. She clamped her hands onto his head, dug her thumbs into his eyes and tried to pry his headdress loose in the hope that it would take a few mechanical parts of his brain with it. It came free at last, the tiny wires on its underside sparking and popping, and the dead skin of Pierce's scalp peeled back beneath it to reveal the top of a metal-plated skull. His eyes fizzled and sent an electric shock into Rogue's hands, which made them spasm and lose their hold. His face went blank for a second, but then his expression of clenched-tooth fury returned and his fingers tightened further around her throat.

It was time for desperate measures. Rogue was weakening, and her arms felt leaden but she forced them to move, forced her right hand to meet her left and to remove its green glove. Her eyeballs had rolled back into her head and she could no longer see, but she reached out blindly, finding metal, metal, metal...*flesh*!

It took only the briefest of contacts, her bare skin to Pierce's, to activate Rogue's mutant ability. His thoughts, his memories, rushed into her head and threatened to overwrite her own. As she struggled to hold on to her sense of self, she could feel her body changing too, taking on the characteristics of his. She didn't know whether to feel disappointed or relieved that his cybernetic augmentations were not part of the deal. Without them, Pierce had no more strength than a normal human being—less than most, in fact—but at least she didn't have to learn what it felt like to have enslaved herself, body and soul, to machinery.

It was hard enough to cope with Pierce's hatred. It was a living thing, a black snake which slithered its way through her mind and left a trail of poison. She hated the X-Men for standing in her (*his*) way, preventing her (*him*) from attaining the power and respect that was due to her (*him*). But her loathing for them was nothing compared to that which she felt for the Hellfire Club. She hated Fitzroy, but she was forced to work alongside him. She had only contempt for Selene, but she (*he*—this was *Donald Pierce*, not her; Rogue would be lost if she forgot that) saw some advantage in serving her as a Black Bishop for the present.

Most of all, Pierce hated the man who had expelled him— twice—from the Hellfire Club's upper echelons. He remembered being hurled from Sebastian Shaw's helicopter, left to die at the frozen heart of the Swiss Alps. Rogue burnt with the all-consuming desire for bloody vengeance against Shaw—and just for a moment, nothing else mattered to her and she was prepared to go to any lengths, do anything to herself, to achieve it.

Then the moment passed and she found herself on the floor, her own personality dominant again, and Donald Pierce was reeling as if out of control, his hands clutched to his head. He steadied himself and revealed his face. It was blank again, his mouth hanging open, and his movements were jerky. He looked like a zombie. It took Rogue a second to deduce that her energy drain had knocked him out, that only his cybernetic limbs and computerized systems were keeping him standing. As his eyes flashed, however, she realized that they were doing more than that. She moved sluggishly, but fortunately he did too, and she was able to avoid an optic blast that tore a hole through the canvas of the broken camp bed.

Pierce's head turned to track her, and Rogue prayed that she could keep dodging him until some of her strength returned.

At that moment, however, a bolt of electricity stabbed down from the ceiling. Pierce was enveloped in a blue corona and one of his eyes exploded. He didn't fall, but his arms fell to his sides and his chin lolled onto his chest. Storm landed beside Rogue and helped her to her feet. "Hurry," she said. "I think we should gain some distance before Pierce has a chance to recover and reboot his systems."

"We're running?" asked Rogue, surprised but not entirely unhappy with the idea.

"I have been in telepathic contact with Phoenix. The White Knight and his followers have already evacuated. We have nothing to gain by prolonging this conflict."

"You've sold me," said Rogue. "Let's go!"

Phoenix was relieved when the last demon fell. She had restricted herself to fighting them hand-to-hand or with her telekinesis, because reaching into their minds—as she had discovered to her cost a year ago—was like plunging into a pit of black bile from which she feared she might never be able to resurface.

Deathstrike's mind, however, was little better. It was cold, and its contents were so fragmented that they were almost impossible to make sense of. Phoenix shuddered with revulsion as she realized that the cyborg's implants had taken over some of her brain functions. She couldn't detect thoughts that were being transmitted through wiring, nor read memories that were stored on hard drives.

Cyclops had a different problem: Wolverine and Deathstrike were fighting at such close quarters, their moves so fast and precise, that it was hard for him to get a bead on the villain without endangering his teammate. He fired one optic blast, which staggered her for a second and gave Wolverine a brief advantage—but before he could target her again, she had recovered, and now she was deliberately using her opponent as a shield.

Phoenix focused her mind upon Lady Deathstrike's foot, pressure building up behind her eyes. It took only a small telekinetic nudge at a critical moment to shift the cyborg's center of gravity. Wolverine did the rest, throwing Deathstrike over his shoulder before she could adjust to the upset. She landed on her back, and Cyclops pounded her with the full power of his eyes. She was still conscious, struggling to rise against the beams of force, until Wolverine launched himself at her in a flurry of fists and claws.

"I could've handled her myself," he said gruffly as he stood over Deathstrike's prone form. Phoenix smiled to herself; it would have been unwise to dispute his claim out loud.

"The X-Men are a team, Wolverine," said Cyclops, tight-lipped. He turned to Phoenix. "What's the situation? Where are the others?"

She had anticipated the question, and was already looking for Storm's mind. She found it, and reported that the African X-Man was leading Rogue, Nightcrawler and Iceman to the surface. "We'll leave through the tunnel," decided Cyclops. "It's best to remain in small groups if Selene's demons are on the prowl. Do we have any idea where this emergency hideout of Sage's might be; this 'Location D'?"

Phoenix was about to answer in the negative when she realized that Wolverine was kneeling beside his fallen foe, his claws poised above her heart as if to strike. Cyclops saw him at the same time; he whirled around and, without stopping to ask questions, stung his teammate's hand with a low-intensity optic blast.

"What the hell are you doing?" cried Wolverine, leaping to his feet.

Cyclops squared up to him. "I was about to ask you the same question."

"That psycho would kill us all without a second thought. You might not be attached to your hide, Summers, but I'm not giving her another chance to scalp mine."

"That's not how we operate, Logan."

"Yeah, yeah, I've heard it all before. 'X-Men don't kill.' But in case you hadn't noticed, this ain't Kansas any more—and desperate times breed desperate measures."

"Not while I'm in charge of this team," snapped Cyclops. "Now sheathe those claws and step away from Deathstrike—and that's an order, mister!"

Wolverine glared at his team leader mutinously, until Phoenix stepped between them. "I think we should talk about this later," she said gently. "Selene knows where we are now. We could face another attack at any moment."

"Jeannie's right," conceded Wolverine. He popped his claws back into their housings, but his eyes were still narrowed and fixed on Cyclops. As the trio of X-Men hurried down the subway tunnel, away from the compromised PATH station, Phoenix heard him muttering under his breath: "But this discussion ain't over yet. Not by a long shot."

CHAPTER 8

A BRIGHT YELLOW light spilled out of the brownstone mansion house and seemed to stain the Fifth Avenue sidewalk. New York was twelve hours behind Hong Kong but, although its night was now giving way to the dark hours of morning, the muted sounds of revelry continued unabated. Membership of the local branch of the Hellfire Club had fallen off under Selene's stewardship, or so the X-Men had heard, but it evidently still held its attractions.

Nightcrawler couldn't understand why. It was well known that the Black Queen was consorting with a demon, and that she had turned the catacombs beneath her new abode into her own personal underworld. She had paraded both facts in front of an unwitting audience on Halloween night, only a month ago, shortly after she had claimed her throne. The Hellfire Club's rich patrons had dabbled with the trappings of diabolism for over two centuries, but this was different. Kurt didn't know how they could even set foot across Selene's threshold, knowing that to do so was to place their souls in jeopardy.

Many of them, he supposed, knew no better: bored billionaires looking for a vicarious thrill, a temporary release from their dull lives, tempted by the allure of the dark. They probably didn't quite believe the rumors or didn't understand the significance of them. They didn't have his experience. Nightcrawler couldn't prove that a Hell existed—although he had faith that it did—but his time with the X-Men had exposed him to many infernal realms that were only too real. He knew what evils lurked in the deepest dimensions, and the idea that foolish men still thought they could play games with such terrible entities scared him silly.

Ironically, most of the people in the Hellfire Club's ballroom at present would probably have fled in fear at the sight of Kurt's own demonic form; either that or attacked him out of blind panic. To remain inconspicuous, he was forced to use an image inducer. This pocket-sized technological marvel cast a holographic field around him, which made him appear human. In fact, thanks to Nightcrawler's tongue-in-cheek humor, it made him look rather like his childhood role model, swashbuckling movie star Errol Flynn.

For the rest of the X-Men, more prosaic disguises were adequate. They loitered inside the perimeter of Central Park, watching the building across the road but looking to the untrained eye like nothing more than a group of friends taking in some fresh air before they went home. They were, of course, ready to shed their outer garments in a second should circumstances call for their "working clothes." They lost more overcoats and hats that way...

"I can't detect any trace of Hank inside the building," said Phoenix.

"That's hardly surprising though, is it?" said Nightcrawler.

Phoenix agreed. "Selene is a powerful telepath herself. She could easily mask his presence."

"We'll proceed on the assumption that she does have Hank in there," decided Cyclops, "until we find proof to the contrary."

"Then I say we move now," said Wolverine, "Shaw or no Shaw."

Cyclops shook his head. "Too many people could get caught in the crossfire."

"If they don't want to get hurt, they'd better have the sense to get out of our way."

"They're innocents, Logan."

"That's relative," contested Wolverine. "No one ever signed up to the Hellfire Club for its charitable works. Anyway, chances are that's why Selene threw this bash in the first place; to keep us from going in there and nailing her till it's too late."

"Wolvie's got a point there," said Rogue. "If we wait for this here shindig to wind up, we could be standing here till mid-morning. Hank might not have that long."

Cyclops nodded. "OK, I accept that—but I'd still like to keep this operation as low-key as possible. I don't want to go in there with all guns blazing."

"What else do you suggest?" asked Rogue. "Walking up to Selene's front door and knocking didn't do you a whole power of good last time."

"And nor did trying to slip in the back way," said Iceman rue-fully. Nightcrawler hadn't been present when four of his team-mates had last confronted Selene, but he knew it had not gone well. The Black Queen's mutant senses and mystical abilities com-bined to make it near impossible to sneak up on her. And this time, she would be expecting visitors. He wouldn't have been surprised to learn that she was watching them at this very moment.

"We've agreed that the Beast is probably being kept on the lower levels," said Cyclops, "where Blackheart can guard him. If we can get down there without disturbing the party guests and keep any combat confined to the catacombs..."

"I believe Logan knows the sewers beneath the building," said Storm. Indeed, Nightcrawler recalled that his teammate had once infiltrated the Hellfire Club's headquarters from below, back when Sebastian Shaw had been its owner.

"Before Selene's renovations, yeah," said Wolverine.

"It might still be the best way to get a group in there," said Phoenix.

"I can assist you there."

For the second time that day, Shaw had approached the X-Men without their knowing it. He had even managed to remain down-wind of Wolverine. He liked to make an entrance; the circus-bred showman inside Kurt Wagner could identify with that. The Black King of Hong Kong had discarded his usual finery and was dressed for action in a simple green padded boiler suit and heavy black gloves, belt and boots.

"About flaming time," grumbled Wolverine under his breath.

"It is precisely one o'clock," Shaw told him with a smirk on his lips and a glint in his eye. "That, I believe, is the time we agreed for this rendezvous."

"You had a suggestion to make?" prompted Storm, forestalling any further argument.

"As I explained at the Pacific facility," said Shaw, "I know this building better than anybody, Selene included. I know all the secret passageways that run through it."

"Can you get us inside undetected?" asked Phoenix.

"Unlikely. But I can make it difficult for Selene to keep track of us once we're in."

"Good enough," said Cyclops. "We split into three teams, then, and converge on the catacombs from three separate points. With luck, Selene won't be able to intercept us all. Wolverine and Night-crawler, you take the sewers; Shaw, I need two more routes."

"That won't be a problem."

"If it's all the same to you, mein Leiter," said Nightcrawler, "I would like to be counted out of sewer duty this one time." He had been thinking of something: a plan to lessen one of the X-Men's immediate worries. He wasn't sure if he liked it. In fact, a part of him hated it—but a part of him, he knew, would take a cynical kind of enjoyment in its execution.

"What do you have in mind?" asked Cyclops.

Storm found it difficult to concentrate on Nightcrawler's explana-tion. Shaw's presence unnerved her too much. In her mind's eye, she could see his face again, hovering above hers, a sole point of light in the darkness. She could feel his breath on her cheek and the muscles of his braced arms against her shoulders. She was buried, but it was all right because he was there. He was talking to her, calming her as he kept the rocks from crushing her. Her savior.

When she looked at him now, she saw a very different person to the one who had invited her to dinner the previous day. He looked somehow taller, demanding attention by his mere presence. Whereas once she had thought him smug in an oily sort of way, she now felt that he exuded confidence. She was waiting, almost with baited breath, to see what he would do next—and when he caught her gaze, she felt a tingle down her spine. She averted her eyes from his, not quite quickly enough. *Goddess,* she thought, *don't let me become attracted to him.*

And a part of her wondered: was it to Sebastian Shaw the man whom she felt drawn? Or was it to his power? The power that he had offered to share with her.

Despite the situation—despite the deadly danger to a teammate and friend—Shaw's offer had remained uppermost in Ororo's mind. She had thought hard about it during the flight back to New York, trying to visualize herself in Hellfire Club robes, trying to work out what that would mean to her and how it would change her life. It hadn't helped her at all. She still had no idea what she would say to Shaw when he put his question to her again.

She looked at each of her fellow X-Men in turn. She knew that if she unburdened herself to them and sought their counsel, they would understand. But a part of her resisted such disclosure, ashamed of her secret longings, of the weakness she could never completely deny. And anyway, would talking to them really make her decision easier?

Her closest friend on the team was probably Jean Grey, Phoenix. In other circumstances, she might have felt able to confide in her. But one thing stopped her: a memory of the X-Men's first confrontation with the Hellfire Club and with Shaw himself.

The Black King had allied himself with one Jason Wyngarde, who went by code name of Mastermind. Wyngarde was dead now, a victim of the Legacy Virus. He was no loss to the world. Over a period of months, this twisted little man had manipulated Jean's thoughts, worming his way into her psyche until he had turned her inside-out. He had transformed her, body and soul, into Shaw's first Black Queen, a creature of pure evil.

Or so it had seemed at the time. The X-Men had learned only later that "Jean Grey" had not been Jean Grey at all, but rather a being—a cosmic entity—that had used her as a template for its newfound physical form. Mastermind had unwittingly unleashed the monster known as the Dark Phoenix, and the universe itself had suffered for his mistake.

The real Jean, of course, hadn't had to live through it all. Unlike Ororo, she hadn't had to see her doppelganger standing at Shaw's side in black leather. Still, she was fully aware of the atrocities committed by the Phoenix force in her name and of the Hellfire Club's role in instigating those terrible events. She had also recently been forced to fight Madelyne Pryor, another dark reflection of herself who had ended up in Hellfire garb. Ororo did not wish to dredge up any more painful emotions for her. And even were she to do so, she already knew what her friend's advice to her would be.

Jean would tell her to decline Shaw's offer. She would point out that the Hellfire Club specialized in the corruption of innocents, as she had good reason to know. Much as she respected Ororo's strength, she would fear that the danger of such an alliance to her would outweigh the potential benefits. In her heart, she would be afraid of losing a friend.

Cyclops would agree with her, at least at first—but then he would lay the image of his lover as the Black Queen to one side and look at the situation again.

Scott Summers, for all that he believed in a dream, was a pragmatic man. He accepted that, to achieve anything worthwhile, it was often necessary to take risks. He would, of course, refute Shaw's accusation that his mentor's goals were unrealistic; however, the suggestion that those goals could best be achieved in a practical way, as if he could create a business plan for world peace, would be enticing to him. If nothing else, Scott would see the advantage of having an X-Man infiltrate one of the Hellfire Club's most powerful Inner Circles. He would share Jean's concerns, but he would also accept Ororo's assurance that she would be careful, that she would not allow herself to be beguiled by its Black King.

Wolverine would react in much the same way, and for the same reasons. It was ironic, thought Ororo, that Logan so often found himself at loggerheads with his team leader. He was the only X-Man who could get under the cool, controlled Cyclops's skin. Perhaps it was because, deep down, Scott knew that they were more alike than he cared to admit.

Conversely, Wolverine's best friend on the team was Nightcrawler, which just went to prove the old adage about opposites attracting. A devout Christian, Kurt Wagner saw no gray areas when it came to the battle between good and evil. In his eyes, the ends rarely justified the means. That wasn't to say he wouldn't empathize with Ororo's dilemma—of course he would—but he would almost certainly opine that it was better to take the Hellfire Club down from the outside than to play Shaw's game.

Iceman would probably agree with him, but Ororo suspected that he would do so more through a youthful naivete, an innocent desire to hold on to a world that had never really existed, than because he shared Kurt's unshakable faith. Was she being unfair to him?

Two for, three against, then. And in Ororo's opinion, Rogue was unlikely to even the tally. Tempted as she might be to side with Cyclops and Wolverine, the Southern X-Man would not be able to forget her own upbringing. Her mother, the shape-changing mutant known as Mystique, had led the Brotherhood of Evil Mutants and had indoctrinated her daughter into the ethic of that terrorist organization. When Rogue had first encountered the X-Men, she had been fighting against them. It had taken her a long time to grow out of Mystique's shadow and to realize that she had the right and the responsibility to ask questions, to make her own decisions in life. Ororo, as she would be forced to concede, was an adult; still, she was all too aware of the pressures that a manipulator like Shaw could bring to bear upon somebody. She would almost certainly remain undecided.

Perhaps if the Beast were here, he would have made a difference. Ever thoughtful and level-headed, Henry McCoy would have cogitated upon the pros and cons of each side of the debate before offering a considered opinion. Until recently, Ororo might have expected him to be cautious, to advise that it was best to keep away from Shaw and all he represented. But then, until recently, she would hardly have expected him to join forces with the Hellfire Club as he had done. The Beast had evidently decided that such an alliance was justified by the needs of the many, the opportunity to achieve a greater good. And in the end, wasn't this the choice that she too was facing? She had the chance to wield some of Shaw's power in a better cause, to accomplish far more than she ever could with the renegade X-Men.

She wanted that power. She wanted it so much that her heart ached for it. But that was the problem. Ororo was afraid of her desire, her need. She feared that, were it to be nurtured, it might grow until it consumed her. And she couldn't help but suspect that, beneath his mask of civility, Sebastian Shaw was hoping for precisely that.

In the end, she realized, it didn't matter what the other X-Men said to her, what advice they might offer. The decision was hers alone, and they would support her whatever she did. If she chose not to join Shaw, then they would say no more about it; only she would wonder if she had thrown away a chance to make a real difference. And if she did join him, if she became his White Queen as he had asked, they would accept that too. They would trust her.

The only question was, could she trust herself?

"And so, the poor naïve insects hurl themselves into the web of the spider."

Selene's crystal ball settled back onto its dais as its picture was swallowed by milk-white fog. She rose from her throne and glided across the room to the alcove in which the Beast was suspended. Hank glared at her in silence. When first he had been brought here, he had taunted her with insults and promises that the X-Men would defeat her as they had before. He had taken advantage of his fragile condition and the fact that she needed him alive. But the Black Queen had ways of torturing a man's soul without endangering his body.

She held his chin in a pale hand and ran her long, red finger-nails through his blue fur. "Ah, my dear Doctor McCoy," she purred, "I know what you are thinking. You act as if subdued, but your eyes are ever searching as your mind plans for an opportu-nity to reverse our situations." The Beast said nothing, and a shadow crossed Selene's face. "I warn you, X-Man, that I will be as quick to punish your dumb insolence as I was your open defiance."

"I merely considered a vocalization of my motives redundant," said the Beast, "given that you have already discerned them with laudable accuracy."

Selene smiled at the compliment. She turned her attention from her captive's chin to his left hand and spoke in a conversational tone. "Your opportunity will not come, of course."

"On that point, we shall have to remain in dispute."

Hank's throat hurt as he spoke, but he had to admit that he was feeling better than he had done for a while. That wasn't necessar-ily a good thing. It had been over twenty hours since his last dose of alien radiation, and the side-effects were beginning to lessen. The super-cell in his body was still mutating, still trying to evolve itself into a match for his affliction, but it could only be hours away from surrendering and being extinguished.

It didn't help that he was secured to the wood-paneled wall of Selene's throne room. His wrists and ankles were securely bound; not by ropes, which he might have been able to break in time, but by wiry tendrils which sprouted from the wood itself. The tendrils were slimy to the touch, and every so often they shifted their grips. He didn't like to ask what they were.

He braced himself now as the tendril around his left wrist extruded something long and sharp from its underside, and punc-tured his skin. Blood trickled onto Selene's waiting finger, and she smeared it onto her tongue with relish. She had done this twice before, apparently gauging the state of the Beast's health by taste alone. No doubt she had concocted a spell to imbue her with just such an ability, for effect.

"Will it be third time lucky, I wonder?" she mused. She rolled her tongue around her mouth and smacked her lips as if sampling a fine wine.

The Beast realized that he was holding his breath, although he didn't know which outcome he was hoping for. His search for a cure to the Legacy Virus had consumed his life of late. A day ago, he would have sacrificed himself gladly to achieve his aim. It was possible that he might yet do so. But Selene had boasted openly about her plans for such a cure. She had talked of an army of mutants, enslaved to her will because only she would have the power to keep them alive.

He remembered a conversation with Moira MacTaggert just over a week ago, although it seemed a lifetime behind him now. He had insisted that it was better to have a cure exist in the hands of an enemy than to have no cure at all. At the root of his argument, he realized now, had been his belief in the X-Men. He had lost faith in himself to find a cure unaided—he had begun to fear, even, that no cure was possible—but he had imagined that, if only that hurdle could be overcome, if only a cure could be found somehow, then no villain could keep it from his teammates for long. Now he was no longer so sure.

What if the X-Men couldn't stop Selene this time? She had allied herself with a demon, after all. Hank had caught only a brief glimpse of Blackheart—a vague impression of a dark face and burning eyes looming over him as he had surfaced from a restless doze—but it had been enough to make his skin itch and his fur stand on end. That was what the X-Men had to face if they were to keep Selene from claiming her prize. What if they failed?

He dreaded to think of the future that he might help the Black Queen to create.

He didn't know how to feel, then, when Selene's expression

darkened. "It is beginning to seem," she said acidly, "that you are not as able as your reputation suggests."

"If you had not deprived me of further treatment..."

"Then the cure would be in the hands of the X-Men and Shaw by now—and what would I profit from that?"

"You're a mutant, Selene," snapped the Beast angrily. "It is in the interests of every one of us to see this disease eradicated!"

Selene's expression softened again as she pursed her scarlet lips in amusement. "Ah, but you see, my friend, my ambitions extend far beyond mere survival. I care nothing for this cure of yours except as a means to an end, a tool to facilitate my conquest of this miserable world." She took Hank's chin in her hand again and grinned, exposing her blood-stained teeth. "Nor, I am sorry to say, will the outcome of your project make any difference to your fate. Succeed or fail, your usefulness to me will soon be at an end."

Rogue hesitated for a second, crouching on the window sill of a second-story office as her eyes adjusted to the gloom inside. She stepped down onto the deep pile carpet, joining Cyclops and Phoenix; the latter had telekinetically unlocked and opened the window from without before levitating her husband and herself into the building.

Cyclops was already feeling his way along the paneled walls, looking for the secret door that Shaw had told him about. It opened with a soft click, and he led the way into the narrow tunnel beyond it. The trio of X-Men tried to move quietly but quickly all the same. They had little doubt that Selene would have sensed their presence already; by the time her grotesque followers reached this room, they intended to be far away from it.

They must have been directly over the ballroom, because the floor hummed with the sound of music and laughter from below. Rogue smiled as the music was abruptly curtailed and the laughter turned into screams. Nightcrawler's distraction, right on time. She pictured him bouncing around the room, perhaps landing on the heads of a few party guests, teleporting from spot to spot in clouds of sulphurous smoke until nobody could be quite sure how many of him there were. He wouldn't harm anybody, of course, but the guests didn't know that. The appearance of a blue-skinned demon in their midst was causing chaos. It would certainly lessen the number of innocent bystanders in the building, and provide a distraction to boot.

Cyclops navigated his way sure-footedly around a labyrinth of passageways until the X-Men emerged onto a landing. It was lit but deserted, so he hurried across it and found another secret panel in the opposite wall. It opened into the side of a vertical shaft, which extended down into the darkness for as far as Rogue could see; certainly far beyond ground level. Curved metal rungs were set into its side at intervals, but the X-Men could make faster progress without them. Phoenix lowered herself and Cyclops into the depths while Rogue followed under her own power.

Black, scummy water filled the bottom few inches of the shaft. Hovering above it, Cyclops slid back another panel but found only a rock wall behind it. One of Selene's modifications, clearly. With a scowl, he curled up his fingers and operated his visor.

The wall was not thick, and it blew apart beneath an onslaught of red energy. Fragments ricocheted around the confined space of the shaft, but Phoenix's telekinesis ensured that none of the X-Men were hit.

The first thing that struck them as they stepped into a tiny, stone-walled cell was the heat. It was dry and oppressive; it wrapped itself around them and filled their lungs as they breathed. Rogue wrinkled her nose in distaste at the distinctive odor of brimstone. She found her eyes drawn to a set of manacles, which were tied by chains to a ring bolted into the floor.

There was a small window, but it was barred and shuttered from the far side. The door was made of thick wood; Cyclops took one look at the sturdy lock before he shot it out.

The trio of X-Men emerged into an enormous, dank cavern. Even the light from its wall-mounted braziers could not dispel the shadows in its distant heights and its myriad nooks and corners.

Dark alcoves and narrow passageways led off in all directions and at various heights, and Rogue counted another twelve doors. She could hear noises—scratching and skittering—but no matter where she looked, she couldn't see what was causing them. She caught only a few vague, disconcerting blurs of movement with the corners of her eyes.

"I'll say one thing for Selene," she whistled. "She sure knows how to stamp her mark on a property. She's given this whole place a makeover in 'Early Inferno' style."

She heard approaching footsteps and readied herself for action. But the new arrivals were only Wolverine and Iceman; they appeared at the mouth of a passageway some five feet above the ground. They dropped down into the main cavern, and the two groups of X-Men met in its center. Storm and Sebastian Shaw arrived together a moment later, and Nightcrawler materialized beside them, having been guided in telepathically by Phoenix.

"I don't like this," said Wolverine, "not one bit. It's too quiet."

"From what I have heard," said Shaw, "these cells are normally in use."

"I presume nobody ran into trouble on the way here?" asked Phoenix.

Storm shook her head. "It's as if Selene intended us to get this far."

"My thinking precisely," said Cyclops, "but let's not look a gift horse in the mouth."

"At least not until it bares its teeth at us," said Nightcrawler.

A flight of crumbling stone steps led up one side of the cavern to a set of huge, metal-studded double doors. "That way?" Cyclops asked Shaw.

"That way," he confirmed.

But before anybody could move, a deep rumbling sound reached the X-Men's ears. The ground vibrated and, for a second, Rogue feared that they were standing at the epicenter of an earthquake. The sound became louder, more savage: it was the clashing and rending of stone, and she realized now what was happening.

The openings in the walls were sealing themselves off; stone was flowing like treacle, gray tendrils joining hands across the gaps but hardening as soon as they had formed their new shapes. The wooden cell doors splintered, cracked and popped out of their frames as the apertures behind them were filled. Even Wolverine was not fast enough to escape in time; he made a start towards the nearest exit but stopped himself when he realized that it was futile. Silence returned to the catacombs as the X-Men realized that they were trapped.

And then shapes began to appear in the wall behind them: patches of darker gray, which grew until they had joined together and resolved themselves into a humanoid form. A gigantic figure was pushing its way through the wall itself. Its body could have been made of stone, except that short black spines grew all over it. Longer spines sprouted from its head like petrified hair, and shadows shifted across a face that was featureless but for a pair of smoldering red eyes. Those shadows seemed to come from within rather than without.

The creature drew itself up to its full height. Its head almost scraped the cavern roof, and the tallest of the X-Men didn't even come up to its knees; it could probably have knocked them all down with one sweep of its spiny tail. Rogue knew that this had to be Selene's demonic consort, Blackheart.

Iceman summed up her feelings perfectly. "We are in big trouble!" he murmured.

CHAPTER 9

PHOENIX TROD with caution as she led Cyclops and Wolverine into an empty basement apartment in Chelsea. Her psi-scans had suggested that nobody was waiting for them—but this was a city of mutants, and those scans had been fooled too many times already. This time, she was relieved to find that they were correct.

The sun was rising, and thin tendrils of cold light pierced the grime on the windows to illuminate a room that had not been used in months. It had not been vandalized, at least, but it had been abandoned in a hurry. Some items remained on its shelves, but there were several gaps. Phoenix sat down on a two-seater couch, and Wolverine flung his torn mask aside and dropped into a chair. Cyclops remained on his feet, pacing. It had been his idea to take cover for an hour or so; if too many people headed for the rebels' secondary base at once, it would attract attention. Nevertheless, he was not particularly skilled at waiting around.

Jean had been keeping a telepathic trace on Storm, so it was a simple matter to contact her again. *I have found the White Knight,* Ororo reported. *He tells me that 'Location D' is an office in a building opposite Battery Park. His people are under instructions to approach it in groups of two or three over a number of hours.* She supplied an address, which Phoenix repeated out loud for the benefit of her companions. She also promised to pass on the information to the rest of the X-Men, and to meet up with Storm soon.

She settled back against the couch cushions and tried to clear her mind. She closed her eyes and concentrated on reaching outwards, feeling her way around New York City for familiar thought patterns. Storm had given her an approximate location for Nightcrawler and Rogue, but it wasn't until she raised her sights above street level that she was able to get a fix on them. They were on a rooftop in the vicinity of Fifth Avenue. She put them in the picture, but learned that they hadn't seen Iceman since he had left the PATH station ahead of them. Nor had anybody seen Shaw since Wolverine's encounter with him in the tunnel.

She continued her search, but found herself distracted by an argument that had broken out between Cyclops and Wolverine. She tried to ignore it.

"And I'm telling you," growled Wolverine, "in a place like this, your precious rules don't apply. It's 'kill or be killed,' and I'm not gonna get myself skewered by some freak like Deathstrike because you want to play at being the big blue boy scout as usual."

"You'd rather we lower ourselves to her level?"

"If that's what it takes, yeah!"

"So, what's your plan, Logan? To take a tip from Fitzroy? Find ourselves a fortress, build up an army and fight some squalid little turf war until there's nobody left in this city?"

"All I'm saying is, we can't afford to be soft. Selene's tough enough on her own; she's damn near unbeatable with Blackheart on her side. We can do without the likes of Fitzroy and Deathstrike getting in the way of what's got to be done. And since we can't exactly have them carted off to the Vault, that just leaves one way of getting them out of our hair."

"I won't take a life until there's absolutely no option," said Cyclops stubbornly.

"Wake up, Summers," sneered Wolverine. "We passed that point as soon as Selene's barrier went up. Some time, if not today, we're gonna have to go back to that witch's lair. We're gonna have to fight her, not just for Manhattan but for the whole blamed world. If she wins—if your squeamishness makes the difference—how many people will die then? Do you think your bleeding-heart conscience can to cope with that?"

Jeannie, came Iceman's voice in Phoenix's mind, *am I glad to hear from you!*

Where are you, Bobby? she asked.

23rd and Lexington. I was following one of our mutate friends, but I don't think she trusted me. She gave me the slip; wriggled away through a sewer grating.

Phoenix repeated the details of the rendezvous point again, not quite able to tune out her husband's voice: "Blackheart must have shown you something. Back in Selene's catacombs, when he tried to bring out our dark sides...what did he show you, Logan?"

"That's none of your damn business, One-Eye!"

"Whatever it was," said Cyclops sourly, "you've obviously learned nothing from it."

Phoenix located Shaw at last, but frowned at the discovery that he was with Storm. She wondered why Ororo hadn't mentioned it. Come to think of it, she had been picking up tension between those two ever since the Beast's kidnapping. Jean didn't like to pry, but she was a little hurt that her old friend didn't wish to confide in her.

"What do you think, Red?" asked Wolverine, snapping her out of her reverie.

It took her a moment to readjust to the physical world. "I can see both your points," she hedged as she tried to order her thoughts. It wasn't the answer that either of her teammates were looking for, so she added tactfully: "I think we need more information. Ever since we arrived here, we've been on the ropes, reacting to one attack after another. I was wondering earlier about the world outside Manhattan Island. I'd like to see it, maybe track down a few people out there. It might help us to gain a little perspective on the whole situation."

Cyclops rubbed his chin thoughtfully. "That's feasible, I suppose. As mutants, we should be able to come and go through the barrier as we please."

"That's just running away from the problem," snarled Wolverine. "People inside the barrier are sick and dying while Selene rations the medicine that could save them. They can't just turn tail and get out of here—and some of them can't afford to sit around while we decide if we want to dirty our hands or not."

"That's not what I'm saying," protested Cyclops.

"It's just that we've lost so many of our friends already," said Phoenix, "and Selene has had a year to plan for our arrival. We don't want to make the wrong move."

"If you want my opinion," said Wolverine, "the only way to make all this better is to stop it before it starts."

"You mean—?" began Cyclops.

"Time travel. Back to where we came from."

Cyclops looked doubtful. "I'm not sure that's a serious option. We've found ways of travelling through time before, but we've always agreed that it's too dangerous. To interfere with our own past is to play with fire, and it might not even do us any good."

"Who's talking about our past?" countered Wolverine. "I'm talking about our present."

"But what if *this* is our present now?"

"I don't accept that. Selene used her hocus-pocus to zap us into the future—a future that, as far as I'm concerned, ain't happened yet. We just need to reverse that spell."

"We can't be sure we actually traveled through time," cautioned Cyclops. "It felt more like some kind of suspended animation; like Selene had shunted us into another dimension for a year, only we weren't aware of it." He longed to be convinced; Phoenix could feel as much through the psychic link that she and her husband shared. He wanted as much as she did to be able to wipe the slate clean, to put right everything that had gone wrong. He wanted a second chance. But he had to be sure. He had to know that it was the right thing to do.

"Either way," said Wolverine, "it boils down to the same thing.

I ain't talking about going back and meeting our past selves, changing their lives, because they won't be around. We're just taking back the year that's been stolen from us."

Scott sat down heavily beside his wife and rested his chin in his hands. "And how do we achieve that? By capturing Selene, I suppose, and forcing her to do as we say?"

Wolverine grinned. "That's one way, sure—but I reckon I've got an easier one."

Jean realized what he was about to say, and the pair spoke in unison: "Fitzroy!"

This time, it was a simple matter to gain access to Avengers Mansion. A detention coil twitched on the ground but lacked the energy to rise, and a gun placement swiveled to target the intruder but the gun itself had been destroyed.

Shaw picked his way through the partially collapsed hallway and into the Avengers' meeting room, where their long conference table with its distinctive "A" logo lay shattered. He had been prepared to wait, but the sounds of movement from an adjoining room told him that he wouldn't have to.

He had been right about Fitzroy: he had always been more stubborn than he was practical. Unable to accept the loss of his headquarters, he had risked returning to it. Shaw found the young mutant lying with his head beneath a curved console, cursing under his breath as his attempts to rewire it went slowly. He had made the mistake of stepping out of his suit of bio-armor, which stood to one side like a silent sentry. Without it, his wiry frame, clad in a form-fitting costume of black and white, looked small. Small and insignificant.

Shaw made sure that he was standing between the boy and the armor before he announced his presence with a polite cough. Fitzroy started and banged his head on the console's underside. He shot out from beneath it, and his eyes widened in alarm at the sight of his one-time employer.

Shaw smiled. "Well, well, what am I going to do with you? My White Rook..."

"Not any more," snarled Fitzroy. "Your time has past, old man. You have no power here."

"Are you sure about that?" asked Shaw conversationally. "Are you sure I couldn't crack your skull like an eggshell now that you don't have your technology to hide behind?"

"I have powers of my own, remember. I can take you." Fitzroy's gaze flicked nervously back and forth between Shaw and the armor, undermining his boast.

"One day, perhaps, we shall test that claim. For today, I have not come here to fight you."

"No?"

"No. I am here to propose an alliance."

Fitzroy sneered openly; he had always been too transparent for his own good. "And what makes you think you have anything to offer me?"

"Perhaps you are content to live as Selene's lackey. I am offering you far more than that: a partnership. We shall seize the New York Hellfire Club from her. I will be its Black King again, and you—you will be my White King." Had Shaw not been such a practiced liar, the words would have choked him. He had gained Fitzroy's reluctant interest, though.

"You're no match for Selene," he said doubtfully.

"In this time period, with her servants around her, perhaps not."Fitzroy's mouth cracked into a grin. "So, that's what you want from me. You need my power to create portals through time and space."

"I wish to return to the past, to the moment from which I was snatched."

"And your friends in the X-Men?"

"They need not know about this. Selene is overconfident. If we can take her by surprise, I have little doubt that the two of us alone can defeat her. We can take the Legacy Virus cure for ourselves.

Imagine what we could do with that power, Fitzroy. We could build a new—a better—Hellfire Club with ourselves at its helm."

Fitzroy was tempted; Shaw could see his internal struggle reflected in his twitching features. But finally the young mutant shook his head. "I don't trust you, Shaw. You expect me to believe you'd share your power, once you had taken what you wanted from me?"

Despite himself, Shaw felt his smile broadening. "You impress me, Fitzroy. I never thought I'd say that. You have grown up a little at last." He hardened his expression. "Regrettably, however, I cannot allow you to refuse me. You will open that portal."

"For myself, maybe, one day," laughed Fitzroy. "Yeah, maybe I *will* go back a year and take that cure. I can be the *Black* King—but if and when I do that, I won't be taking any passengers with me. And right now, old man, I'm enjoying myself far too much here."

"Then you leave me no option," said Shaw softly, "but to use force."

He made no move to carry out his threat. He waited for his nervous opponent to take the initiative. Fitzroy ran at him, his hands outstretched; he only needed to touch Shaw to begin to drain his life force from him. Shaw, however, struck like lightning, and Fitzroy reeled with the impact of a powerful punch to the head. Shaw pressed his advantage, leaping forward and gripping the front of Fitzroy's tunic. He threw him, spinning him so that he lost his orientation and fell. His head glanced off a console, and blood seeped from the resulting gash.

Shaw stood astride his fallen foe, satisfied with his easy victory. Fitzroy looked up at him groggily, and Shaw was about to speak when he heard a clanking noise from behind him.

He whirled around in time to see that the empty suit of bio-armor had raised its left hand towards him. He was staring down the huge circular barrel of a blaster weapon from the future, and he could see fire flashing in its innards.

He couldn't leap out of the way in time. He was caught in an explosion of searing pain—but more agonizing still was his own disgust at himself for not having seen this coming. He had already been told that Fitzroy had upgraded his armor over the past year; why hadn't he allowed for the possibility that he might be able to control it remotely?

His kinetically-charged body withstood the attack, but he was dangerously weakened. The armor lurched towards him, its long metal claws raised, and he barely staggered out of its way as it made a swipe for his throat. Then Fitzroy reared up in front of him and assailed him with a barrage of furious punches. He was an unthinking fool—and for that at least, Shaw was grateful, as the blows replenished some of his spent energy. He threw Fitzroy away from him with less force than he would have liked, and turned to face the bio-armor. It raised its blaster again but Shaw moved first, shoulder-charging it. It rocked but remained on its feet. It clamped a metal gauntlet onto his shoulder and he was dismayed to realize that he no longer had the strength to break free. He curled his foot behind its leg and bent all his remaining reserves to the effort of trying to trip it. At first it appeared that he would be unsuccessful—but then, to his surprise and satisfaction, the bio-armor tumbled backwards and crashed to the ground. Shaw almost fell too; he kept his knees from buckling by willpower alone.

While he had been occupied, a new combatant had joined the fray. He had realized some time ago that Tessa—or rather Sage—had followed him from the subway station. Out of curiosity, he had chosen not to challenge her. He had waited for her to show her hand. She must have cut off Fitzroy's psychic connection to his armor. She had also engaged him in physical combat, keeping him from pressing his advantage against his foe. Shaw was interested to see that she had picked up a lot of new moves since her days as his assistant. Unfortunately, Fitzroy denied her the time she needed to concentrate, to strike at him with her mind. Conversely, he was able to use his own mutant abilities to devastating effect.

Sage struggled to break his hold on her, but it was too late. Drained of energy, she passed out, her slim body hanging limply by the wrists until Fitzroy chose to drop her.

By that time, Shaw had crossed the short distance between them, pulled the young mutant's arm up behind his back and looped his own arm around his throat from behind. "Try doing that to me," he snarled in Fitzroy's ear, "and I'll snap your neck like a twig!"

The Technomancer thought hard about that before demonstrating the characteristic lack of courage on which Shaw had been counting. "What do you want?" he squealed.

"A portal," said Shaw.

"To the past?"

"Not yet. There's somewhere else I have to go first. And before you even think about betraying me, boy, think about this: I'll be taking you with me."

He recited an address, and Fitzroy obligingly tore a hole in space for him. The once and future Black King stared into it suspiciously, although he knew that he wouldn't be able to see past the maelstrom of clashing energies which rendered its surface opaque.

He took one final look at the fallen Sage before he stepped through the portal. She was unconscious, but her breathing was regular. She would recover, provided at least that nobody else happened upon her while she was defenseless. She had endangered herself for his sake: a year ago he would have expected such loyalty, but in this time, this place, he hadn't been so sure of it. Perhaps he had misjudged her. But then, the very fact that he couldn't divine her motives was enough to change everything. He had trusted Tessa once, in a way that he had trusted only one other woman in his life. He could do so no longer.

The decision to leave her behind was harder than he could ever have expected. But he made it all the same.

The silence of West 25th Street was broken by the sound of a spluttering starter motor as it failed to jolt a reluctant engine to life. Storm sat in the passenger seat of an abandoned yellow taxicab and watched as the man behind its wheel attempted to turn the ignition again with a short piece of wire. The White Knight clicked his teeth in frustration as his makeshift tool slipped between his fingers, not for the first time.

"Battery Park is downtown, is it not?" said Ororo.

"It is," confirmed the White Knight. He was leaning forward awkwardly in the confined space, straining to reach for the fallen wire.

"Then how is it that I found you heading uptown?"

"I have other business to attend to before I rejoin my group."

"And may I inquire as to the nature of that business?"

"You may not," said the White Knight shortly.

"If you still expect me to forge an alliance with you, you will have to be a little more forthcoming than that."

He froze with the wire poised over the ignition again. He turned to look at Ororo, who returned his gaze evenly. "I suppose Wolverine identified me at the station?" he said.

"As did I," she said coolly.

The White Knight nodded to himself as if amused. Then he took hold of the fabric of his white mask and pulled it off over the top of his head. Ororo was not at all surprised to see the face of the rebels' leader revealed. "You have not changed," she said.

Sebastian Shaw smiled. "Oh, my dear Miss Munroe, I have changed far more than you could ever imagine."

"I wondered for a time how you could appear in two places at once," said Ororo. "I arrived at a conclusion this morning. You are the same Sebastian Shaw who fought Selene with us, I believe. You are the same Shaw who arrived in this city, this time period, yesterday."

"Indeed. I remember it well."

"And yet those memories are of events which, for you, are a year past."

He inclined his head slightly, accepting the truth of her assertion.

Ororo's voice hardened. "You betrayed us! You came here as the X-Men's ally, but you saw a chance to claim Selene's power for yourself and you took it. You traveled back in time, probably to the very moment at which she sent us away. You abandoned us, Shaw. After all your fine words, your promises, you abandoned me!"

"I can assure you," he said, "that no personal slight was intended."

"Is this your idea of trust, then? Is this how you would treat your Lords Cardinal?"

"Let us not forget, my dear, that you never accepted such a role. Your allegiances are still first and foremost to the X-Men, and I could ill afford to involve them in my plans."

"And what were your plans for me, Shaw? Did you think that, given more time, you could have won me around to your way of thinking? Did you imagine I could ever be persuaded to turn my back on my friends, to compromise my ethics?"

"On the contrary, it is that very strength of character that I most admire in you."

Ororo let out a bitter laugh. "I know the true worth of your hollow words now, Shaw."

"Believe me or not," he said, "I have held you in nothing but the utmost regard since you first served on our Inner Circle; a grudging regard at first, I will admit, but a genuine one nonetheless. I regret that I had to leave you behind—but had circumstances been different, had things gone according to my plan, then you would have arrived in this future to find it very different indeed."

"To find you sitting on Selene's throne, no doubt."

"And my offer to you would still have been open," said Shaw quietly.

Ororo stared at him, trying to pierce his inscrutable expression. She considered herself a good judge of character, but something about Shaw dulled those senses. No matter how much her intellect and experience told her he could not be trusted, her instincts—her heart—longed to believe otherwise. She wondered if he made everybody feel this way.

Suddenly, Shaw stiffened and his eyes widened. A pack of six Hellfire Club demons had turned into the road in front of them—

and, even at several blocks' distance, they had seen that the cab was occupied. As they lumbered towards it, Shaw muttered something under his breath and fumbled with his wire again. Ororo stilled his clumsy arm with her left hand as, with her right, she slid a lock pick out of her belt. She reached over and slipped it into the ignition, manipulating it deftly. It took three attempts—but, thanks to her expertise, only a few seconds—for the engine to catch, whereupon Shaw took off the handbrake and stamped hard on the gas pedal.

"I suggest you put on your seatbelt," he said as Ororo was flung back by the sudden acceleration. She hurried to comply. Shaw had no need of such a safety measure; his mutant ability would protect him from any knocks.

He aimed the car squarely at the demons, his eyes gleaming and his lips curling into a sadistic smile as he picked up speed. They scrambled to get away from him, falling over each other in the process. Ororo winced as the cab's front wheels bounced over a fallen body to the accompaniment of an unearthly howling and a sickening squelching sound.

A demon had leapt onto the hood and sprawled itself across the windshield. Shaw couldn't see where he was going, but his demeanor hadn't changed. He was enjoying this. He slammed on the brakes and threw the steering wheel hard left. The cab's back tires screeched in protest as they were dragged around in an arc, and the demon squealed too as it was flung into the road. The vehicle had turned a full one hundred and eighty degrees, and Ororo could see the fallen creature pulling itself up in the rearview mirror. Shaw reversed over it.

The four remaining demons had been loping after the cab but they froze now, their faces elongating in dull horror as they saw that it was facing them again. Shaw jerked the stick into neutral and revved the engine, for no reason that Ororo could see other than to taunt them. One of the demons turned and fled, but the other three dared to come closer.

He drove at them again, veering right to follow two of them as they dived onto the sidewalk. He hit one, ramming the glass door of an office building and driving the startled creature into the narrow lobby before him. The windshield shattered and Ororo threw up her hands to protect herself from flying glass. The hood buckled and steam hissed out from beneath it.

The engine wheezed and groaned but held out. The fifth demon climbed onto the roof of the cab via its trunk, and the sixth tried to follow it. Shaw reversed suddenly and crushed it against the burnt-out shell of an old Dodge on the opposite side of the road. Ororo braced herself against the dashboard as her belt snapped tight across her chest. Shaw spun the wheel again and headed east, but the final demon refused to be dislodged. Ororo started as its claws punctured the roof above her head and started to peel back the metal. She closed her eyes and concentrated, summoning a crosswind that caught it by surprise. It fell past her side window, screaming in anger and frustration.

Shaw drove around Madison Square and stopped the cab on Park Avenue South. In the aftermath of his adrenaline rush, he looked tired and gray, and suddenly Ororo could believe that he really was older—much older—than the Shaw she had arrived here with. He leaned his forehead against the steering wheel, his breathing ragged.

"We should abandon the car," said Ororo softly. "It's too conspicuous."

He shook his head as if it were too great an effort to speak. He made coughing, spluttering sounds as if unable to quite clear his throat. He looked pale. It took him a few seconds to compose himself enough to sit up again. "I have a long distance to travel," he said weakly.

Ororo looked at him suspiciously. "Sebastian," she said, "do you have the Legacy Virus?"

He avoided her gaze. "I have been trying to conceal the symptoms. My followers look to me to give them hope, and I would not wish to see them demoralized."

"How...?" she began, but she tailed off, realizing that no words were careful enough.

He answered the unspoken question anyway. "I contracted the disease one year ago. Selene infected me herself. It is in its final stages now. I am near death."

"I'm sorry," said Ororo. It sounded inadequate, but she reminded herself that Shaw's cause was not hopeless. A Legacy cure did exist now, even if it was not yet free for all. "You have not been receiving treatment, have you?" she deduced.

"I will not humble myself before that witch."

"You would rather die than accept her handouts of medicine?"

Shaw's eyes flashed. "Count yourself lucky, wind-rider. You have not seen a fraction of what I have had to see. Can you imagine what this past year has been like for me? I crossed the time barrier itself to prevent all this from happening. Selene and her pet demon defeated me. I was infected—but worse still, I was humiliated. I was forced to watch as this world came into existence around me all over again!"

"It is little wonder you wish to strike against her as soon as possible."

"I have waited a long time for the X-Men—and my younger self—to return."

"But surely she will have prepared for just such an attack from you?"

Shaw shook his head. "I have ensured that the Black Queen thinks me dead. She is aware of our movement, but she does not appreciate the extent to which we are organized. She will anticipate resistance from the X-Men, of course, but we can still strike earlier and in greater numbers than she expects. We can gain the advantage of surprise over her."

"And then what, Shaw? What happens after you have reclaimed your precious Hellfire Club? You have already demonstrated that your word cannot be believed."

"I have no taste for Selene's brand of mischief; you must see that, at least."

"But you do have a taste for power. You may lower the barrier around Manhattan Island—you may even keep your promise to distribute the Legacy cure—but how are we to be sure that we are not merely exchanging one type of avaricious would-be dictator for another?"

"That, my dear Miss Munroe," said Shaw coldly, "is your decision to make."

"Then you leave me with no choice." Ororo took a deep breath, steeling herself for what had to be said. "A year ago, Shaw, you offered me the post of White Queen in your Inner Circle. I have given the matter much consideration—and I have decided to accept."

Sebastian Shaw was an expert at disguising his feelings. There was something very satisfying, then, about the expression of incredulity that spread across his face now.

"You need not look so surprised," said Ororo. "Even after Selene has been usurped, it will be necessary to repair the damage she has done. The Hellfire Club, with its extensive resources, could lead that effort. We could work together to rebuild this city."

Shaw spoke at last. "No," he said.

"No?" Ororo's stomach sank. She had convinced herself that she was making a bargain of necessity, but now she felt as if she had had a lifelong dream crushed.

"Under other circumstances..." Shaw took her hand in both of his, and his sad eyes suggested that he actually meant what he said and that he wanted, needed, her to believe it. "In a different time, dear lady, I would have been proud to have you stand at my side. We could have been unstoppable, you and I."

"Then why—?" she began.

He silenced her with a gentle finger to her lips. "Even I cannot always choose my path in life. What I do now, my sweet, strong Ororo, I can only do alone."

"There is no other way?"

"Regrettably not. The course of my future has already been plotted. I know I have done nothing to deserve your trust, Ororo, but I must beg you for it this one time."

They sat in silence, then, for what seemed like an age. Ororo's insides were churning and she felt that there were so many things she ought to say but she couldn't think of a single one of them. In the end, she climbed out of the cab without another word. Shaw didn't spare her a backward glance as he put the battered vehicle into gear and drove it north, away from her.

She didn't move until long after he had disappeared from sight.

And even then, she couldn't explain to herself why she had let him go.

A pack of demons had caught Iceman's scent, and he couldn't shake them off.

He had outpaced them in his traditional manner: by skating along a thick slide of ice, condensing each fresh section out of the air as he reached it. The problem with this was that it left a very clear frozen trail for his pursuers—and they were nothing if not persistent. As he stopped for a breather, they emerged from the shadows again. He frosted the ground beneath their clawed feet to throw them off-balance, but he didn't stop to press his advantage. He was too badly outnumbered, and he remembered all too well how his last solo encounter with Selene's infernal servants had ended.

He had been heading east ever since he had left the PATH station, and now he found himself on FDR Drive. This highway, more than any other, ought to have been bumper to bumper with rush hour traffic, but it was as eerily deserted as the rest of the city. Beyond it, Manhattan Island gave way to the East River, and Iceman was startled to see that he was a lot closer to Selene's mystical barrier than he had realized. The shifting white shell arced down in front of him and disappeared into the placid water just a few hundred yards offshore.

He smiled as a thought occurred to him. Only mutants could

pass through the barrier, right? So, if he went around the *outside* of it rather than the inside, then the demons would be unable to follow him. He could make his journey in safety and reenter the quarantined island at its southern tip, right on top of Battery Park and the rendezvous point.

An angry howl behind him hastened his decision. With a cheery wave and a cry of "See you around, suckers!" Iceman formed another ice slide and propelled himself along it, leaving the perplexed demons standing. He cringed in anticipation as he hurtled towards the barrier, but there was no pain, not even a suggestion of resistance, just a touch of dampness and a slight tingling sensation. It was like sliding into a fog bank. He was enveloped by a white shroud...

...and as it lifted, he was hit by the cold light of the full winter sun, bright in the eastern sky. He flinched from it, shielding his eyes with one hand, and suddenly he was aware of a gigantic figure above him. It swooped down towards him, and his jaw dropped in alarm as he realized what it was.

It was humanoid, but large enough for its questing fingers to wrap themselves around Bobby Drake's slender body if he let them. It was made of metal, tinted in shades of maroon and light blue. Iceman half-leapt, half-tumbled out of its reach, but a powerful fist shattered his slide like glass and sent him into free fall. The East River filled his field of vision and he braced himself for impact. Instead, he was suddenly jerked upward as if on strings. He rolled over and saw a giant blue hand poised above him. A circular orifice on its palm had slid open, and the air rippled as an invisible tractor beam did its work. He tried to block the hole, but the robot's other hand emitted a blast of concentrated heat, which melted his ice plug before it was fully formed. His armor was beginning to turn to water; it was all he could do to maintain it, and even this was a losing battle.

It was all over in seconds. The robot's steel fist closed around Iceman's waist, holding him in an unbreakable grip which shattered the top layer of his protective coating. For a second he stared helplessly into its impassive, angular, flesh-toned parody of a face; a face that was all too familiar to him. He had been captured by a Sentinel: a machine built solely for the purpose of tracking down and eliminating mutants.

And then it exhaled a sweet-smelling gas, and the world pulled a slow fade to black.

CHAPTER 10

MS. MUNROE? Ms. Munroe, are you listening to me?"

Ororo Munroe blinked and, for a second, she had no idea where she was. For some reason, she had been thinking about the X-Men's battle with the demon Blackheart. It was odd, she thought, that it should have come back to her at this moment and with such startling clarity. She had almost been able to smell the brimstone in Selene's catacombs, feel the fetid air against her cheeks and the stone beneath her feet.

It occurred to her that she couldn't quite recall how the battle had ended. Just for an instant. But that didn't matter now. It was all such a long time ago anyway.

She was sitting behind a polished walnut desk in an executive office on the top floor of the Storm Investments building in New York City. Her desk. Her office. Her building. The exquisite décor was enhanced by a selection of carefully arranged flowers: exotic breeds imported from around the world, some of her favorites. Without her regular attention and the blessing of her elemental powers, many of them could not have survived in this climate.

A man was seated across the desk from her, regarding her with rheumy eyes and a frown. He was dressed in a neat blue business suit. Ororo started. "I do apologize, Mr. Ambassador," she said, flustered. "My mind must have...wandered for a moment." She cleared her throat in embarrassment and looked at the papers in front of her, frantically trying to recall the topic of conversation.

"We were discussing the irrigation program?" the dignitary reminded her.

"Ah, yes, yes of course."

He leaned forward urgently, exposing a bald patch on the top of his head. "Ms. Munroe, I can hardly impress upon you enough how important this project is to my country. Overseas aid can only go so far as long as it is targeted at short-term relief. With this grant, our people can become self-sufficient in a matter of years. We can..."

Ororo had located a money transfer order. She took an elaborate quill pen out of its holder, looked at the form for a moment, then added another zero to the figure upon it and signed her name with a flourish. She slid the form across to the ambassador, whose eyes widened as he saw it. He hardly knew what to say, but Ororo accepted his gushing gratitude with a gracious smile as he backed out of the room, almost trembling with excitement.

She rose and walked across to the window, luxuriating in the feel of her red silk dress against her skin. She basked in the glittering lights of the city, which stretched out below her towards the East River. People teemed along the sidewalks; she couldn't make out their individual details from this height, but she felt an almost proprietorial warmth towards them all. Most of them didn't know it, but she had improved their lives in a thousand small ways.

She had created a better world.

Sebastian Shaw was alone in a white void. It stretched for as far as he could see in all directions, even below him. It looked and felt as if he were standing on thin air.

He knew it couldn't be real. A moment ago, he had been in the catacombs beneath the New York Hellfire Club building, the X-Men at his side. He concentrated, exerting the mental defenses that telepathic allies like Tessa and, in her time, Selene herself had taught him how to build. He pivoted slowly, squinting as if to pierce the blankness and make out the real world beyond it. To his aggravation, he saw nothing.

He completed his circle and recoiled in shock to find Blackheart standing beside him. The demon's charcoal features were recognizable even though he had reduced himself to Shaw's size and clad himself in a dapper black suit. Shaw composed himself, galled at having shown weakness in front of a foe. He suppressed a scowl at the sight of a gold trident pin on Blackheart's tie. Selene had bestowed upon this creature the rank of New York's Black King: a rank that Shaw himself had once held, and would hold again. The fact that Blackheart eschewed the Club's traditions by wearing modern clothing was a further slight against him.

"What do you want from me?" he asked, determined not to show trepidation.

"From you?" rumbled Blackheart. "Nothing that you have not already forfeited."

Shaw smirked mockingly. "I assume you are referring to my immortal soul. Do not insult my intelligence, demon. I accept that you have power here, and over your own physical realm—but I am not superstitious enough to believe that it extends into an afterlife."

Blackheart inclined his head, apparently unconcerned. "As you wish. In any case, I choose not to waste my time with such as you; not when I have had delivered into my grasp the souls of seven noble heroes, ripe for the corrupting."

"The X-Men."

Blackheart extended an upturned hand towards Shaw. His featureless face betrayed no emotion, but Shaw was sure that the red glow of his eyes had intensified. "I thought you might care to accompany me on a guided tour of their nightmares."

He didn't wait for an answer. He turned and opened a door that wasn't there, creating a widening crack in the nothingness, which he stepped through. Out of curiosity more than anything, Shaw followed him into a small, brick-walled cell. A shaft of golden sunlight fell through a high, barred window, bringing with it bird-song and the promise of a brighter tomorrow. But the shadows around the light were dark and dank.

Wolverine was chained to the far wall, spread into an X shape by the manacles that bound his wrists and ankles. Cyclops was trying to free him, but the metal resisted his optic blasts.

"It's no good," said Wolverine. "You've got to get out of here without me."

"I'm not leaving you," insisted Cyclops.

"The X-Men's leader," observed Blackheart, his words apparently heard by nobody but Shaw himself. "A man who has devoted his life to the pursuit of an impossible dream."

"A stubborn man," said Shaw. "Strong-willed."

"But not incorruptible. Nobody is incorruptible." Blackheart moved to Cyclops's side, and suddenly the X-Man reacted to him as if seeing him for the first time. There was no sign that he could see Shaw, however, and Wolverine simply lolled in his restraints.

"What do you want, Blackheart?" snapped Cyclops, his fingers closing reflexively on the palm controls for his visor.

"I have a proposition for you, Scott Summers."

"Forget it!"

Blackheart sighed. "So impetuous...you might at least hear what I have to say before you dismiss it."

"Whatever it is," said Cyclops, "I'm not interested."

"Not even in the fulfillment of your most cherished ambitions; of your mentor's dream?" Blackheart spoke the words casually, but Cyclops's pose changed. He stiffened almost imperceptibly. "I talk of a world in which your kind are recognized as equals, in which they can live their lives openly and freely without fear of persecution. I am talking about eradicating anti-mutant sentiment from the hearts and minds of humanity forever."

"And you'll expect something in return, of course."

"Of course. Is that not fair?"

Cyclops shook his head. "I don't do deals with your kind."

"You will find that a demon's word is his bond."

"But there's always the small print to worry about, isn't there!"

"No small print this time," said Blackheart. "No hidden clauses. I will expect full payment in advance for my services. After that, your obligation to me will be at an end."

"What kind of payment?"

"Kill Wolverine!"

Cyclops just stared.

"He is weak," said Blackheart, "chained. You will never have a better chance."

"What makes you think I *want* a chance to commit murder?" spluttered Cyclops.

"Come now." Blackheart laid a hand on the X-Man's shoulder, but it was shaken off before he could guide him into the shaft of sunlight. "Why don't you look out of the window?" the demon purred. "Why don't you look at the world that could be?" Indicating Wolverine, he said, "Do you really imagine that this psychopathic runt could fit into a world like that? It only takes one snake to bring down a paradise."

"So that's your offer, is it?" asked Cyclops hotly. "You'll make my dream come true by slaughtering anyone who might possibly disagree with it?"

"Just one death," said Blackheart. "You have my word on that."

"It's one too many."

"Are you deaf or something, Summers?" The interjection came from Wolverine, who suddenly seemed aware of what was happening in front of him. It occurred to Shaw that he probably wasn't real, just a gruesome trapping in a scenario created for his teammate. "Didn't you hear what the man said? This is everything you want, everything we've ever fought for. One life in return for thousands, probably millions, spared."

"It isn't worth the price," said Cyclops obstinately.

"To you, perhaps," said Wolverine scornfully. "You're weak, Summers. You talk the talk all right, but when it comes down to it, you don't want to dirty your pure lily-white hands."

"Think carefully, Scott Summers," said Blackheart. "Few people are offered the chance to wish for world peace. All I ask is one stained soul to amuse me throughout a lonely eternity."

"But you don't mean Wolverine's soul," said Cyclops shrewdly. "You mean mine."

"Indeed I do."

Blackheart turned away then, and beckoned to Shaw to follow him as he walked straight through the wall beside the shackled Wolverine. Shaw lingered, looking at Cyclops, who continued to ignore his presence; he was staring at the window from which the light came, and his expression was torn by painful indecision. He took a step towards the light, but could go no further. He couldn't let himself see what was outside that window.

"If he was asking you to lay down *your* life," his teammate taunted him, "you'd do it like a shot." Cyclops's only reaction was to clench his fists tightly. "Kill me!" bellowed Wolverine. "For God's sake, Summers—for the world's sake—*kill me!*"

Disconcerted, Shaw hurried through the intangible wall, and emerged onto a busy New York street. Blackheart was waiting for him.

"He won't do it, you know," said Shaw.

"I know," said Blackheart.

"Then why—?"

"The claiming of a soul is a lengthy process. Seeds must be planted. Scott Summers may not accept my offer now, but in the years to come he will dwell upon his failure to do so. He will wonder if he made the noble choice or merely the craven one. I have made him that little bit more likely to accept a similar, smaller compromise in the future."

"I see." Shaw couldn't help but smile despite himself.

"It is easy for men to forget that the lesser of two evils is still an evil."

A ripple of fear had spread through the shoppers on the sidewalk. Some people gasped in horror, while others had started to run. A young woman raced through Shaw without either seeing or feeling him. The disturbance was centered upon the opening of a narrow alleyway, and he could hear the sounds of a violent battle from within.

Blackheart gestured toward the opening. "Perhaps you would like to see more?" he said.

Ororo didn't remember leaving her office. She didn't remember taking her private elevator down to the street, where her limousine and its chauffeur were waiting. She didn't remember being driven the few blocks uptown to the Hellfire Club building, and she certainly didn't remember walking the familiar route to her suite therein and changing into her elegant white robes. But that was probably because she had done all those things so many times before.

She admired herself in a full-length, gilt-edged mirror, and a smile came to her lips. But it froze there as she was struck by a blade of doubt beneath her breastbone. For a dreadful moment, she felt as if she were floating on the outside of her body looking in, and she was screaming in impotent silence at the sight of what she had become.

"It suits you."

She started at the unexpected voice. Another figure had appeared in the glass beside her: a redheaded woman, dressed in the leather bodice and cloak of the Hellfire Club's Black Queen. Ororo turned to greet her best friend in the world, Jean Grey.

"I only wish I could be as sure," she said.

Jean smiled. "Oh come on Ororo, what would you rather be wearing? Yellow spandex?"

"The X-Men..." murmured Ororo, and something cold slithered down her spine.

"The X-Men did a lot of good," said Jean, "nobody's denying that. But the time came to move on, and you know it."

"I...I know, but..."

"You're one of the most powerful people on this planet, Ororo. You were worshipped as a goddess! We've both been blessed with incredible abilities, and what did we do? We wasted those gifts on never-ending battles with the likes of Magneto and the Brother-hood of Mutants, and why? What did we gain from it? We never changed anything important."

Ororo nodded thoughtfully. "I remember how frustrating it could be at times."

"Look at how much we've accomplished since we joined the Hellfire Club," said Jean. "I still remember a time when Congress were debating a Mutant Registration Act."

"How could we forget?"

"Today, they're talking about new laws to prevent anti-mutant discrimination in the workplace—and they're likely to be passed."

"Because there are mutants in Congress now," said Ororo. She sounded as if she had only just realized that fact, but she wasn't sure why. She had always known it, hadn't she?

"And the Hellfire Club were instrumental in putting them there."

"Yes," she said distantly. "Yes, I remember." Another thought occurred to her, and she frowned. "Although I am not entirely comfortable with some of our methods."

Jean shrugged. "A few dollars in a few back pockets, a few words in the right ears about certain indiscretions...what differ-ence does it make in the long run?"

"You are saying that the ends justify the means?"

"I'm saying that history will judge us on our results." Jean grinned. "Anyway, it could have been much worse. When Moira MacTaggert ran for election, Sebastian wanted to assassinate her opponent. If not for you, he would have done it."

"I talked him out of it?" Why was it so hard to remember?

"Just like you made him fix a fair market price for the Legacy cure," said Jean. "You make a good team, our White King and Queen: Shaw's ruthlessness tempered by your compassion."

Ororo was becoming more and more confused. "Sebastian is the...*White* King?"

"Of course. He deposed Selene, my predecessor as Black Queen. He had to take the opposing color to hers; Hellfire Club rules. Ororo, are you OK? You don't look yourself."

Ororo smiled bravely and tried to shake off her strange mood. "I am fine," she said. "I was just reflecting on how many things have changed for us."

"But for the better, I hope," said Jean.

"I hope so, too."

The alleyway was strewn with the garishly clad bodies of fallen criminals: some of the X-Men's most persistent super-powered foes, mutant or otherwise. Shaw had made it his business to be aware of such people; he could put names to all the masks and to most of the faces beneath them. He was both disturbed and oddly proud to see his own face among them.

Only a few villains remained standing, but they were losing badly. They still outnumbered their single opponent, but he was knocking them down with ridiculous ease. The teleporting Vanisher was taken out by a kick to his chin; the colossal and reputedly unmovable Blob fell next. A flurry of punches to the head of the Living Pharaoh concluded the uneven combat.

Nightcrawler's yellow eyes glowed with satisfaction as he surveyed the results of his handiwork.

"Kurt Wagner," said Blackheart, unseen and unheard by the object of his scrutiny. "Gentle, kind and chivalrous to a fault. And yet, even within such a man, there lurks a savage."

"I would be impressed," said Shaw, "if I thought he was in control of his actions."

"To an extent, he is. I have only exacerbated his worst emotions: his anger, his arrogance." Blackheart gestured toward the German X-Man with a stony hand. Nightcrawler had drawn a rapier from a scabbard attached to his belt. Its thin blade was stained with old blood. He stepped over two fallen villains and placed his two-toed foot on the chest of another. Shaw was not amused to see that it was his own simulacrum.

"You have defeated us," panted the ersatz Black King, his voice rendered hoarse by the tip of the rapier against his windpipe. "What more do you want?"

"Repent!" said Nightcrawler. "Confess your sins and pray for forgiveness."

"N-never."

"Then I dispatch you to God's judgement, and may He have mercy on your blemished soul." Nightcrawler placed both hands upon the rapier's hilt and drove its blade down hard. His victim's arms and legs thrashed helplessly as he gargled on his own blood. Shaw winced at the sight of his own slaying in effigy.

"I have always thought it a delicious irony," said Blackheart, "that the darkest sins of mortal men are so frequently committed in the name of a benevolent higher power."

"Nevertheless," said Shaw, "I fail to see how this will serve to corrupt the X-Man. When he returns to his senses, he will be revolted by what you have made him do."

"I have reminded Kurt Wagner that his own Bible advocates divine retribution, the punishment of the guilty, a crusade against the enemies of his God." Shaw detected a hint of amusement in the gravelly voice. "That is, if you choose the right passages to believe." Blackheart clicked his fingers again, and the alleyway began to fade away.

It was replaced by a bedroom, decorated with posters of movie swashbucklers. A wooden crucifix hung above the head of the bed—and beside it stood Nightcrawler, whose position and stance hadn't altered as the world had reshaped itself around him. The demon clicked his fingers, and the X-Man became aware of his surroundings. He sank onto the bed and played nervously with a smaller silver cross, which hung on a chain around his neck.

"To Kurt Wagner, the events we have just seen are already a distant dream, a fading memory. He is in a different world now: a world in which the X-Men's enemies have either turned to the path of righteousness or perished for their sins. He is wracked with guilt, but that will lessen. He will spend time with friends who would have been killed by those enemies, discover a world in which humanity has not been made paranoid by the actions of a misguided few. He will be treated as a hero, and he will wonder—

oh, he will deny it to himself, he will resist the idea, but he *will* wonder—if he did the right thing after all."

Shaw could hear a crowd outside the window. They were chanting Nightcrawler's name, and cheering for him. The X-Man looked pained: he covered his goblin ears with a pillow, but Shaw wondered how long it would be before the ex-showman succumbed to the lure of fame and adulation. "Another seed planted," he said with grudging respect. Blackheart didn't acknowledge the compliment. He left the room by its door, and Shaw followed him out onto the forbidding surface of an alien planet.

The ground beneath their feet was composed of a fine crimson sand, but they left no tracks in it as they walked. Blackheart took a seat upon a large red rock, the top of which had been flattened by erosion. Standing beside him, Shaw followed his line of sight upwards. At first, he could see nothing. The sky was an inky black, bereft of stars. If this world had a sun at all—if it was not just a barren lump of rock cast adrift in the cosmos—then this face was turned away from it. There was no wind—the sand lay undisturbed—but the air must have been bitterly cold, if only he could feel it. Almost certainly, thought Shaw, the planet possessed no atmosphere, and yet he could breathe.

He waited with studied patience, staring into the frigid depths of infinity—and a minute or so later, the light show began.

It was small at first: a few sparks in a distant corner of the sky, like a fireworks display on the far side of town. But as its unseen source drew closer, it became ever more impressive, until Shaw's field of vision was filled with fiery streaks and swirls of yellow, orange and red. The display followed no pattern, or at least none that he could discern, but its ebbs and flows were a thing of beauty and, although he could hear nothing, he felt as if Creation itself were singing to him. He could have stayed there and watched the pyrotechnics forever. He could have lost himself in their mesmeric wonder. But to do so would have betrayed a weakness. So he tore his gaze away from the warm colors and back to the cold face of his demonic guide.

"I assume you created this scenario for one of the X-Men," he said.

"She is at the heart of the flames," said Blackheart. "She controls them, or so she believes."

"Phoenix," guessed Shaw.

"I have taken a slightly different approach with her." Blackheart stood, clasped his hands behind his back and began to amble back across the sand as if enjoying an evening stroll. His strides, however, were deceptively long, and Shaw had to make an effort to remain at his side rather than at his heels. The door through which they had come was still there, a white wooden rectangle hanging incongruously in midair.

"Your former associate Madelyne Pryor complicated matters," the demon continued, "when she confronted her doppelganger with her greatest fear: the fear that she holds within herself the potential for great evil. She hoped to exacerbate that fear, to consume her opponent with it, to drive her to despair. The result of her failure is that Jean Grey is stronger, more sure of herself, than she has ever been. I could have made her fearful again, but I decided that the opposite course of action might bear sweeter fruit."

They came to a halt in front of the white door. "Nobody lives in this part of the galaxy," said Blackheart, "and nobody ever will. Jean Grey can unleash her powers without thought of consequence. I have made her as much a slave to her gluttony as Kurt Wagner was to his own baser instincts. She does not control her actions any more than he did, but she will not remember that. She will only recall the intoxicating sensation of release, of channeling forces through her frail human body that could save a universe or lay waste to it."

"A sweet temptation indeed," murmured Shaw.

"Rarely have I beheld such power as hers," said Blackheart, "and yet her subconscious mind represses it. She unlocks her potential in stages only as she feels prepared to cope with each one. Imagine, then, what might happen if the dim recollection of a forbidden pleasure coaxed Jean Grey—unwittingly, of course—into hastening that process."

Shaw didn't need to imagine it. He had been present when Jason Wyngarde had unleashed the Dark Phoenix, and the memory made him shudder.

"You see, my friend," said Blackheart, "her fears were well justified. Great power always carries with it the potential—the likelihood, I believe—of corruption. If your associate achieved anything, then it was to make Jean Grey try to deny that. In this case, it was she who planted the seeds, and I who have provided the sustenance to make them grow."

The demon opened the door and walked through it, but Shaw lingered a little longer on the dead planet. He was unable to resist glancing back over his shoulder at the burning sky. And in so doing, he saw that a recognizable shape had coalesced out of the flames.

It was the shape of a phoenix.

Ororo must have made her way downstairs to the underground chamber in which the Hellfire Club's Inner Circle met. She recognized the joyless, candlelit surroundings in which her fellow Lords Cardinal had gathered, and the uncomfortable feel of the rigid, straight-backed chair beneath her. She had never liked this dark, dusty room in which dark, dusty deeds took place, and she only half-listened to the droning reports of self-important men as she waited for the latest interminable meeting to end.

From the Black side of the long council table, Jean Grey sent her a telepathic flash of reassurance. She knew that Ororo would rather have been putting the world to rights in a more direct fashion, but that way had been proved ineffective. Much as both women disliked the time-consuming strictures of politics, they had good reason to endure them. They could settle for slow but lasting gains or they could lose everything.

Her gaze was drawn to the strong profile of Sebastian Shaw, who sat to her left, resplendent in his clean, fresh, white garb. He rewarded her attention with a secret smile.

"I wondered if our White Queen might wish to attend to that matter in person?"

Ororo was suddenly aware that the speaker—an anonymous fat company director who held the post of Black Rook—was looking at her, his eyebrows raised in expectation. She dismissed the sudden bizarre feeling that she had never seen this man before in her life, and tried to remember what he had been saying.

"Given," the Black Rook prompted her, "that she was a member of the X-Men before their unfortunate...demise, and that she is now a respected businesswoman."

It took a second for those words to sink in. Then the world began to spin around Ororo; so much so that she found herself holding on to the table for support. Dimly, through the blood that rushed to her ears, she heard Sebastian attempting to rescue her. "Miss Munroe does not yet feel ready to issue a public statement," he said. "It is still too soon."

But the fat director was not to be put off. "I still think it would be prudent to act now," he said, "to quell the rumors that the X-Men were terrorists—and indeed that the Hellfire Club were instrumental in their downfall."

"If only they had not been so arrogant," sighed a White Bishop—a middle-aged woman—to the far side of Shaw, "so stubbornly sure that they alone occupied the moral high ground."

It was too much. Ororo let out her pain, her confusion, her disbelief in a single explosive cry of "No!" She buried her face in her hands, but she didn't have to look to know that all eyes had turned towards her. She composed herself and rose, not meeting any of those eyes, staring at the wooden tabletop instead. "If you would excuse me," she murmured, "I have had a very trying day and I am not feeling myself. I am going upstairs to my quarters."

She pushed back her chair and walked stiffly out of the chamber, aware of the heavy silence that followed her. As soon as she was out in the hallway, freed from the scrutiny of her peers, she broke into a run.

* * *

Blackheart had guided Shaw through the personal scenarios of another three X-Men.

Rogue had been first; the Black Kings had found her alongside Mystique and the Brotherhood of Evil Mutants. She had committed appalling crimes and reveled in the heady thrill of being able to get away with them, to take what she wanted from life. When the X-Men had opposed her, she had rushed into combat, laughing, relishing the chance to prove herself. And Blackheart had explained that this was no fabrication, but rather a series of memories. He had plucked them wholesale from Rogue's mind, and left them unchanged.

"Many mortals feel nostalgia for their childhood," he had said. "Mutants, more than most, have reason to yearn for a simpler, happier time. This woman—Rogue, as she now calls herself—has repressed that natural desire. She has buried her past, denying to herself that she could ever have been that person. I thought a small reminder might be in order."

Iceman too had been forced to relive the past; in his case, the day that anti-mutant fascists had taken out their blind hatred on his father. This time, however, Blackheart had allowed him to get home in time, to stop the thugs before they could do serious injury. Except that they had seemed unstoppable. They had refused to stay down, shrugging off whatever he had thrown at them, coming back and hitting his father again and again with their baseball bats, breaking his bones. He had put them down again, harder and harder, and even Shaw had been impressed as this youngster—this most overlooked of the X-Men—had unleashed his full powers, the genetic potential that had rarely been tapped in the real world.

In the end, however, Iceman had had no choice. Blackheart had enhanced his righteous anger just a little—until, for the love of his family, for the life of his father, he had resorted to lethal force. Shaw had left him on his knees on his parents' front lawn at the center of a vast, sprawling translucent ice sculpture. A dozen corpses had been scattered around him, suspended in various twisted positions by the ice. He had been cradling his father's battered but living body, and tears had frozen on his cheeks.

Wolverine, in contrast, had always been prepared to kill when necessary, and so Blackheart had pushed him one step further. He had presented the wildest of the X-Men with a succession of dilemmas in Virtual Reality, the solutions to which were always the same. Wolverine had been happy to extend his claws into Magneto's heart, secure in the knowledge that he was saving the world. He had become no more reticent when required to execute a multitude of villains who didn't make their intentions plain with colorful costumes. He had showed some hesitation when dealing with the fairer sex, but only a little: he had still done what, in his mind, had had to be done. But he had balked at last when faced with a child, a girl no more than three years old. She had riveted him to the spot with her huge, imploring eyes as, with one hand, she had played with the strands of her long, blonde hair.

The other hand had rested on the trigger device of a nuclear weapon.

For a time that, to Wolverine, would seem like an eternity, he had roamed the radioactive wasteland that had once been his world. He had surrendered to his feral instincts, scavenging for food, defending his pitiful lair, because it had been too painful to think, to regret. He had cursed himself a million times over for his hesitation, his weakness. Like his teammates, he would not remember all the details of his dream when he awoke. But in Blackheart's judgement, he would be marginally less likely to err on the side of caution again.

Shaw had begun to wonder about the fate of one particular X-Man. He had said nothing, but he had begun to suspect that Black-heart was deliberately saving the best show for last. As he finally stepped into an opulent bedchamber, then, he knew who he was likely to find there.

The room was hung with white satin drapes, trimmed with lace. It was decorated with Victorian ornaments and paintings in pristine condition. Storm lay beneath the sheets of a majestic four-poster bed and, as Shaw drew closer, he saw that she was weeping into her white pillow. A familiar trident logo was embroidered upon the pillowcase in gold thread. "I suppose I ought not to be surprised," he said.

"When I looked into Ororo Munroe's soul," said Blackheart, "I saw that she was already engaged in a struggle against temptation. Her heart is divided over your proposal to her. I thought I might mitigate in your favor."

"Why?" asked Shaw suspiciously. "Why assist one of your enemies?"

"More than most men, Sebastian Shaw, you should appreciate that today's enemy could be an ally tomorrow. We have similar goals. It might even be that you are more able to achieve them than my current...partner."

Shaw was flattered but still wary. He was ready to issue a cynical rejoinder when Ororo's eyes flicked open—and, to his surprise, she saw him.

"Sebastian!" she gasped. Sitting up, she hurriedly wiped her face with her hand. White sheets slipped away from a negligee that was near transparent and, being a gentleman, Shaw averted his gaze. Then Ororo said: "I have been waiting all night for you to come to bed!" and he found himself staring at her, nonplussed.

"You have done a commendable job thus far," said Blackheart in his ear. "I offer you the chance to finish it. She is confused. You need only offer reassurance and she will be yours."

"I was thinking about the X-Men," said Ororo, "wondering if things might have been different if...had I not..." She swallowed, took Shaw's hand and pulled him down to sit on the bed beside her. He perched on its edge, feeling awkward. Only now did he realize that he was no longer wearing his green combat suit, but rather a white jacket and breeches. He looked for his demon guide, but Blackheart had faded into the shadows, leaving only a hint of brimstone in the air.

It would have been so easy to deceive her. In her vulnerable state, she would believe his lies. He could have had his new White Queen. It was what he had planned. So, why did he falter?

Partly, it was because of Blackheart. It was because Shaw felt that his own game had been wrested out of his control, and that the only way to win it now was not to play. But it was also because of her, because of Ororo Munroe. He had been truthful with her about most things. He admired her, respected her strength, and yet here she was, her spirit abused and broken, begging him for validation. She deserved better. He didn't want to win her like this.

He tried to take a hold of himself. Blackheart's methods may have been more obvious than his own subtle brand of manipulation, but did that make them worse? Sebastian Shaw had not built a business empire by refusing to take a prize that sat so easily within his reach.

"Tell me I did the right thing, Sebastian," Ororo pleaded. "Tell me I did not make a grave mistake when I pledged my allegiance to you and to the Hellfire Club."

And for one of the very few times in his life, Shaw didn't know what to say.

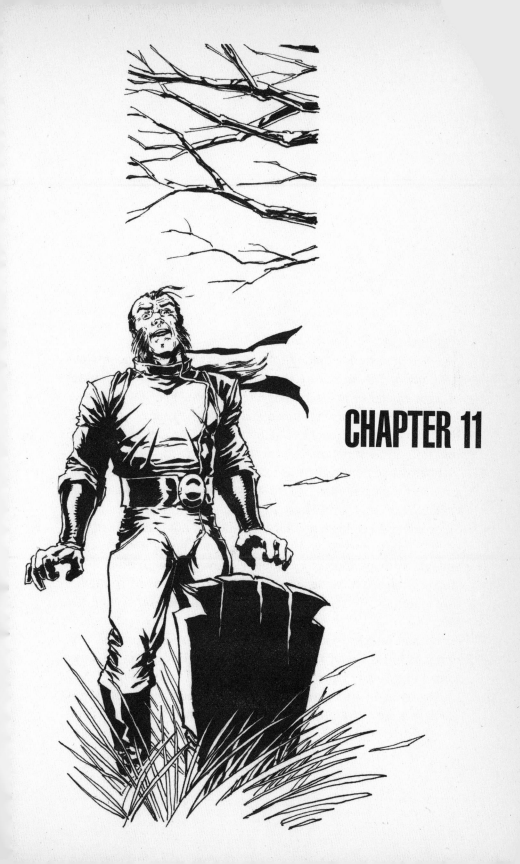

CHAPTER 11

SEBASTIAN SHAW was tired.

He had trudged along for ten blocks with the unconscious body of Trevor Fitzroy slung over his shoulders, ducking out of sight whenever he heard movement. As much as anything else, his constant and unaccustomed state of nervousness was beginning to tell. But he couldn't allow anybody or anything to keep him from his destination. Not this time.

Fitzroy had done as he was told. The portal he had opened from Avengers Mansion had led to the northern tip of Manhattan Island. With only an address to go on—and with neither he nor Shaw having seen his target location—he had not been able to pinpoint it more precisely. However, he had brought them close enough. Perhaps too close, thought Shaw. The butterflies in his stomach refused to settle, and he ached with a mass of contradictory emotions. He scowled, annoyed with himself for feeling like this.

He had attacked Fitzroy from behind, knocking him out with one punch. He would need him again soon. Until then, he didn't intend to take any risks with his treacherous former Rook.

The wrought-iron gates of the cemetery had almost rusted shut. The lawns were overgrown and weeds encroached upon the pathways. Among the headstones, paper-wrapped bunches of dead flowers decayed. If this place suffered from neglect, however, then at least it had been spared the wanton destruction inflicted upon Midtown. Shaw wondered how long it would be before mutant gangs took over the streets here too, pushed northward by the search for sustenance and fresh victims.

Reeva Payge's directions had been vague, and it took him a wearying hour to find the right grave. When he finally set eyes upon it, it was with a mixture of relief and a plunging sensation in his stomach. He let go of Fitzroy, who fell into a heap on the frost-hardened turf.

There was no headstone, just a simple wooden marker. The grave's occupant had been an exceedingly wealthy young man, but his friends had been forced to bury him in secret, in a hurry. Shaw's legs felt weak as he forced them to approach the makeshift memorial. He resisted the urge to kneel, listening instead to his own breathing as he stood and looked at the carved name and dates until time no longer had any meaning to him. Then, at last, he spoke.

"Hello, Shinobi," he said in a husky voice. "Hello, son. It's been a long time."

When Iceman saw the kindly face of Doctor Moira MacTaggert hovering over him, he thought for a blissful instant that he was still in his room beneath the Kree island, that Hank was still alive and everything could still be all right.

He struggled to sit up, not fully awake yet, not even aware of his surroundings. He just wanted reassurance, some confirmation that the events of the past day had been no more than a bad dream. Instead, he felt Moira's hands pressing him down into a threadbare mattress. White walls closed in around him and, aware of an itch around his neck, he felt for it and found something cold and metallic. The memory of his defeat by the Sentinels crashed into his mind, too vivid and painful to have been a simple nightmare.

There were two guards on the door, clad in green and golden armor, armed with blasters.

"Easy, Bobby," said Moira, "you've had a wee bit of a shock. Your body needs time to throw off the effects of the anaesthetic gas."

He was breathing heavily. His throat was dry. His skin was slick with sweat, and he had become dehydrated. He tried to replenish himself by drawing fresh moisture from the atmosphere, but no matter how he tried, nothing happened. It was the collar, he realized, inhibiting his mutant powers. "Where am I?" he croaked.

"In hospital. Don't worry, you're getting the best of care."

He glanced at the guards. "I preferred the old nurses' uniform."

"You're under strict quarantine." Moira put a glass of cold water to his lips, and he sipped from it gratefully. "Just be glad you're not showing any symptoms of the Legacy Virus," she said in a conspiratorial tone, "or they might have killed you before you even reached me."

"'They'? Who are 'they'? Who runs this place?"

"The U.S. government."

Of course. It made sense. Iceman's own government had used Sentinels to deal with the "mutant problem" in the past. And if they couldn't reclaim Manhattan Island from Selene, then neither could they ignore the situation there. They had to attempt to contain it, at least.

A memory shook itself loose inside his head. He wasn't sure where it had come from. He was being manhandled out of the back of a large white van, each arm taken by an armored guard, neither of whom seemed to care what they knocked him against or how hard. His head lolled, his neck feeling like a worn-out spring. He was staring at a sky made gray and heavy by the threat of rain, thinking how strange it looked. It took his cotton wool brain several seconds to realize that he had become used to seeing the stark white ceiling that Selene had placed over New York City.

A shape loomed before him: a building, dark and forbidding, its lines drawn harshly across the dull background. He was being carried towards it, his nostrils filling with the scent of rusted iron. The image of a barbed wire fence was imprinted upon his thoughts, but he didn't recall seeing such a thing.

There was a tender spot on the back of his head. Dimly, he recalled hearing, as if from the far end of a long tunnel, one of his guards shouting: "The mutt's awake!" And that was where the snatch of memory ended, in an explosion of pain and color.

"Great," he sighed, "so I'm in some kind of internment camp for mutants."

"Until your trial," said Moira, "yes."

"My trial for what? For being born different? And I thought it was bad enough for our kind *inside* the barrier."

"It's not what we dreamed of, that's for sure."

"Not even close."

"Selene was sending mutants out from the city, Bobby, to infect people with Legacy. The Sentinels patrol the outside of the barrier to keep it from happening again."

"You mean they want to keep us penned up inside," Iceman retorted. "And you, Moira—I can't believe you're working with them! What happened to your principles?"

"I'm doing all I can!" Moira's raised voice drew the attention of the guards. She smiled to reassure them before continuing in a tone that was softer but no less urgent. "I'm the resident doctor here, Bobby. I do my best for everyone who comes into this camp. Most of them are infected, but these days I can prolong their lives by a year or more. So yes, I work for the government—but that doesn't mean I make their policies for them or condone them. I'm a Legacy sufferer myself; in some eyes, that makes me no better than my patients."

Bobby's anger turned to despondency at this reminder of his friend's condition. "You haven't found a cure yet?" he asked, although she had already told him the answer.

Moira shook her head. "I'm doing my best. I've tried to recreate Hank's findings—but without the data from the Kree computer, there's just too much guesswork involved. It's still my top priority.

It's the only way I can think of to make things better. There are mutants in New York City who don't want to be there. If they weren't dependent on Selene to keep their symptoms at bay, they could leave."

"What, and spend their lives in prison?"

"While they're inside the barrier," said Moira, almost pleading, as if trying to convince herself as much as him, "it's easy for the media to paint them as dangerous villains. If they were out here to put their own case, we could convince the world that they're the victims in all this. And if they were no longer infected, the government would find it much harder to justify detaining them. We could start to turn things around."

Bobby clenched his fists in frustration. "If we could only get that cure from Selene..."

"Enough people have tried."

"Maybe," he said, his lower lip protruding stubbornly, "but not the X-Men."

He hadn't realized how tired Moira had looked until hope dawned across her features and washed away the lines of hardship. She glanced over at the guards and lowered her voice again, sounding overcome. "You mean, all seven of you...the X-Men who disappeared a year ago, with Sebastian Shaw? I hardly dared hope...I thought you might be alone..."

Bobby Drake saw a glimmer of Moira's old passionate fire, and it made him smile for the first time since he had arrived in this time period. "We're back, Moira. We're all back!"

Sebastian Shaw was swimming through a sea of painful memories.

He wasn't accustomed to looking back across the forty-plus years of his life; he had survived this long, come this far, by focusing himself upon the future. But now his eyes glazed over until he was no longer aware of the wooden marker before him, of the cemetery itself. He saw only the surly, defiant face of his dead son, heard only the angry words of days long past. He saw the poor steelworker who had forged a multi-billion-dollar empire with his bare hands, and he asked himself what it had all been for.

Shaw had only ever loved one woman, and she had died in his arms. He had almost forgotten what it was like to be held, to confide in somebody, to feel the simple warmth of companionship. He had built for himself a world in which such things had no place. His relationships were handled like chess games. He engaged with others only for the purpose of advancing his own position, and he always knew that their eyes were on the grand prize too. Nobody could be trusted. They would all betray him in the end.

For the first time since he had plotted the course of his life in the sweltering heat of a Pennsylvania steel mill, Shaw asked himself if he had taken the right path.

Lost in such anguished thoughts, he failed to hear the approach of his enemies until it was too late.

He was alerted, in the end, by Trevor Fitzroy's death rattle: He must have been stirring from his unconscious state when Lady Deathstrike had impaled his heart upon her adamantium claws. The brash young upstart was no loss, of course, but he took with him Shaw's only hope of escape from this miserable world. He felt the all-too-familiar ache of despair at seeing his plans crushed, and a surge of irrational anger toward Shinobi for delaying him here, for reaching out beyond the grave to frustrate and disappoint him again.

Deathstrike was crouching over Fitzroy's corpse, a euphoric grin on her face. Shaw turned his back to her. Now that he was listening for them, he had heard footsteps behind him. He was not surprised to find himself facing Donald Pierce.

"I didn't think you were the family type, Shaw," sneered the cyborg. He glanced at Shinobi's grave. "Don't worry, I can arrange a father-son reunion."

"Is that the most original threat you can come up with?" asked Shaw mildly.

Pierce scowled. "I don't need threats. I've waited a long time for this moment, Shaw. I'm going to crush the life out of you with my own cybernetic hands."

"You always did lack imagination," said Shaw. He sounded bored, but it was a bluff. He was trying to rile his foe into making mistakes as Fitzroy had done. It would be harder with Pierce, but not impossible. He was strong in physical terms but weak in all important respects. He had allowed himself to become consumed by jealousy and hatred. All Shaw had to do was coax those emotions to the surface.

"You never thought much of me, did you Shaw? You never thought I was good enough for your old boys' club." Shaw shrugged in a deliberately provocative manner. Pierce took two steps closer to him. "You left me to die!"

"I gave you a chance," said Shaw. "You failed me. You weren't good enough."

"I proved myself a better man than you. What have you got now, Shaw? You've lost your precious Hellfire Club; you've lost everything!"

"Rather that," said Shaw, "than play the role of lapdog to that treacherous witch."

Pierce bristled. "I am a Black Bishop, a member of the Inner Circle. We rule this city!"

"You're a liability, Pierce," spat Shaw. "I realized that; Selene will too, in time."

"A pity, then," said Pierce coldly, "that you will not be around to see it."

Shaw had been prepared for the telegraphed attack, but he was distracted by the sudden realization that Deathstrike was immediately behind him. She had sneaked up on him without him hearing her. He moved almost too late: an energy blast from Pierce's eyes sizzled past his ear, and he felt its heat wash over him. He threw himself at his former colleague, bruising his shoulder as he collided with what felt like solid metal, unable to absorb the kinetic energy of his attack because he had created it himself. Pierce was staggered, but Shaw couldn't unbalance him. The Black Bishop broke his hold and hurled him away. He expected to feel Lady Deathstrike's claws across his back, but she made no such move.

This was a personal vendetta for her partner, and she was leaving him to fulfil it. For now.

Pierce bore down upon Shaw: he was reaching for his throat with steel fingers, trying to throttle him. But unable to get a grip on his writhing foe, the frustrated cyborg resorted to using his fists instead. That was just what Shaw had wanted.

In less fraught circumstances, he would have let the blows bounce off him and taunted his ineffectual attacker. Right now, however, he needed every advantage he could get. He reacted as if hurt, hoping that Pierce wouldn't stop to realize the truth. He made a show of pretending to fight back but he was really biding his time, storing the power that was being fed to him. He could feel it crackling in his cells: it almost hurt to keep it contained.

When finally Shaw did strike, it was with a fully-charged uppercut, which cracked Pierce's headset and sent him somersaulting head over heels and skidding across the dry mud on his back. He anticipated Deathstrike's reaction to that. He turned and dropped to his haunches as she sprang at him. Her claws whistled over Shaw's head, but she adjusted her tactics before he could retaliate. She was a more intelligent fighter than Pierce: she denied Shaw the brute force that would only strengthen him, but her claws thrust closer, ever closer, to his chest and he knew that his powers couldn't stop her from cutting out his heart.

He tried to push her away from him, but she used her martial artistry to turn his bodyweight against him. Shaw crashed to the ground, and Deathstrike threw herself upon him. But that was her first mistake. She may have been aware of his abilities intellectually, but in the heat of battle she had expected him to react like anybody else upon being felled. She had expected him to be winded, to give her that vital instant in which to penetrate his defenses. She learned her folly as her chest was greeted by a punishing kick.

She recovered quickly, but Shaw had time to stand and prepare himself for her next lunge. They grappled again, and her claws stabbed through his purloined combat jacket, between his ribs. He absorbed the kinetic component of the blow, but Deathstrike had four razor-sharp points of adamantium resting against his skin, and she eased them into his flesh. The pain brought tears to his eyes, but he blinked them away and seized her right arm before she could retract it. At last, he could put his superior strength to use. He didn't know if the limb was real or artificial, but he tried to wrench it out of its socket all the same. Deathstrike couldn't break his grip, so she slashed at him with her free hand. Her claws, sapped of their momentum, could not cut deep, but they left parallel marks across Shaw's knuckles.

His left hand was afire, but he clung to his opponent stubbornly. With his right hand, he reached behind her back, took her right shoulder and twisted her around, using her as a shield as Pierce, now balancing groggily on his knees, unleashed another optic blast. His scarred face lengthened in horror as he saw that his partner had taken the brunt of his impetuous attack. With Deathstrike dazed, Shaw flexed his supercharged muscles and snapped her back.

Flinging the broken cyborg aside like a sack of garbage, he turned his attention to his lesser but more hated foe. Pierce ran at him with an incoherent scream but, confident of victory now, Shaw too allowed himself to surrender to his raw emotions. Fitzroy was dead. This miserable half-man had stolen his only chance to reverse his misfortune, to take the source of Selene's power from her, and why? For the sake of some pathetic vendetta; because Donald Pierce had never been able to accept the fact that he wasn't good enough. A hot well bubbled up inside Shaw's chest, only given more heat and force by the Black Bishop's hydraulically-powered, metal-reinforced punches. Engulfed in a red mist of fury, he lashed out again and again, not caring if his fists impacted with steel or flesh, not caring even as the steel began to crack and the flesh to liquefy beneath his knuckles.

Shaw didn't recall the moment at which Pierce fell. He wasn't consciously aware of pounding a fallen foe. He didn't realize for a time that he was weakening, no longer invigorated by his enemy's blows. It was only as his body discharged its last iota of stolen energy—or perhaps some time after that—that the red mist receded. He could see the gray world around him again, see Pierce's battered corpse at his feet, and he felt cold and sick.

Across the dead silence of the cemetery, he heard the sound of a slow handclap.

The White Knight was walking through the headstones towards him. He had removed his mask, but it took Shaw a moment to accept what was revealed as a consequence: a face that he was more accustomed to seeing reversed in mirrors.

"Bravo!" said the leader of the rebels. "I wasn't sure you could beat both Pierce and Deathstrike alone. Sometimes I forget how driven I once was."

Shaw didn't know how it could be, but he was facing himself—or at least a good facsimile thereof. His mind cycled sluggishly through the possible explanations: could this be a trick on Selene's part? A clone or a shape-shifter?

He didn't want his doppelganger to know that he had the advantage over him—so, instead of the obvious question, the important one, he asked: "How did you find me?"

The White Knight—the other Sebastian Shaw—halted a few feet in front of him. "I came here too," he said, "when I was your age. I was hurt, and I allowed my emotions to rule me, to divert me from my path. I don't know what I was thinking."

"I wanted to see where my son was buried," snarled Shaw.

"As I recall," said the White Knight smoothly. "But to mourn for an heir who was lost to us a long time before he died, or to dance on his grave?" He held up a silencing hand. "No, don't bother to say anything, Sebastian. I never did work out the answer to that question."

Shaw was beginning to realize what must have happened. "You went back, didn't you?" He narrowed his eyes suspiciously. "You made Fitzroy open a portal for you."

His future self inclined his head in confirmation.

"Then...your past isn't mine. In your past, Deathstrike couldn't have killed Fitzroy."

The White Knight's eyes were dark, and a faint smirk was poised upon his lips. Shaw shouldn't have been surprised that he could read nothing in the older man's face; he had practiced that same inscrutable expression himself.

"Pierce couldn't have found you here," he concluded. "Why would he? We're a long way from the subway station, and nobody could have followed me through Fitzroy's portal."

"I hoped it wouldn't come to this," said the White Knight quietly.

"You told Pierce where to find me, didn't you?"

The White Knight smiled a humorless, ironic smile. "I suppose I ought to have known better by now. We never could rely upon that ineffectual madman." He reached inside his clean white jacket and produced a gun. Shaw eyed it warily. Ordinary bullets couldn't harm him, of course: they lost their impetus in the instant that they hit him, and fell to the ground without breaking his skin. But his future self knew that.

"I designed this gun myself," he said. "It fires special pellets: they adhere to their target and inject a payload of thousands of nanoscopic organisms into the blood. Our mutant power can't stop them. Once they're inside your body, they'll burrow into every one of your cells—and then they'll explode. It's a gruesome but relatively quick death."

Shaw licked his dry lips as his doppelganger leveled the weapon at him. He had to buy time to think. He had never before faced a foe whose abilities, intelligence and ambitions he considered the equal of his own. He thought he might die this time. "You and I are not the same person," he said with cold contempt. "I do not accept it. I would never bow down before the likes of your Black Queen."

It was a guess, but the White Knight's reaction told Shaw that it was right on target. "Once, I believed the same," he said with a heavy sigh. "I thought I could win the game alone, but I have paid a high price for my hubris. My dreams of power are long gone; for the past year, I have done only what it took to survive. I have played the role of the dutiful Black Knight."

"Selene is expecting tonight's attack, isn't she?"

"She orchestrated it through me. It will be her final victory, her chance to rid herself of the remaining opposition to her rule."

"Then why are you here?" cried Shaw. "I was about to leave this time, to fulfil my destiny, to become...you." The words almost stuck in his throat. "You've changed your own history—and if you fire that gun now, you'll kill yourself as surely as you kill me."

"That," said his future self, "is precisely my intention."

He thumbed the safety catch off the gun and squeezed the trigger.

Lady Liberty lay facedown in New York harbor like a drowned woman. Her torch had been shattered as if the dark water had extinguished its flame. Her former pedestal still reached for the sky, but it looked thin and fragile against the harsh white background of the barrier.

The sight made Cyclops ache inside. He almost wanted to cry, if only to let out the pain, but he wasn't sure he could. After all he had been through, he was experiencing a kind of emotional fatigue. It sapped at his resolve and he knew that, for his team's sake, he had to fight it—because they would probably be feeling the same. He had to inspire them, set them an example, lift their morale. The leader of the X-Men couldn't afford the luxury of feeling.

He shouldn't have let the broken statue draw his attention. He dragged his gaze back to the deserted sidewalk beneath him. He stared through the horizontal slats of the window blinds and tried to penetrate the lengthening shadows. His heart leapt as he heard a clattering sound, but it was only a rusted tin can blown by the gathering wind.

He turned back to the others with a dour expression and a shake of his head. "No sign of anybody else out there."

"It has been almost ten hours since we fled from the subway station," observed Storm.

"And at least two since anyone showed up here," said Wolverine. "It's beginning to look like we're all that made it."

"I still can't find Iceman," reported Phoenix. "I've scanned the entire area between here and 23rd Street and Lexington, where I last had a fix on him. Either he's taken a very long detour or..." She didn't have to complete the sentence. Even Jean Grey couldn't detect a dead mind.

"Widen the search," said Cyclops, "and see if you can find any trace of Sage or Shaw." He glanced at Storm and corrected himself: "Either of the Shaws."

The White Knight's secondary base had turned out to be a seventh-story office suite that had once belonged to an insurance company. It offered an excellent view of the surrounding area, and therefore—assuming a sensible watch system—advance warning of an enemy approach. Cyclops had stationed sentries at the windows accordingly, but he was still worried that anyone unable to fly could too easily be trapped up here by an attack from below. He had sabotaged the elevators himself and instructed the young mutant Lightshow to create the illusion that the stairway had collapsed. Nobody had questioned his right to give orders: with their leader absent, the would-be rebels had had little to say for themselves. As far as Scott could tell, none of them had combat experience—and though their spirits hadn't been completely crushed by Selene, they were still frightened of her.

The six X-Men had gathered in a small corner office to discuss their next move in private.

"I doubt we'll see the younger Shaw again," said Storm.

Phoenix nodded thoughtfully. "If what he told you is true..."

"And we've no reason to believe a word he says," put in Wolverine.

"He was being honest with me," said Storm firmly, "I'd stake my life on it."

"If what Shaw told you is true," repeated Phoenix, "then his younger self has probably left this time period by now."

"How?" asked Nightcrawler.

"Fitzroy," grumbled Wolverine.

"So, do you think Shaw took him along for the ride?" asked Rogue. "Because if not, if Fitzroy's still here, then what's to stop us from getting hold of him ourselves?"

Cyclops shook his head. "If we were destined to follow Shaw, I think we'd know by now."

Wolverine sneered. "Bull! Far as I'm concerned, you make your own destiny. I'm not gonna roll over and die just 'cos you think that's what we're supposed to do."

Cyclops tightened his lips and refused to rise to the bait. "The fact remains that, even before Shaw went back to the past, we could already see the effects of what he would do there. But we've seen and heard nothing of our own future selves."

"So, whatever we do," said Storm, "we won't get the opportunity to follow him."

"Unless we fought Selene a year ago and she killed us all," said Nightcrawler with a shiver.

Rogue groaned. "I hate all this time paradox stuff. It gives me a king-size headache."

"You're guessing," said Wolverine. "We can't know for sure what's going to happen."

"Of course not," said Cyclops, "and if we do encounter Fitzroy, we should make every effort to capture him alive. But until then, I think our most realistic option is to take down Selene in the here and now. We can worry about the rest later."

"I agree," said Phoenix, "but it's not going to be as easy as all that, is it?"

"Shaw—the White Knight—and Sage said they had a plan," said Storm.

"But they ain't here, are they!" said Wolverine. "And I doubt they confided in any of those poor mooks out there."

"Even if they do show up now," said Rogue, "can we still trust them? I mean, now that we know who this so-called 'White Knight' really is?"

"It's a good question," said Cyclops. "Shaw could be planning to lead us all into a trap."

"Even if he is not," said Storm, "he has admitted that his goal is to take Selene's throne for himself. Do we wish to be instrumental in handing him that kind of power?"

Cyclops was surprised that she, of all the X-Men, should have made that point. It hadn't escaped his notice that Ororo had been distracted of late. She had also spoken up for Shaw on more than one occasion. The pair had spent a lot of time together: Shaw had saved Ororo's life, and now he had apparently confided some of his secrets in her. Scott knew he ought to trust his teammate, and he didn't want to invade her privacy, but he would have to start asking questions soon. Unless, as now seemed likely, she was beginning to realize that she didn't know the erstwhile Black King as well as she had thought she did.

"Do we have a choice?" asked Nightcrawler. "We need his organization."

"If only for their numbers," sighed Cyclops.

Wolverine grinned. "Cannon fodder, you mean?"

"No, Logan, that's not what I meant. Shaw's people can keep the Hellfire Club's demons occupied while we go after the bigger fish." And some of them, Cyclops knew, would die, because they were ill-prepared and ill-equipped for a mission like this. He told himself that they were fighting in a good cause, that they had chosen to follow a dream despite their fears.

"So it's agreed, then?" asked Phoenix. "Siding with Shaw is the lesser of two evils."

"For now, at least," murmured Nightcrawler.

Cyclops looked up as the office door opened. Standing on the threshold was the White Knight: he must have entered the building from its rear, unseen by the sentries. Either that or he had countermanded Scott's instructions to report any sighting of him to the X-Men. He had obviously been in a fight: his expensive suit was disheveled and torn, its white fabric marked with grass stains. He was no longer wearing his white mask. His face was not bruised but it was red from exertion, and his black hair was plastered to his head.

"You have made the right decision," said Sebastian Shaw with quiet confidence.

Wolverine had been perching on the edge of a table; now he got to his feet, glowering at the newcomer, his fingers twitching. "We'll need more'n your word for that, pal."

"Then let me see if I can allay your worries," said Shaw. He gestured toward the outer office. "If you would care to join us, I am about to hold a briefing."

"We're still an X-Man down," said Phoenix. "Iceman hasn't arrived yet."

"And nor has your pet computer," said Rogue, "unless she's with you?"

Shaw's habitual smirk slipped for a second, and a shadow passed across his eyes. "Several of our members are missing, Sage and Iceman among them. We have no alternative, I'm afraid, but to consider them dead. We have work to do."

Iceman strained with all his might, trying to create the tiniest sliver of ice inside his inhibitor collar. If it could melt in there, perhaps short out the mechanism....But it was no good. It felt as if there were a hole in his brain, like his captors had cut out an important part of him. They might as well have amputated one of his limbs.

The armored guards raised their blasters as the door slid open, relaxing again as Moira MacTaggert re-entered the white room. "I did what I could," she said, sitting on the edge of Bobby's bed. She gave a wistful shrug. "I don't know if it'll do any good."

"It has to," he insisted. "You told your boss-man about the attack on Selene, right?"

"It would have helped if you'd known more details."

"I just know it's going to be some time tonight."

"They've thrown a lot of resources at the barrier already," said Moira. "The Avengers, S.H.I.E.L.D., the Fantastic Four...they've all tried and failed to break through it."

"I know that—and I know it's a long shot, but if they can try again tonight, just hurl everything they've got at it. . . . At the very least, it's got to distract Selene. It's got to give our side an advantage. I mean, hasn't it? She can't fight on that many fronts at once, can she?"

"I explained all that to Gyrich," said Moira. "I'm just not sure that . . . well . . ."

Bobby pouted. "In his eyes, you mean, the X-Men are no different to Selene."

"Something like that," she said with an apologetic smile. Bobby didn't know how she could be so calm about it. But then, he reminded himself, she had had a year to get used to all this, to accept her own helplessness in the face of a worsening situation. She had probably grown so used to being disappointed that she had had to make herself stop hoping too hard.

She lowered her voice so that the guards wouldn't hear her. "But I spoke to somebody else."

"Who?"

"Let's just say I still some useful contacts, and I don't mean inside the government. With a bit of luck—and assuming they're in town—the Avengers should be hearing about our little problem within the hour, even if Gyrich won't talk to them himself. Somehow, I can't picture him standing up to Captain America, can you?"

Iceman grinned. "You're a miracle-worker, Moira." But his newfound exuberance was dampened as his thoughts returned to his own situation. "If only we could get a message to the others. . . . I suppose there's no point in asking if Gyrich agreed to let me go?"

"I'm sorry, Bobby. All we can do now is wait, and keep our fingers crossed."

Storm stood at the back of the meeting room, watching and listening closely as Sebastian Shaw gave instructions to his ragtag army. He used all the materials to hand, writing names on a whiteboard as he divided his troops into strike teams and displaying plans of the Hellfire Club building on an overhead projector. He conducted a mission briefing as if it were a presentation to a group of bankers, but even Cyclops could find no flaws in his plan.

The rebels—Storm counted thirty in all, plus the unmasked White Knight and the six X-Men—filed towards the staircase in apprehensive silence. Shaw watched them go with an unreadable expression; Ororo hung back, waiting until only he and she remained in the room. Then, as Shaw made for the door, she blocked his path and eased it shut behind her.

"I am going to ask you a question, Shaw," she said. "And for once, I would like a direct answer. No lies, no obfuscation, just the truth. Do you think you can manage that?"

"For you, dear lady, anything."

"I have met two versions of Sebastian Shaw in this time period. Which are you?"

Shaw smiled to himself as if at some private joke. He avoided Ororo's gaze for a few seconds and, when he looked at her again, his expression was deadly serious. "I am, as you have no doubt surmised, the younger version." He spread his arms and looked down at his white suit. "I am wearing this costume for the first time."

"And what happened to the original White Knight?"

"He was working for Selene," said Shaw grimly.

"That does not answer my question."

"She has been pulling the strings of this so-called rebellion from the start."

Ororo was alarmed. "Then she knows our plans? She will be expecting our attack."

"She is expecting *an* attack," said Shaw. "I have made a few alterations to my...predecessor's tactics. Chief among them is a small matter of timing."

Ororo nodded. "That explains why you were so insistent we strike as soon as possible."

"The Black Queen thinks she has several more hours to prepare," said Shaw. "She has lost many of her Inner Circle, but soon she will have more followers around her, more mutants desperate to do her bidding in return for extending their wretched lives."

"How can we go into battle," said Ororo, "when we cannot trust our own leader?"

Shaw's eyes gleamed with a zeal that she had never seen in them before. "This is our last chance, Ororo—our only chance—to take that witch by surprise. We have to do this!"

And then he seized her shoulders and, inadvertently she was sure, paraphrased his own future self's words to her. The words that he had said just after he had lied to her.

"I need you to trust me, Ororo, just this once. Do you think you can do that?"

CHAPTER 12

THE BLACK Queen's crystal ball was relaying the X-Men's torments to her in soft focus. For several minutes now, she had been transfixed—and the Beast had found it just as hard to tear his gaze away from the unsettling pictures. Whether by accident or design—and he suspected the latter—the ball hung in the air at just the right angle for him to see every detail of the scenarios that Blackheart had created for his friends.

Right now, he was looking at an image of Bobby Drake. He looked small and frightened against the austere surroundings of an oak-paneled courtroom, dressed in a black suit two sizes too large for him. He was facing a barrage of hostile questions, stumbling over his words as he tried to defend himself against multiple charges of homicide. He testified that he had acted only in the defense of his father, but nobody wanted to hear it. He was forced to repeat his claim again and again, his frustration boiling over into righteous anger at his unfair treatment. Hank knew that, even as Bobby protested his innocence to the court, so too was he insisting to himself that he had done the right thing.

Selene waved a hand, and the scene was shrouded with mists. When they parted, Bobby Drake had gone and Kurt Wagner stood in his place.

Nightcrawler had become the swashbuckling star of a major Hollywood movie, and a host of familiar faces surrounded him at the lavish premiere. Among them, Hank recognized John Proudstar: in the real world, he had joined the X-Men at the same time as Kurt and had taken the code name of Thunderbird. He had been killed during one of his first missions. Also present was Illyana Rasputin, the younger sister of sometime X-Man Colossus, whose life had recently been lost to the Legacy Virus. But even though Kurt appeared to be having the time of his life, he wore a distant, troubled expression, and it looked to Hank like was simply going through the motions. He wasn't yet ready to accept this new world.

"If you expect the X-Men to bow to your tawdry theatrics," he said, heartened, "then you have evidently learned little from your past defeats."

Scowling, Selene sent the crystal ball back to its dais with a flick of her fingers. As she stood and glided across the room to her captive, her red lips twisted into a smile again. "Ah, my dear, dear Beast," she cooed, "your health must be improving for you to dare speak to me in such a manner. I must confess, I have almost missed your foolish bravado."

"I expect you will see all the—" Hank began, but the rest of his words were lost to a gasp of pain as Selene's eyes flashed and something twisted inside his head.

"I may let Blackheart have some fun with you too, before I kill you. I wonder what form your dream would take? Perhaps you could learn what it would feel like to have your bestial side take over, your intellect repressed." Hank could feel her cold eyes in his mind as she sought out his greatest fear.

"Or I could become something even more unspeakable, like you," he snarled.

"Enough jollity!" Selene snatched the Beast's left hand, and once again he felt his blood being pricked from his veins by one of the tendrils that held him. She turned away from him so he couldn't see her reaction as she licked the viscous fluid from her fingers.

When she turned back, however, there was no disguising her delight.

"It appears I have underestimated you, my friend," she said. "You will be pleased to hear that your disease has gone into remission—which means that your life's work is complete at last. The super-cell that will cure the Legacy Virus is present in your bloodstream."

Hank had dreamt of this moment for a long time, but he had never pictured it quite like this. He ought to have felt relieved, triumphant even. Instead, he just felt sick.

"Sadly for you," said Selene, "it is of little use to me in there."

"Listen to me, Ororo! It is important that you listen to me."

Sebastian's tone was urgent. He had taken Ororo's arms in a grip like steel, and he was shaking her, his teeth clenched in grim determination. It was the last thing she had expected, and she tried to pull away from him. "You're scaring me, Sebastian. Is something wrong?"

"Everything about this place is wrong."

"I don't understand."

"None of this is real, Ororo. Remember the Hellfire Club. Remember the Beast and Selene and the Legacy Virus. Remember Blackheart!"

"I...I remember. But that was all such a long time ago. Sebastian..."

"Then how did you escape from him?"

The White Queen stared at her White King blankly. She remembered asking herself the same question a few hours ago. She had dismissed it then as unimportant. But Sebastian Shaw had a talent for finding her weak points. He had always known what she was thinking. He had always been able to turn her life upside-down with words that had to be—but couldn't possibly be—true.

"You didn't escape from Blackheart, Ororo," he persisted. "You're still there, in that cavern beneath the Hellfire Club building. The X-Men are still there. *I'm* still there. The last few years have been an illusion, played out in a few short minutes. Listen to me!"

He let go of her, and Ororo suddenly realized that she was exposed. She drew the bedclothes up around her shoulders. She was looking at Shaw in a different light now, all the fears and uncertainties of the past returning to haunt her. "I…I don't know if I can trust you…" she stammered as two worlds collided inside her head.

He stood and straightened his white jacket, appearing calmer now that he had begun to get through to her. "If I intended to deceive you, Ororo," he said, "I would have played my part in this scenario as Blackheart planned. It is still my fond hope that you will accept my offer to become my White Queen in reality—but this is not how I wish to achieve that goal."

Ororo felt as if she had been distracted from a pressing problem for a few minutes only for it to return to her with crushing force. She remembered Shaw's offer to her, and she knew now that she had not given him an answer. That was why she had been unable to shake off her nagging doubts, why she had needed somebody to tell her that everything was all right.

She didn't belong here. She hadn't chosen this life. Not yet. Perhaps not ever.

She blinked, and suddenly she was back in the cavern, back in her costume, and the Hellfire Club and the White King and Storm Investments were only parts of a fading dream. The rest of the X-Men stood around her, frozen like waxwork figures in battle-ready positions. Of their demon foe, there was no sign.

"Their souls are imprisoned as were ours, on a plane beyond this one."

Storm jumped as Shaw broke the silence. She hadn't realized that he had returned with her. She felt a sudden rush of embarrassment. She had invited him into her bed. She hadn't been in her right mind then, but the scenario that Blackheart had created for her had not been conjured from nothing, it had been based on her own hopes and fears. The demon had taken her most private dreams and shown them to the very last person who should ever have seen them. She couldn't even look Shaw in the face any more. She felt violated.

"I can see that," she said irritably. She formed a cloud beneath the high roof of the cavern and brought down a shower of rain, blasting the cold water into her teammates' faces with a horizontal wind. It was the quickest way to bring them back to their senses—but the concentrated, violent expression of her powers was also calculated to relieve her frustration.

"I had no choice!" moaned Iceman under his breath as he came round. Wolverine dropped to his haunches and popped his claws as if expecting trouble, relaxing only a little when he saw where he was. Nightcrawler looked heavenward and offered a thankful prayer.

Storm didn't have to explain what had happened. Cyclops's only question as he took in his surroundings anew was: "What happened to Blackheart?"

"He was not here when I awoke," she said.

"Looks like Old Stone-Face has popped out and left us to it," said Rogue. "He probably didn't expect us to break out of his little psychodramas so quickly."

"I don't like it," said Wolverine. "Smells like a trap to me."

"He wouldn't be the first big bad villain to underestimate the X-Men, sugar."

"Either way," said Cyclops, "the Beast's situation leaves us with no choice. Trap or no trap, we have to keep going until we reach Selene's throne room."

He set off at a run, leading the way up the stone steps which, according to Shaw, had once provided access to the lowest level of the Hellfire Club building proper. The door at their head had been destroyed now, of course, and a stone wall stood in its place.

For the X-Men, however, it was hardly an insurmountable problem.

As Cyclops set about the barrier with his optic blasts, he was unaware that he was being observed. Selene's crystal ball had

leapt from its dais in response to a signal that the Beast had neither seen nor heard, shooting across the throne room to slap into
the Black Queen's gloved hand. Captor and captive alike had
watched in silence as Shaw had revealed the truth to Storm,
whereupon the scene had changed and they had witnessed the
X-Men's awakening.

The Beast's heart soared. "Reluctant as I am to resort to recrim-
inations," he said, "I did attempt to impress upon you the likelihood of this contingency." It was no longer just a matter of
expressing "foolish bravado" as Selene had put it; this was one
thing he could still do to aid his teammates. The longer he could
keep her distracted, angry with him, the less time she would have
to spend preparing for their arrival. He even resumed his struggles
against the tendrils at his wrists and ankles. He was still woozy
from his radiation treatment, but the knowledge that his system
was finally winning its own fight against the Legacy Virus was a
powerful tonic. He could feel his strength returning.

Selene did not react to his taunt. She dismissed the crystal ball
and remained standing with her back to her prisoner for several
long seconds. When she did turn to face him again, he knew that
something was wrong. Far from looking disappointed or angered
by her setback, the Black Queen's face was alight with glee.

"My dear, dear Doctor McCoy," she said, "how willfully you
contrive to misunderstand. I have not even the heart to punish the
insolence of one so naïve, so blissfully unaware of the nature of
things. Do you truly believe that a handful of pitiful mortals could
outwit the offspring of the Prince of Lies himself?"

"I believe your diabolical partner was met with stronger resistance than he had anticipated. Whoever could have guessed that
our friend Shaw has a conscience after all?"

Selene laughed contemptuously. "I know my old Black King as
well as anybody," she claimed, "and he acted precisely as my new
King and I expected he would."

The Beast said nothing. He was pulling so hard against his bonds
that the muscles in his arms and legs ached, but it was to no avail.

"Blackheart's intention was not to corrupt Shaw," said Selene, "for his soul is, after all, already stained beyond all hope of redemption. Even his decision to tell Storm the truth was motivated by a selfish desire to assert his independence from us. Rather, we have given an enemy cause to doubt his own motives, his very self. We have weakened his resolve. I have control of the New York branch of the Hellfire Club; Shaw will not rest until he has taken it back from me. Today, my consort has lessened the possibility of such an outcome."

"Why not just kill him if he's such a threat to you?"

"Oh, I have not finished with Sebastian Shaw. Not yet."

As she spoke, Selene walked into another alcove. She emerged with a large glass container, which she placed on the stone floor at the Beast's feet. He estimated that it would hold about a gallon of liquid, and he shuddered as he realized what it had to be for. He tried to keep his captor engaged in conversation, to delay her.

"Nevertheless, he did insert the proverbial spanner into your plans for Storm."

"On the contrary," said Selene, "Ororo Munroe now believes that there is a noble side to Sebastian Shaw's nature. She is closer than ever before to accepting his proposal. Your teammate is strong-willed, my friend: she could never have been brainwashed into joining Shaw's Inner Circle, at least not for long. How much more satisfying, then, to see her make that decision of her own free will? How sweet the taste of a heroic soul thus compromised?"

Hank was still trying to think of an answer to that when he felt a prickly pain all over the back of his body. The tendrils were extending their needles—or thorns, or whatever they were—into his skin again, but not just into his wrist this time. He gasped, and tried to arch himself away from them. He felt as if he had lain down on a bed of nails. And now he could feel the needles drawing blood, draining his newly restored vitality from him.

Selene pressed her fingers against the wall beside Hank's shoulder. He couldn't see what she was doing, but when she pulled her hand away she was holding a length of tendril, which became a loop as she teased it towards her. Then she leaned forward and, in one quick, feral motion, tore the squirming tentacle apart with her teeth. Blood gushed from both ends of the ruptured pipeline, and she gave them each a savage yank, pulling them further out of the wall until they reached down into the glass container. The Beast watched in numb horror as his own blood was pumped sluggishly into the receptacle. It was filling at an alarming rate.

"I must apologize for my unseemly haste," Selene smirked, her lips and chin red, "but as I'm sure you'll appreciate, this precious fluid has to be placed in a refrigeration unit as soon as possible. After all, we wouldn't want your super-cell to conclude its work and extinguish itself before I can isolate and duplicate it. Not after all your hard work."

"That cure belongs to Mankind, Selene," insisted the Beast through gritted teeth.

The Black Queen laughed. "You are very much mistaken. The cure belongs to me now—and to ensure that it remains that way, I will of course be draining *all* the blood from your malformed body." She nuzzled Hank's chin with her knuckles, almost affectionately. "Oh, I know that, strictly speaking, I don't need it all—a small sample ought to be enough for my purposes—but you see, my dear Doctor, I am a hoarder by nature. If I want something, then I'm afraid I have to be the only person who has it—and I have to have it all."

"You're psychotic!" spat the Beast.

"I knew you'd understand," purred Selene.

The stone wall was thick, but it began to crack under the force of Cyclops's repeated blasts. Storm stood a little way behind her comrades, lost in silent contemplation. She was dwelling upon the dream that Blackheart had created for her, but the precise details of it were proving ever more elusive. She chased them around her memory, but they twisted and flickered and slipped through her mental grasp like shadows.

She did remember that the dream had been full of warmth: not only the physical warmth of a well-heated, sumptuous Hellfire Club apartment, but the more satisfying inner glow of achievement, of knowing that her actions had improved lives. And then there had been a more intimate warmth, the warmth that came from sharing her bed with another person.

In contrast, real life felt cold. Despite the close heat of the catacombs, she felt as if her skin were breaking out in goose pimples. She was worried for her teammates, about what Selene might have planned for them. She feared that the Beast might already be dead. And she dreaded the prospect of a Legacy Virus cure under the sole control of the Black Queen.

For as long as she had been with the X-Men, it had been like this. Professor Xavier dreamt of a better world—but the would-be architects of that dream were forever on the defensive, forced to react to new and deadlier threats. They always seemed to be fighting somebody, but rarely did they gain from it; the best they could hope for was to safeguard what they already had. Sometimes, they couldn't even do that. Sometimes, a friend fell or the public were given fresh reason to distrust those who weren't like them. Sometimes, they couldn't even stop a madman from achieving his goal; a madman like Stryfe, the mutant from the future who had unleashed the Legacy Virus upon his own past in the first place.

There had to be a better way than this.

Ororo shook herself out of her introspection, sensing Shaw's eyes upon her. She returned his concerned look with a weak smile. She still felt a little awkward around him, although she could no longer remember why. All she did know was that he had passed up the opportunity to take what he wanted from her. He had done the honorable thing, and saved her again.

And then there was no more time for thinking. Rogue stepped forward to complete the job that Cyclops had begun; she shattered the weakened obstruction with three resounding blows. Storm brought up the rear as the X-Men clambered over the wreckage to find themselves at one end of a long, narrow hallway. The floor was carpeted and the walls were hung with paintings. Ororo saw four closed doors and was alarmed to realize that she knew what lay behind each of them, even though she had never been through them. Thanks to Blackheart, this building felt like a home to her. But it was a home that had been invaded.

At the far end of the hallway, a spiral staircase snaked upwards. Waiting at its foot were eight demon creatures in Hellfire Club uniforms.

Storm summoned and redirected the air currents from the cavern behind her, and a fierce wind whistled past the X-Men. It gained strength as it rushed along the passageway and picked up Wolverine, who was already racing to the attack. He allowed himself to be carried by it and approached his foes like a cannonball, claws outstretched. Some of the demons came forward to meet him, but the wind had acquired the force of a hurricane and it scattered them like tenpins. They tried to pick themselves up, but Wolverine was already in their midst. By the time his teammates had reached him, all but two of the demons were back on the floor, leaking black blood from deep wounds. Cyclops felled the first with an optic blast, while Phoenix picked up the second telekinetically and smashed it into a wall.

The X-Men mounted the staircase almost without missing a footstep. More demons were charging down towards them, and Cyclops's eye-beam struck out again and again. The few creatures that were able to get past it were dispatched by Wolverine's claws or Rogue's fists—and any demon which tried to throw itself at the advancing heroes from one of the higher balconies found its direction suddenly and painfully reversed by Storm or Phoenix.

They attained two more floors in this fashion, but their foes seemed numberless and, although they weren't strong, they were extremely persistent. They reached the highest basement level—the one on which Selene's throne room was located—but once there, they found that they could go no further. A veritable horde of demons had been lying in wait for them, and they attacked from every direction, too many for even the X-Men with their varied powers to repel. Within seconds, they were engulfed.

Leering, yellowed faces pressed in around Storm, and she could no longer see past them to aim a lightning bolt or direct a strong wind. Fortunately, the X-Men had been trained not to rely solely upon their mutant abilities, and Ororo was particularly skilled in hand-to-hand combat. The close quarters even worked partially to her advantage as she could use her attackers as weapons against each other, felling several of them at a time.

At Phoenix's telepathic prompt, the X-Men fought their way to each other and formed themselves into a circle, their backs together so that they couldn't be struck from behind. Try as they might, the demons couldn't get past their ring of defense; they hammered and kicked and scratched and bit at their enemies, but the X-Men remained standing and returned each blow with greater force. More demons fell, cut by adamantium claws, beaten down by telekinesis or blasted with ice darts, and their ranks began to thin out at last. Storm knew it was only a matter of time before the vile creatures were defeated.

Time, unfortunately, was the one thing they didn't have.

"My demons are no match for the X-Men, of course," said Selene. "Your friends have proved their capabilities—not to mention their sheer determination—on many occasions."

"Then...why...?" croaked the Beast.

"Oh, we wouldn't want to give them any more cause for suspicion, now would we? I have to give the impression, at least, that I am trying to keep them away from my sanctum. I would hate them to know just how eagerly I anticipate their arrival."

"Such confidence...has been your...downfall...before..."

"You talk as if the outcome of this encounter is in doubt. Believe my, my dear Beast, it is not. When the X-Men reach this room, they will activate the magical glyphs with which I have marked the door. They will be transported one year into the future." Selene smiled. "Oh, I could have chosen glyphs that would have exploded in their faces—but you self-appointed do-gooders have an unfortunate reputation for being hard to kill. And my Black King desired another chance to stain their oh-so-pure, noble souls."

She paused as if awaiting an answer, but the Beast was too weak to give one.

"Of course," she said in a softer, mocking tone, "even if I was wrong, it would be of little consequence to you, my friend. Your teammates are already too late to save your life."

As an X-Man, the Beast was used to fighting against impossible odds. He had no intention of accepting his death until it had become an immutable fact. But he had to admit to himself that, short of a miracle, Selene was almost certainly right. He felt light-headed and empty, and it was an immense effort just to keep his eyelids raised. Unable to concentrate, he had no option but to follow his thoughts as they drifted back to happier times. He smiled to himself as he recalled his first day at Professor Xavier's School for Gifted Youngsters, his nights on the town with Bobby and the acceptance he had found with the Avengers.

But the good memories were blotted out by the specter of the Legacy Virus, by the interminable days and nights he had spent working to wipe its blight from the world. More than anything else, Hank felt cheated. Even if the X-Men couldn't save him, they would not stop fighting. They would take his blood, his cure, out of Selene's hands if they could. But he would never know the outcome of that struggle. He would die without knowing what his own legacy to the world would be: whether he had eased the suffering of millions as he had intended or simply made the Black Queen more powerful.

Selene's voice stirred him from his half-awake dreams. "I believe your friends have arrived," she said. "You might even be able to say goodbye to them if you are quick enough."

The door burst open, and Hank felt a momentary surge of elation as the first of the X-Men, Cyclops, raced into the throne room.

Wolverine was right behind him, and the Beast could see Rogue and Phoenix at his heels.

Before any of them had taken three steps, however, a chill wind whipped through Hank McCoy's fur and the raw scent of ozone hit his nostrils.

There was a sudden flash of black light...

CHAPTER 13

CROWD OF mutants had gathered outside the Hellfire Club building on Fifth Avenue. They made for a pathetic assemblage in their filthy rags, bowed and defeated, their eyes mostly downcast. They jostled quietly for the best positions, their sleeves rolled up in anticipation, and the weakest of them were pushed out into the road and up to the edge of Central Park.

Selene's demon agents moved among them, carrying syringes from which they injected single measures of the Legacy Virus cure. The mutants shuffled and raised their hands in the hope that they would find favor, that their pains would be eased for a few days. Inevitably, some of them were overlooked. Some of the demons delighted in holding out full syringes in front of beseeching eyes and then squirting their transparent contents wastefully into the air before moving on. More than one mutant groveled in the dirt, trying to lick up the remnants of the life-prolonging elixir before they seeped into the concrete.

But nobody dared to complain. Nobody even dared to offer a plea. The mutants accepted their lot, because to do otherwise would have drawn the attention of the Black Queen.

Selene stood in the doorway of her mansion house at the head of a short flight of steps, framed by a stone archway into which were set two trident symbols. And she drank in the suffering of her loyal subjects.

She probably shouldn't have been here. She had other matters to attend to. Her Black Knight would be leading her remaining enemies to her soon. But she enjoyed this so much: what use to her was power over others if she couldn't at least witness the demonstration of it? And after tonight, after she had turned her sights beyond the restrictive confines of Manhattan Island, she might have little time for this small pleasure.

She raised a hand suddenly and flared her nostrils in mock anger—and although she had cast no spell, an electrical aura crackled through the crowd and all activity ceased. Selene walked slowly down three steps, savoring the attention, and fixed her gaze upon a skinny mutate whose flesh practically hung from his skeleton. He had just caught the attention of a demon, and a needle was poised above his bare arm. But the transcendent joy in his expression froze and turned to dread as his mistress pointed a long fingernail at him.

"This creature here," said Selene coldly, "has taken more than his ration. He has been injected once today; now he thinks to steal somebody else's share."

The mutate was almost in tears. He was shaking his head vigorously, his lips forming words that emerged as a barely audible squeal. "No, mistress, I didn't, no, please..."

Selene clicked her fingers dispassionately, and her demons closed in around the trembling wretch. He found his voice at last and screamed as he disappeared beneath a pile of their foul, decaying bodies. The other mutants shrank away as far as they could from the grisly scene: even those who might have felt sympathy for their fellow didn't wish to share his fate.

The demons withdrew, leaving a torn and twisted corpse on the ground. They would toss it into a dumpster later, some distance away; Selene liked to keep the area around her home clean. For now, at a nod from her, the weekly ministrations were resumed.

She had no reason at all to believe that the mutate had been guilty of the crime of which she had accused him. She had picked him out of the crowd at random. It didn't matter: his example would prevent others from becoming bold, from taking enough of the cure to rid themselves of their affliction altogether. She might not be able to oversee future handouts in person, but her presence would be felt nonetheless.

She returned to her doorway and watched impassively for a minute longer, until she felt a sudden tingle at the base of her skull. A psychic alarm signal. With a frown, she turned her thoughts inward and confirmed her suspicions. Two enemy groups, over thirty mutants in all, were moving fast—some faster than others—through the sewers beneath her building.

The rebels' attack had begun early.

She sighed. Irritating as this turn of events might be, it wasn't entirely unexpected. She had always known that Shaw might betray her, or that his plans—the plans that she had approved—might be overridden by the X-Men. It was against just such an eventuality that she had erected another mystical barrier inside the first, extending three blocks in each direction from her mansion house. This second barrier was invisible and intangible to all—but it recognized the heat signatures of known dissidents and alerted its creator to their proximity.

The two rebel groups had crossed the barrier at the same time, which suggested that they were fully aware of its presence and had coordinated their approaches.

Selene narrowed her eyes and surveyed her surroundings. Three blocks downtown, light glinted off something on a rooftop. She glared in its direction for a few seconds, unable to discern anything more. Realizing that she was frowning, she rearranged her features into a more confident expression. Then she whirled around and swept back into the Hellfire Club building with a deliberately unhurried gait.

The rebels were immediately below her now, but Selene wasn't worried. Her Black King was aware of their presence too—and she could sense that he had already intercepted them.

* * *

Wolverine felt an overwhelming sense of déjà vu as he waded through the familiar labyrinth of New York City's sewer system with Rogue and fourteen of the White Knight's mutant followers behind him. He couldn't help but remember how the X-Men's last battle in Selene's catacombs had turned out, and the thought made the hairs on his back stand on end.

When he estimated that he was within a few feet of Selene's mystical sensors, he held up a hand behind him, wincing as his team splashed to an excessively noisy halt. From far above him, Phoenix was maintaining a telepathic link between the X-Men, and Wolverine let her know that he was in position. A minute or so later, he received confirmation that Cyclops's team were also ready. He dropped into a crouch and snapped: "OK, let's go!"

He heard Rogue's voice behind him: "I hope you're ready for this, sugar!" And then, her full weight struck him in the back and propelled him into the air. He caught his breath as the tunnel walls streaked past him; his feet were dangling over black water as he hung by his armpits in his teammate's grasp. He was barely aware of running footsteps receding behind him as the other mutants obeyed instructions and followed as quickly as they could. It didn't matter how much noise they made now; Selene already knew they were coming.

They took a sharp right turn into a rough-hewn passageway, and then into another. Thankfully, the White Knight's information proved accurate—the layout of Selene's catacombs hadn't changed—and they emerged into a large cavern, just as Wolverine had a year ago. Less than a minute had passed since he and Rogue had tripped the alarm—but to his dismay, Blackheart was waiting for them.

"Is this the best opposition your leaders can muster? The psychotic killer and the thug? Your souls are practically mine already." The demon was in his "stone monster" form, almost as tall as the cave itself, but Wolverine didn't let that faze him. The plan was to hit him hard and fast, and that was exactly what the two X-Men did.

Rogue delivered what Wolverine liked to call a "fastball special," he tucked his arms and legs into his stomach as she hurled him at Blackheart's head, unfolding himself at the last instant to aim his claws at the Black King's eyes. Blackheart flinched away from him, which if nothing else was a telling—and in its own small way, satisfying—reaction. It was a reaction, unfortunately, which also left Wolverine in free-fall. As he tumbled past Blackheart's left shoulder, he reached out and caught hold of it, almost wrenching his own arm out of its socket. Looking up, he saw the demon's right hand poised above him, about to swat him—but at that moment, Rogue slammed into Blackheart's ankle.

If she had hoped to fell him, then her effort was in vain. The demon's leg was like a granite pillar, and she rebounded from it with a pained expression. Ignoring his own pain, Wolverine hauled himself up, unable to shake the impression that he was attempting to climb a mountain during an earthquake. Far below him, Blackheart's thick, spiny tail swung around and swiped the still-dazed Rogue off her feet.

Wolverine had dragged himself onto Blackheart's broad shoulder, and he leapt at the demon's face again. But a giant hand plucked him out of midair, and he was hurled across the cavern to collide first with a rock wall and then with the ground. Had his bones not been laced with adamantium, his spine would surely have been shattered; as it was, he was badly bruised and the breath had been knocked out of him. His healing factor needed time to do its work—but Blackheart was already towering over him again, and he had to force his protesting muscles to move. He rolled aside as a blast of energy exploded from the demon's fingertips. It narrowly missed him, but he wasn't sure he could avoid a second such attack.

"Ah," rumbled Blackheart, turning away from the fallen X-Man, "at last, this game promises to become worthy of my time."

Wolverine's team of resistance fighters had arrived. Almost simultaneously, Cyclops and Storm had burst into the cavern from the opposite side, at the head of a second team. In a moment, the area was filled with heaving bodies; some of the White Knight's followers were attacking Blackheart directly, while others were simply running interference. No one of them was a match for the demon, but the plan was to confuse him with their numbers, to keep him off-balance and unable to take the initiative.

To this end, a group of four mutates raced up the stone staircase that led to the Hellfire Club's basement levels and their real target, Selene. Blackheart saw them before they got halfway, and collapsed the stairs with a wave of his hand—but the mutates had been chosen for their flying abilities, and they kept on going. As Blackheart concentrated on forming some of the debris from the staircase into a barrier between them and the door, he left himself exposed to a lightning strike from Storm. It seemed to hurt him, but he shook off its effects in a second, and there was a gleeful tone in his gravelly voice. "Come then," he bellowed, "pit your mortal powers against the son of Mephisto—but be there thirty or three hundred of you, it will make no difference in the end. Mine is the power of evil itself; the power of every sin committed or malicious thought harbored upon this tainted world. My strength is limitless."

He was probably right, thought Wolverine. But then, it wasn't necessary for the X-Men and the rebels to defeat Blackheart; they simply had to keep him occupied while their third and final strike team did its job.

He had found his second wind now, and he was about to rejoin the battle when a familiar blue and yellow-clad figure emerged from the chaos in front of him. At the last possible moment, he sensed that something was wrong. Cyclops triggered his visor, and an optic blast pounded into the ground where his teammate had just been standing.

"You're pointing those eyes in the wrong direction, mister!"

"You heard what Blackheart said." Cyclops's jaw was set determinedly, and he unleashed another blast, which Wolverine only just managed to evade. "This is all your fault. You and everybody else like you. Every time you lose control, every time you take a life, you feed him. You increase his power." His voice was rising in pitch, becoming almost hysterical.

"You're in my way, Summers!" growled Wolverine—and as he spoke, he realized that Scott Summers had *always* been in his way. The X-Men could have made a real difference but for their timid leader, always preaching restraint, always ensuring that their work was left half-done. They had defeated villain after villain—but the villains always came back. Their continual presence made the world a darker and darker place, and *it was all his fault.*

Wolverine had been fighting all his life. But now, with a sudden blinding clarity, he saw that he had been fighting the wrong people.

Cyclops had reined in his emotions. Tight-lipped, his voice trembling, he said coldly: "If we're to defeat Blackheart and Selene, you have to die first. I see that now."

"And if we're to do the job properly, it'll have to be without you holding us back."

Wolverine took the brunt of the next optic blast in his chest, but he had braced himself for it. His teeth gritted, he fought his way forward through the beam of ruby force until he was almost within a claw's reach of his opponent's throat. At that point, Cyclops switched tactics and leapt forward to punch him on the chin.

A red mist descended in front of Wolverine's eyes, and he howled with pure animalistic rage as he launched himself at his one-time friend.

"She's seen us," said Nightcrawler.

He lowered the binoculars through which he had just seen Selene look directly at him before smiling, turning and walking back into her building. He turned to Shaw, who was standing on the rooftop behind him, still dressed in the garb of the White Knight but unmasked. But for the wind ruffling his hair, he remained perfectly still. His hands were clasped behind his back, but his rigid body and solemn expression belied his casual pose.

He didn't seem unduly concerned at the news, but Kurt thought he detected a slight twitch in a muscle beneath one of his eyes. "Do we still have a telepathic lock on her?" Shaw asked quietly.

Beside him, Phoenix nodded. Her eyes were closed, her brow furrowed in concentration, and she answered in a strained voice. "She's moving down the hallway. She's in no hurry."

"Then we proceed as planned."

Nightcrawler nodded and took a deep breath, steeling himself for what was to come. He reached out to the final two members of the five-strong assemblage: the young mutants whom he knew only by the code names of Lightshow and Booster. They took hold of his three-fingered hands, and Lightshow in turn tugged gingerly at the hem of Shaw's jacket.

"She's at the top of the stairs," murmured Phoenix as Shaw linked her arm with his. "She's going down them."

"Excellent," breathed Shaw. "Excellent!"

"Shouldn't we go in now?" asked Nightcrawler. "Since we've had the good fortune to catch Selene above ground..."

Shaw shook his head. "On the ground floor, she has too many places to run, and too many demon agents to defend her."

"But Blackheart..."

"...will be kept occupied long enough for us to do our job," said Shaw confidently.

Nightcrawler accepted his decision. Shaw had explained in his briefing that he considered Selene's throne room the best place to confront her. She would be cornered there, and Lightshow could block the door with a solid hologram to prevent her minions from reaching her. Kurt concentrated on visualizing the corridor outside the room, on the first basement level of the Hellfire Club's mansion house. He was certain that he could remember it well enough to teleport into it without the risk of materializing inside a wall. He was less certain, however, that he could take four people with him. Normally, even a tandem 'port placed great stress upon the bodies of both him and his passenger. He prayed that Booster's power to augment the mutant abilities of others was all it was reputed to be.

The boy couldn't have been more than thirteen or fourteen years old, and his thin, acne-scarred face was ashen with apprehension. Nightcrawler hated the thought of taking him into combat, but there was no other option. He tightened his grip on Booster's hand; he had expected to feel an energy surge, but there was nothing.

Suddenly, Phoenix cried out and clutched her hands to her head. Her legs buckled, and only Shaw's firm hold on her arm prevented her from falling to her knees. With difficulty, Nightcrawler resisted the impulse to break the chain and rush to her side. "What is it?" asked Shaw brusquely, with no hint of sympathy.

"Selene...detected my presence in her...mind," Phoenix panted. "She...expelled me."

"You've lost her?"

Phoenix nodded weakly. Shaw turned to Nightcrawler. "Take us in," he ordered, "now!"

Nightcrawler screwed his eyes shut, gritted his teeth, held his breath and teleported.

To his relief, it didn't hurt at all. The five mutants arrived at their destination with an ear-deadening burst of imploding air and a larger than normal billow of smoke. They were midway between the door of Selene's throne room and the staircase upon which she had last been detected, only a few seconds ago; however, as the smoke began to thin, Nightcrawler saw to his dismay that there was no sign of the Black Queen.

"She can't have gone far," insisted Shaw, a hint of worry entering his tone at last.

"I can't locate her," reported Phoenix—and Nightcrawler could see from her expression that the very effort of using her psychic abilities was hurting her.

"Keep scanning," rapped Shaw, "and keep us linked." Phoenix nodded bravely. "Lightshow and Booster, check the stairs; Nightcrawler, the throne room."

"Jawohl, mein Herr," acknowledged Nightcrawler with only a touch of resentment. As Shaw hurried past him to search the rest

of the floor, he teleported again, solo this time. *Remember,* Shaw's voice said inside his head, relayed there by Phoenix, *if we can't find Selene, a sample of the Legacy cure is the next best thing.*

He began to search the deserted throne room.

Selene crept along the carpeted corridor to where Phoenix stood, thinking herself alone. In her mind's eye, she could see the tendrils of psionic force emanating from the X-Man, slipping easily in and out of the ceiling, walls and floor as they searched for their quarry. The Black Queen could not have shielded her thoughts by force of mind alone—she had to admit to herself that Phoenix was the more powerful telepath—but she had other means at her disposal. A simple cantrip had rendered her undetectable to all senses, psychic or otherwise.

She waited until she was at her foe's shoulder before she dropped her cover.

Phoenix detected her presence almost immediately and whirled around, alarmed.

Selene smiled, and hit her with a devastating mindbolt for which she was totally unprepared. She didn't even have time to scream, let alone issue a warning to her friends. Her brain shut itself off, her eyes rolled back into her head and she crumpled. The Black Queen left her lying on the floor, catatonic, staring into nowhere.

She almost bumped into two of Shaw's younger idealists as she reached the stairs. The pair cowered from her, terrified; Selene could sense their thoughts as they tried to contact their leader, and their despair as they realized that their link to him had been broken. She brushed past them, considering them unworthy of her attention—but as she headed downstairs, to her surprise, her way was barred by a brick wall. She attempted to remove the obstruction, but frowned as she realized that she couldn't manipulate its molecules as she could those of most objects.

She turned to look at the young mutant called Lightshow, an eyebrow raised. "It appears I have underestimated you, my friend," she purred.

At that, both boys turned and ran. But it took no more than a thought on Selene's part for the carpet itself to trip them. As they fell in a tangle of arms and legs, she bludgeoned her way through Lightshow's pitiful psychic defenses, took control of his mind and compelled him to lower his barrier.

Less than a minute later, she unbolted and opened the heavy wooden door that led into the catacombs. She stood at the head of the collapsed staircase and looked down upon a scene of chaos, savoring the heady concoction of anger, fear and confusion that her consort had unleashed. Blackheart was playing with the emotions of his erstwhile attackers, overwhelming them with feelings of hatred and jealousy and turning them against each other. Even some of the X-Men had succumbed to his influence. Rogue was on her knees weeping, and Selene sensed that she was consumed by self-loathing for the sins of her past. Cyclops and Wolverine were locked in hand-to-hand combat, neither giving any quarter, and it was surely inevitable that one would kill the other. She looked forward to it. She might even leave the victor alive, to nurse his paralyzing guilt in her nightmare chambers.

Storm, on the other hand, was still very much active. She had created her own weather system in the cavern, and thick black clouds obscured its roof altogether. Blackheart was actually beginning to reel beneath a sustained onslaught of wind, rain and lightning. Selene had never seen the wind-rider unleash her elemental fury with such abandon before, and the sight was breathtaking. Focused as Storm was on staying out of her target's reach, however, she was vulnerable to an attack from behind.

Selene encased her in stone, enjoying the X-Man's terror as a brittle shell hardened around her. As Storm fell from the sky, the Black Queen gathered up the debris of the staircase and returned it to its old formation.

With the X-Men no longer a threat, Blackheart turned his attention to the rest of Shaw's ineffectual band of rebels. He downed at least a dozen of them with one sweep of his arm, then he gathered up six more in his hands and crushed the life out of them. They mustered what resistance they could, striking back with feeble punches and sparks of bio-energy, but they never stood a chance.

Selene swept regally down the restored stone staircase, her lips twisting into a smirk at the knowledge that her victory was assured.

Jean Grey's consciousness was a guttering flame in a black void. She was fighting to keep it lit, to hold back the shadows that threatened to engulf it and snuff it out forever. But then, unexpectedly, the flame was fanned. It grew into a roaring fire and exploded triumphantly into a birdlike shape, which dispelled the darkness.

And Phoenix awoke with a gasp to find the young mutant Booster kneeling beside her.

She flashed him a grateful smile, realizing that he must have amplified her powers and enabled her to fight back against the effects of Selene's attack. Her head was no longer aching, but she was suddenly, shockingly aware of everything and everybody around her in minute detail. She felt as if she were seeing the world in a new light, and understanding it at last. Without having to search for them, she knew where each of the X-Men were, and what they were going through. She was on a different plane, hovering above them, watching them from a great distance as they went through their flat, three-dimensional lives. She was tingling with power, but the sensation reminded her of something else—a faded dream from, it seemed, a long, long time ago—and the tingle became an icy shudder.

She narrowed the focus of her senses, sifting out relevant information from a tidal wave of thoughts. She entered the minds of Cyclops, Wolverine and Rogue and reasoned with them gently, helping them to regain control over their artificially heightened emotions. She calmed Storm's fear at being entombed again and allowed her to see herself from the outside, so that she could call down lightning with pinpoint precision and shatter her stone prison.

And then she felt something else: a series of psionic shock waves rippling through the ether. Phoenix didn't know what was causing them at first—but then, through Wolverine's eyes, she saw Selene stiffen and wince. On a hunch, she allowed her mind to drift away from Manhattan Island—and there, beyond the Black Queen's barrier, she touched the thoughts of a vast assemblage of heroes, some familiar to her, some less so. The Avengers, the Defenders, the Fantastic Four, the Thunderbolts...the list seemed endless.

It could have been a coincidence, of course, that they had chosen this moment to launch an all-out attack upon the barrier—but Phoenix thought she detected the hand of her missing teammate, Iceman, in this fortuitous turn of events.

Selene's distracted, she told the rest of the X-Men and the remaining rebels simultaneously. *We'll never have a better chance than this to take her down!*

"I won't have the blood you shed on my conscience any more!"

Cyclops blasted his opponent square in the chest and sent him flying backwards. Before Wolverine could regain his balance, Scott closed the gap between them and leapt on top of him. The pair rolled over and over on the ground. A set of claws whistled past Cyclops's ear—a little too close for comfort, but he was sure that his teammate knew what he was doing.

Selene's buying it, Wolverine reported via the newly reestablished telepathic link. *She isn't even glancing our way; thinks we're too busy knocking hell out of each other to worry about her. I'm gonna throw you forwards and right in three...two...one...*

Wolverine's foot struck Cyclops in the stomach—but, prepared for the blow, he rolled with it, closer, ever closer, to his real target. Impatient as he was to make his move, to bring this to an end before anybody else had to die, he knew that the timing of his attack was crucial. Thankfully, Rogue and Storm were airborne again, drawing Blackheart's attention and ending his massacre of Shaw's less able followers for now.

Shaw himself had just been teleported into the cavern by Nightcrawler. He walked calmly towards Selene, his hands held up in front of him in a conciliatory gesture. "I trust we aren't too early?" he said with a wry smile. "You appear to be coping well enough, in any case."

Selene looked confused and uncertain of herself. "Stay back, Shaw," she warned. "I don't know if I can trust you."

But Shaw kept coming. "My dear lady, you know you can always count on my loyalty—just as I could always count on yours."

His eyes hardened and he leapt for her throat, but she saw the attack coming. She waved her arms, and the ground reared up in front of her to form a shield. With a telepathic yell of *Now!* Cyclops spun around and aimed an optic blast at her back. To his astonishment, it passed straight through her, leaving her unharmed. She turned, just in time to meet a charge from Wolverine. For all her powers, she wasn't a match for him in close combat—and yet somehow, he ended up on his back on the ground beside her.

"She's cast some sort of illusion spell," he cried. "She's about six inches to the right of where you think she is."

Cyclops adjusted his aim accordingly—but before he could fire again, Selene's eyes flashed and she took control of the molecules in his mask. She tightened it around his head so that his visor folded in upon itself, its ruby lens cracking beneath the strain, and his eyes were sealed shut. Blinded and helpless, he tore desperately at the constricting cloth.

He could still sense the others through the telepathic link. He knew that Nightcrawler had joined the assault on Blackheart, but he feared that even three X-Men couldn't hold out against the demon for much longer. He was proved right when, to his horror, Kurt teleported too close to his adversary and was seized by a stony hand. Blackheart dashed the X-Man against the wall and let him drop. Cyclops shared the pain of his shattering impact, and his heart sank into his stomach as he felt the light flee from his teammate's mind.

Rogue was the next to fall, so distraught was she at the fate of her friend that she misjudged a turn and flew into a crushing blow. Only Storm now stood between Blackheart and his beleaguered Black Queen. Wolverine, in the meantime, had reached Selene, but she was manipulating the very adamantium in his claws to bend them back upon themselves. He howled like a wounded animal, and Cyclops felt sick as he realized why. Selene had no power over organic matter; the bones inside the metal could not bend with it, they could only break.

The door to the Hellfire Club building flew open again, and a horde of demons in blue and red costumes began to pour down the stone steps into the cavern.

You must keep at her, insisted Phoenix from afar. *She's trying to maintain her barrier and fight off my telepathic attacks. She's stretched too far. She's weakening!*

Jean had included Shaw in the link, and Scott could feel his hatred, his tightly focused rage and the unshakable determination that drove him as he finally laid hands upon the woman who had usurped his throne. "You'll never betray me again," he spat. "You'll never humiliate me. I won't let you shape my destiny!"

Beneath a barrage of kinetically charged punches that would have shattered concrete, the Black Queen fell at last.

Cyclops hurled aside the tattered remnants of his mask and donned a pair of ruby quartz spectacles from a pouch on his belt. They wouldn't give him as much control over his eye-beams as his visor did, but at least he could see again through their red-tinted lenses.

The demon agents were halfway down the steps now. He raised his glasses and stunned the first two; as they fell, they also brought down the creatures behind them. He had delayed the arrival of reinforcements by vital seconds.

Lowering his sights, he saw Shaw's hands closing around Selene's throat. He saw the madness in the former Black King's expression and sensed his intention to kill his tormentor. Narrowing his eyes, he stung Shaw's fingers with a low-powered burst of energy.

"It's over, Shaw," he said. "Leave it."

Selene made no move to rise. Her pale face was bruised and she was sporting a cut lip and a black eye. Shaw glared at Cyclops, but he didn't renew his attack; whether this was because he recognized the truth of the X-Man's words or simply because his mutant power wouldn't protect him from a full-strength optic blast, Scott couldn't tell.

Blackheart had seen that Selene was down, and he gave an almighty roar. He strode across the cavern, his footfalls shaking the earth and bringing down trickles of dust and pebbles from the roof. Storm tried to blind him by gathering clouds around his head and placing him at the center of a torrential rainstorm, but he pressed on regardless. She assailed him with bolts of lightning, so powerful that they took chips out of his hide; they evidently caused him pain, but Blackheart shrugged them off like insect bites. The surviving rebels could do no more than scramble to get out of his way before they were stepped on.

Cyclops stood over the Black Queen, his back to the approaching leviathan, and fingered the frame of his glasses. "You've lost, Selene," he said sternly. "Call off your demons—all of them—or I'll finish the job that Shaw started."

"Give me the word, my Queen," said Blackheart, suddenly looming over his shoulder, "and I will crush this brazen mortal to dust." Cyclops swallowed his fear and concentrated on maintaining his grim expression. He didn't know if he could carry out his threat or not, but he had to make Selene believe it. He had to make her believe that even the son of Mephisto couldn't act fast enough to prevent him from killing her.

To his relief, Storm, Wolverine and Shaw joined him; between them, the quartet formed a threatening circle around their enemy as she climbed to her feet. Selene pivoted slowly on the spot, looking at each of their faces and perhaps reading the thoughts behind them too. By the time she stood eye to eye with Cyclops, she was obviously convinced. She raised her right hand and clicked her fingers twice, and the creatures behind her turned and shuffled away up the staircase in single file. Blackheart shrank down to human size, although Cyclops remained acutely aware of the demon's malevolent presence beside him.

Selene smiled. "Congratulations, Mr. Summers," she said. "You have won the game. Manhattan Island is yours."

"This wasn't a game to us, Selene."

"Nevertheless, my barrier has fallen—and the human champions of this world are even now fighting their way towards us."

"There's one more thing," said Cyclops. "We want the cure to the Legacy Virus."

Selene shrugged as if it no longer mattered to her. "The spoils of a war well fought," she said. "Very well. Your wife has plucked its location from my mind anyway. I should have had the foresight to kill both her and the power amplifier when I had them at my mercy."

"You've been responsible for quite enough deaths already," said Cyclops tersely.

"I have, haven't I?" said Selene brightly, beaming with pride. "A shame it had to end like this. Still, there will be other games."

"Not for you there won't," growled Wolverine.

Phoenix sent a telepathic warning of what was about to happen, but Cyclops received it too late. He had been watching his defeated foe so closely that he hadn't anticipated his teammate's sudden action. He didn't have time to do anything but curse himself for his momentary lapse as Wolverine pounced and drove a set of claws into Selene's back.

The Black Queen stiffened as three adamantium tips emerged from her chest in a spray of blood. For a tense, interminable second, nobody moved or made a sound.

Selene's eyes were wide, her red lips tight and her face even whiter than usual. She looked down at the claws as if the impaling of her heart upon three spikes were no more than an inconvenient surprise for her. But then, her centuries-old body crumbled, losing definition in an instant as it collapsed into a pile of fine ash. A moment later, gravity caught up with her black Hellfire Club costume and it fell too, beating her remains up into a choking gray cloud.

Wolverine was left standing with an arm outstretched, his claws extended and a gleam of malicious satisfaction in his eye. He returned Cyclops's look of disbelieving horror with a lopsided grin and a cheerful wink.

And Blackheart let out a howl that sounded like the clashing of continents.

In the moment before the demon dispensed bloody retribution, Cyclops heard Wolverine's telepathic voice in his head: *Just wanted to test a theory. If our distracting Selene helped to bring her barrier down, I wondered what other spells might just wear off if we could take her out of the picture altogether.*

Blackheart was growing again, and drawing back a huge fist, but time had slipped a groove and everything was moving in slow-motion. Cyclops turned his head, the simple movement seeming to take an age, and he saw that everything and everybody around him was picked out in negative. And then the images blurred and changed, and he was somewhere else.

Somewhere he had been before...

CHAPTER 14

NIGHTCRAWLER WAS trying to run forward, but something held him back. Everything around him was black; he couldn't see where he was going and he didn't know why, but he knew he had to get there. His teammates were around him, but they too were moving as if through treacle. They were picked out in negative like images caught on a strip of film. He had experienced something like this before, but he couldn't remember when.

Blackheart had killed him. That much, he did remember. Was this, then, an afterlife? If so, then everything he had believed in was wrong. His chest swelled with dread and the only thought he could hold on to was that none of this could be true, that he had to get through it, had to keep on running until he had torn himself free of this damnable black light...

And then the colors of the world inverted around him, and he caught his breath and almost tumbled forward as he burst back into reality and found himself in Selene's throne room. He saw the Beast, unconscious, strung up by his wrists in an alcove, his blood trickling into a glass container, and he saw the Black Queen standing by her throne. A smile of triumph had frozen on her pale face, and a horrified look had begun to dawn in her eyes.

It took Nightcrawler a second to work out where and when he

was, and to adjust to the fact that he was no longer even bruised from his encounter with Blackheart. Even the tears in his costume had vanished, and his teammates also seemed to be in better shape than when he had last seen them. Sebastian Shaw, he noted, was back in his green combat suit rather than his white Hellfire Club attire. He didn't know what had happened since his...since he... while he had been asleep, but somehow, thank God, the X-Men had been given a second chance.

They had been returned to the place and time from which Selene had expelled them, as if they had never left. And evidently, she was surprised to see them. Which was just as well, because Nightcrawler's teammates were every bit as confused and disoriented as he was.

Wolverine was the first to act, but Selene was only an instant behind him. She brought up her hands, and the air in front of her shimmered. The Canadian X-Man bounced off a transparent but no less solid mystical force field, but by now Rogue and Cyclops were running at their black-clad foe from each side. Selene gestured again, and the flames of a dozen black candles streaked towards her and formed themselves into the shapes of leering demons. Storm took to the air and doused the infernal creatures with a localized but fierce rainstorm; the flames hissed and guttered but were not completely extinguished.

Even as Nightcrawler leapt forward, Selene pointed over his head; he turned to see that she had animated the door through which he had entered the room. It cracked and squealed as it strained to loose itself from its hinges, reaching out and coiling strands of wood around Iceman, Phoenix and Shaw. It took all of Nightcrawler's agility to keep himself from becoming similarly trapped. Even entwined, however, the X-Men weren't helpless. Phoenix's eyes turned red as she engaged Selene in a psychic struggle, and Iceman unleashed a barrage of snow upon the fire demons.

Seeing that the tide was turning against her, Selene shrieked three words that sent a chill down Nightcrawler's spine: "Blackheart—to me!"

Shaw had already broken his bonds, and Rogue was running to help Iceman and Phoenix. Nightcrawler teleported to the ceiling and looked down on the field of battle, awaiting an opportunity. The room began to shake with the sound of approaching heavy footsteps, and he knew that he only had seconds before Blackheart arrived and all was lost.

With the fire demons quenched, Cyclops, Wolverine and Storm rushed Selene from three directions at once. She clenched her fists, set her jaw and repulsed her attackers with a wave of pure psycho-kinetic force. While the Black Queen was thus occupied, Night-crawler dropped onto her shoulders, wrapped his legs around her neck and teleported with her.

He appeared in the Hellfire Club's ballroom, reeling from the strain of the tandem 'port. He was glad of the fact that he had emptied the room of bystanders, an age ago now it seemed.

Where are you, Kurt? came the voice of Phoenix in his head.

One floor straight up, he responded. He had remembered that Blackheart was confined to the lower levels of the building and he knew that, so long as the X-Men could keep Selene up here, she would be denied the support of her deadly ally.

Even alone, however, the Black Queen was too powerful for him. She let out a howl of rage as she reached up and seized Nightcrawler's legs. At the same time, he felt her cold, baleful presence in his mind, battering down the rudimentary psychic defenses that Professor Xavier and Phoenix had helped him to build. He lost his grip on Selene's neck, and she threw him to the floor. Winded, he was unable to teleport away as she raised her hands, her fingers crooked, and he felt a searing agony inside him as if she had set light to his soul.

"You dare to challenge me, little goblin?" she shrilled. "I have ruled empires. I have seen civilizations rise and fall. I have preyed on the weak since time immemorial."

"Really? I must...say, you don't look a...day over..." Night-crawler grimaced, unable to complete the taunt. He had never felt pain quite like this before, but he refused to surrender to it. He bit down to keep himself from screaming, his fangs cutting into his lower lip. He clung on to his last slender thread of consciousness and forced his trembling hands to reach out, to take Selene by the throat. He couldn't let her go, couldn't let her return to the basement and Blackheart, couldn't let her win this time. He had seen the unholy future that she would build upon such a victory, and he refused to let it happen again.

Blinded by pain, he almost didn't notice that the floor was shaking beneath him until at last it erupted in a scarlet haze. The pain ceased abruptly as he and Selene were flung away from each other, and he rolled aside as a black-clad figure hurtled past him.

There was a jagged hole in the floor, created as Nightcrawler now realized by Cyclops. Storm had already flown up from the throne room below, and Wolverine, Iceman and the team's leader himself were close behind her, carried aloft no doubt by Phoenix.

As the X-Men closed upon their foe, Kurt Wagner allowed himself to pass out at last.

The throne room was still shaking, and Rogue feared that Blackheart might burst through the wall at any moment. She tried not to think about it, tried not to think about what he had done to both her and Kurt in that terrible future. A friend was in danger, and she had to save him.

"Hank! Hank!" she shouted, slapping the Beast's cheeks gently with her gloved hands. "Come on Hank, it's me, Rogue. Can you hear me? You've got to wake up!"

It was no good. He was well and truly unconscious, still breathing—albeit shallowly—but hanging like a dead weight from the wall. Rogue remembered Selene's boast that she had killed him shortly after the X-Men's departure. She knew now how it must have happened. She couldn't remember offhand how much blood there was in the average human body, but the glass container at the Beast's feet had to have taken most of his fill. It was impossible to tell if his skin was pale beneath his blue fur, but he was certainly looking gaunt.

Rogue took hold of him around the waist and tried to tear him free from the tendrils that held him and were draining him. She wasn't sure if this was such a good idea, but she suspected that there wasn't time to approach the operation more delicately. The tendrils were stubborn, though, and she resorted to feeling for them over the Beast's shoulder and plucking them out of his back one by one. To her frustration, they squirmed and writhed like snakes and implanted themselves in him again. The blood in the glass container was still rising.

She was relieved when Phoenix came to her aid: as Rogue wrenched each tendril loose, Jean flattened it against the wall telekinetically to prevent it from striking again. Finally, the Beast collapsed against Rogue, who hauled him across the room and out of danger.

"I'm keeping his wounds sealed," said Phoenix, her face grim with concentration, "but he's lost a lot of blood already. We've got to get him to a hospital." The room was vibrating so fiercely now that Rogue could hardly hear her, but she caught the gist of her words.

She bundled her unconscious teammate into Phoenix's arms. "You go ahead!" she shouted over the shriek of protesting stonework. "I've just thought of something I have to do." Phoenix opened her mouth as if to argue, but there was no time. The door had returned to its original shape after Selene's departure, but now it collapsed inward with a heavy thud as Blackheart strode into the room.

He was shorter than when Rogue had last seen him, but no less imposing for his diminished stature. In any case, his petrified hair still scraped the top of the doorway—and as he entered the throne room, he grew to fill its full height. "Jean, get Hank out of here!" Rogue yelled, and she rocketed toward the stony-skinned demon. He struck out with blinding speed and knocked her out of the air with a casual sweep of his hand. As she crashed into the debris of the fallen ceiling, the demon leapt at Phoenix, who was levitating herself and the Beast toward the upper floor. Rogue's distraction had given her a second, but no more; fortunately, it was enough. Blackheart made a swipe at the escaping X-Men, but howled as his fingers slammed into an invisible barrier where the ceiling had once been.

For a moment, Rogue dared to hope that the demon had forgotten about her. She crawled quickly over to the container that held the Beast's stolen blood. She picked it up and held it to her chest even as Blackheart rounded on her, his eyes blazing furiously.

She didn't pretend to understand half of what the Beast had told her about his work on a Legacy cure—but she knew that, if the Black Queen wanted his blood, then it could only be for one reason. And having seen the future, she knew that this was no false hope: the cure would really work this time. That was what she had come back for. Now, Rogue was holding the means by which mutantkind—perhaps the whole world—could be saved.

If only she could get it out of this place alive.

For one devastating instant, Phoenix had felt Blackheart's rough fingers against her leg, and her heart had plummeted. She had repelled the demon's hand telekinetically and tried to speed her upward progress, knowing that her mind was no match for his great physical strength. But then, miraculously, she was in the Hellfire Club's ballroom and he was howling at her from below. She thanked her lucky stars for Daimon Hellstrom and his containment spell, and prayed that Rogue would find similar fortune. She desperately wanted to turn back for her teammate, but there was nothing she could do for her now.

She could only hope that the same was not true of the Beast. His body felt cold in her arms, and her mental probes detected only the slightest spark of activity in his brain.

The X-Men had managed to drive Selene away from the hole in the floor, away from the restricted reach of her demonic ally. However, the battle was by no means over. From Jean's vantage point, it looked as if the whole room had turned against them. The Black

Queen was fighting back fiercely, and every molecule of her surroundings had been reshaped and bent to her iron will. A table had reared up to keep Wolverine's claws away from their target; a bronze bust had come to life and fastened its teeth onto Cyclops's arm; Storm was finding it difficult to remain aloft as her own cloak wrapped itself around her and tried to suffocate her; and Iceman was kept off-balance as the very floorboards at his feet tore through their carpet covering and snatched at his ankles.

Phoenix started as she realized that Nightcrawler was lying unconscious in a corner; his body had blended in with the shadows, and she hadn't seen him at first. However, he didn't appear too badly hurt.

Her path to the door was blocked, and she had no desire to drag the unconscious Beast into the melee. However, the ballroom's leaded windows looked directly out onto the street. Jean reached out with her mind and tore the animated bust away from her husband; it had probably been modeled after a famous composer or a politician, but now its metal face was twisted with hatred and unrecognizable. It glared at her in apparent anger as she smashed it through the nearest window and created a new exit for herself.

It was dark outside, and relatively quiet. Phoenix was confused for a moment, but then she remembered how little time had really passed since the X-Men had stood in Central Park, shortly after midnight, and planned their attack. In fact, there were more people around than she would have expected. She saw clusters of men in evening dress and women in elaborate gowns, and she realized that the Hellfire Club members whom Nightcrawler had scared out of the ballroom had not gone too far. Perhaps they had even been plucking up the courage to return to the building when she had made her appearance.

The sight of a costumed mutant hovering above the Fifth Avenue sidewalk with her blue-furred companion cradled in her arms was the last straw for many of them. As some people stared agog, others simply turned and ran. A drunken man hollered something about "muties," and his lady companion hushed him fearfully and dragged him away.

A distracted driver steered his vehicle into the back of another; a third driver steered around the blockage and onto the opposite sidewalk in his haste to get away; and, upon seeing what lay ahead of her, a fourth stepped on her brakes and threw her car into reverse.

Phoenix was used to such reactions—she even understood the fear from which they were born—but they still hurt. She tried to ignore them as she hurried southward, her mind bearing most of the Beast's weight, alarmed and slightly drunk pedestrians scattering before her. She set eyes upon an empty yellow cab, but the cabby saw her too and put his foot down, studiously ignoring her. Phoenix took control of his mind and forced him to stop. She hated using her powers like that—to enforce her will upon another human being, she believed, made her no better than many of the X-Men's foes—but a life was at stake.

She floated the Beast into the back seat of the cab and leapt in after him. "This man needs a hospital," she said, "and fast!" With a modicum of hope, she returned control of the cabby's mind to him. He shot his seatbelt and made to open the door and flee.

"If that's the way it has to be..." she sighed as, reluctantly, she retook the strings of her puppet.

A second later, the sound of squealing tires pierced the night air as the cab raced off on its mercy dash.

Rogue was staring at Blackheart. She couldn't help it. She was screaming inside, telling herself that she had to move, had to *get out of here*, but his red eyes filled her world and she couldn't control her muscles, couldn't turn her head, couldn't move her arms or legs, couldn't tear her gaze away from him. She was mesmerized, rooted to the spot by a primal terror that fried her nerve endings and set off a clamor of alarm bells inside her brain.

He was playing with her emotions again, she realized—and that knowledge, she hoped, would make her able to resist him. She tried to override her feelings with logic, to retake control of herself. If anybody could do it, she told herself sternly, she could. Every time she used her mutant ability, every time she stole the thoughts of another person, she had to fight to assert her own personality. Surely this was little different?

The demon extended one hand towards her. He was taking his time, enjoying her fear, and that proved to be his mistake. Willing herself with every fiber of her being to move, Rogue took to the air even as Blackheart unleashed a torrent of molten lava from his fingertips. She couldn't help but look back over her shoulder, her heartbeat quickening as the white-hot fluid hardened into a misshapen lump on the ground.

She aimed to fly over Blackheart's shoulder and through the hole in the ceiling, but he was too fast for her. He reared up in front of her again, and she was forced to make a rapid course correction. Stone fingers snapped at Rogue's heel as she hurtled out of the throne room through the doorway, the heavy glass container of blood still clutched to her chest.

She rocketed down the basement corridor, her speed turning the wooden panels and paintings on each side of her into pastel-colored blurs. She didn't dare look back, but she could neither hear nor sense Blackheart behind her. She had expected to gain a second or two as he reduced himself in size to follow her, but this total disappearance was unnerving.

She slowed down to round a tight corner, and suddenly he was in front of her again, at the foot of the staircase that would have taken her beyond his reach, hunched up to fit his gargantuan body into the corridor. Briefly, she considered trying to plow through him, but she had tried something similar before with disastrous results. Instead, she pulled up short just as she was about to hit him. She executed a sharp right turn and darted off down an adjoining passageway. But this time, she was too slow.

Blackheart caught hold of her, his hand encircling both her ankles. He yanked her backwards and slammed her into the wall. It was all she could do to keep hold of her fragile cargo. She tried to pull herself free from his grip, but the demon's fingers were exerting such pressure that they threatened to crush the bones in her feet to paste. She considered using her power against him as she had against Pierce—but she knew instinctively that she wouldn't be able to cope with any part of this evil creature inside her. He would overwhelm her.

And then Blackheart swung Rogue like a baseball bat, and she saw the opposite wall of the corridor coming towards her but she couldn't stop herself from hitting it face first.

And the container shattered in her arms.

She let out a scream of frustration as she tumbled to the floor in a shower of glass and blood. For all she knew, the Beast was probably dead and his life's work, his hopes and dreams, were soaking into her costume. Blackheart loomed over her, and she wanted to lash out at him, to make him pay for what he had done, but she knew it would do no good. Instead, she picked herself up, her furious eyes fixed upon him as if she were about to attack...

...and then she dived between his legs, took flight to avoid a swipe from his tail and flew as fast as she could up the stairway. She emerged onto the ground floor sweating and shaking, her costume plastered to her chest and her legs unsure if they could support her weight. But she thanked her lucky stars that she had made it at all, that her desperate maneuver had apparently taken her demonic foe by surprise.

Or perhaps, she thought, with the cure destroyed, he had simply had no reason to detain her any longer.

The sounds of battle still echoed around the throne room, although the combatants themselves were no longer visible through the hole in its ceiling. As Sebastian Shaw emerged from his hiding place behind the Black Queen's throne, he let out a quiet sigh of relief. He had risked much by staying behind and taking cover when the X-Men had left; had Blackheart not been distracted by Phoenix and Rogue, then he could have lost his life. However, much of

Shaw's prosperity had been built upon his willingness to take such risks in the name of progress.

Alone now, he pulled a purple drape from the back of the throne and laid it across the seat. The floor was strewn with slush left by Iceman's attack upon one of the fire demons; Shaw filled his cupped hands with the half-melted ice and dropped it onto the velvet. Then he removed one of his padded gloves and popped open a compartment in his belt, from which he produced a small, thin vial. He held it gingerly between two fingers as he strode over to the alcove in which the Beast had been held.

It was unfortunate that Rogue had escaped with the Beast's blood, but the ultimate prize was not yet out of Shaw's reach. Slimy green-brown tentacles grew out of the wooden wall; most of them hung limply as if dead, but a few still thrashed about defiantly. He seized one of them in his gloved hand, being careful to avoid its barbed end, and gave it a sudden, savage tug. It tore, leaving him with a length of about eight inches. As he had hoped, a trickle of blood seeped from the tendril's severed end. He held it over the vial and closed his gloved fist around it until he had squeezed it dry. Then he stoppered the full container with a rubber cork and, discarding the dead tendril as he returned to the throne, he pressed it into the ice. Donning his glove again, he ladled another scoop of slush on top of it before wrapping the whole bundle inside the velvet drape and gathering it into his arms. His makeshift icepack would serve, he hoped, to keep the blood fresh until he could get it to a refrigerator.

Fortunately, before he had met the X-Men in Central Park, he had had the foresight to plan a quick retreat. He activated a signaling device on his belt, knowing that his personal assistant Tessa would be standing by to receive the signal and to home in on its point of origin. Indeed, from her point of view, she would have waited only an hour or two for his call.

The thought of Tessa gave Shaw pause. She hadn't betrayed him yet—not in this time period—and perhaps she never would. But he had been wrong about her. He had seen a side of her that he had never imagined could exist, and it had left him disconcerted. He couldn't think of her, couldn't trust her, in the way that he once had.

He had nobody now. Perhaps he was destined to remain alone.

But there would be time for such troubling thoughts later. For now, it was enough to know that Tessa would serve him as she had always served him before. Shaw slipped out of the door, pausing in the corridor outside to listen for sounds of movement. He heard nothing, but he knew that Rogue had turned to the left with Blackheart on her heels, so he headed to the right, picking his way through the unconscious and dead bodies of the Black Queen's vanquished demons. While Selene was occupied above ground, he would make a surreptitious exit through the catacombs and the sewers beyond them.

When next he entered this building, he swore, it would be as its owner again.

In the ballroom, the battle was almost over. Wolverine knew when an opponent was defeated, and Selene had been on the defensive for minutes, still fighting with all her might but losing ground. She ripped up more floorboards, forming them into a barrier as nails flew at the X-Men like shrapnel. They stung Wolverine's cheeks and made him blink, but no more than that. "Watch out," he cautioned the others, "she's trying to get below ground again."

Cyclops had already realized that: he aimed a series of staccato blasts at Selene's feet, forcing her to skip back from the hole she had made. Storm lifted her into the air, where she kicked and squealed in impotent fury as Iceman plugged her would-be escape route.

Wolverine fought his way through the hovering floorboards as Storm dropped the Black Queen into his path. She screamed out loud as he lunged for her, his claws coming a hair's breadth from gutting her. He had planned it that way, of course—there was no need to kill her this time—but he took a certain pleasure in imagining Cyclops's reaction to the near miss.

In dodging his attack, Selene had left herself open as he had planned. Cyclops concluded the battle with a stunning optic blast, which knocked the sorceress off her feet. Wolverine was on top of her in an instant, his claws at her throat. "It's all over, sweetheart!" he growled. "Make one move, or say anything that sounds like a spell, and I'll cut out your voice box!"

"Easy, Logan," said Cyclops, "she's beaten."

Wolverine glowered at him; he was about to make a remark about being patronized when Iceman spoke in a quivering voice: "I wouldn't be so sure about that."

The menacing figure of Blackheart had appeared in the doorway. Iceman tried to keep him there by forming a block of ice around his feet, but the demon simply strode through it like a ghost. "I thought we decided he couldn't come upstairs," protested Bobby, backing away.

"We did," said Cyclops tersely. "Wolverine?"

"Can't smell a thing," said Wolverine with a grin, "and believe me, that sucker gives off some stink. We're looking at a projection."

"Indeed," said Blackheart calmly, coming to a halt before the wary mutants. "With my physical body bound to the underground levels of this building, I can send only my astral form into this room. That form is sufficient, however, to inform you that there is no longer a reason for us to fight."

"What do you mean, Blackheart?" snapped Selene from her prone position.

"The Beast, my Queen, has been rescued—and the Legacy cure has been lost."

"If this is a trick—" began Cyclops.

"It's no trick, Cyke," came a despondent voice from the doorway. Blackheart stood aside to reveal Rogue. She hobbled into the room as if her feet were causing her pain. The front of her green costume was stained by a large dark patch, which Wolverine identified by its smell as dried blood, and she wore a miserable expression. "I'm sorry, y'all. I tried my best to save it."

"Then it seems," said Selene with a tight smile, "that Black-heart is correct. The prize has gone; the game is over. None of us have anything to gain by prolonging this confrontation." Her old arrogance was returning, and she pushed Wolverine's claws aside and got to her feet. He glared at her, a growl in the back of his throat, but he did not move to stop her. Perhaps she would give him a reason, just one good reason, to put an end to her threat forever.

"Are you satisfied now, Selene?" asked Storm. "Because of your greed, nobody will benefit from the cure. Our kind will be as shunned and persecuted as ever."

Selene looked at her with cold contempt. "Get out of my building!" she said curtly.

"For now," said Wolverine, "gladly. But if the Beast dies, you can bet we'll be back."

The Black Queen turned away from him and swept towards the door at a dignified pace. Perhaps mindful of her recent defeat, however, she said nothing to provoke him further.

Blackheart's astral form faded away, leaving the four X-Men standing in glum silence. For long seconds, the only sound they could hear was the background hum of New York's nighttime traffic, carried into the ballroom on a cool breeze through the window that Phoenix had smashed. Then Nightcrawler shifted and groaned, and Cyclops went to tend to him.

"Where's Shaw?" asked Iceman suddenly.

Wolverine shrugged. "I haven't seen him since we moved the fight up here. He must have stayed behind in the throne room."

"You don't think he could have been captured?"

"No great loss if he has. Let Selene have her fun with him."

"No!" said Storm.

Wolverine looked at her, his brow furrowed, but the exclamation had not been meant for him. Ororo was already running past him, following in Selene's footsteps out into the hallway. However, she turned not towards the stairs but towards the doors that led out onto the street. Cyclops rose from Nightcrawler's side and called out her name in concern, but Wolverine dissuaded him from following her with a raised hand and a shake of his head.

"Leave her," he said. "It looks to me like she's got some unfinished business to deal with."

CHAPTER 15

SEBASTIAN SHAW scrambled out of the sewers in a back alley-way, a few blocks to the south of the Hellfire Club's mansion. For the sake of his dignity, he was glad that nobody was around to see him. The droning sound of helicopter blades would certainly have attracted the attention of any onlookers.

His assistant had arrived to collect him with her usual immaculate timing: even as he replaced the manhole cover, she was lowering the chopper into a hovering position above him. The end of a rope ladder fell beside him, its metal rungs clattering against each other as it unfolded itself. He clambered onto it and, sensing Tessa's telepathic presence, confirmed to her that he was on board.

The helicopter rose again as Shaw climbed the ladder towards it. He made awkward progress, only able to cling to the rungs with his left hand as his right still cradled the vial in its velvet wrapping. Nevertheless, he proceeded with the confidence of one who knew that even a fall from this height wouldn't hurt him.

Incoming at eleven o'clock, Tessa warned him. *It appears we have company.*

By now, Shaw had been lifted above the lights of New York City, and it took him a moment of squinting into the black sky before he discerned a flying cloaked figure. Storm.

He reached the top of the ladder and hauled himself through an open hatchway to find Tessa waiting for him. She was clad in full Hellfire Club regalia, her black hair piled up and held in place by pins. She gave him her full attention, waiting for his instructions.

He looked at her for a long moment, a hundred thoughts and images clashing inside his mind so that even he could not be sure what he was thinking.

At last, he brushed past her without so much as a nod of acknowledgement.

"Deal with the X-Man," he said gruffly.

The dark shape of the helicopter pulled away into the night, and Storm knew that Shaw had to be on board. She increased the ferocity of the wind that carried her, flying faster and faster. She pushed herself to her limit as if trying to outrun the uncomfortable fact that she didn't know why she was pursuing the Black King at all. All she did know was that, back in Selene's ballroom when she had realized that he must have fled, her stomach had performed a somersault. She was acting on instinct, surrendering to the part of herself that couldn't bear the thought of him leaving her like this. After everything they had been through, everything they had said to each other. . . . She had to see him again.

And maybe, when she did, she might finally know what she wanted to say to him.

Sebastian does not wish to speak with you.

The rebuttal popped into her mind unbidden—placed there telepathically, she deduced, by Tessa. She ignored it. She was closing in upon her target.

This vehicle is equipped with armaments, persisted Tessa. *Come closer, and I will be forced to take defensive measures.*

Storm formed a response in her thoughts. *I am not leaving until I have spoken with Shaw.*

Your business with him is concluded.

I do not think so. Your employer made me an offer.

You do not belong in the Hellfire Club, Ororo. Storm was surprised to "hear" Tessa using her first name, and more surprised yet when she detected a genuine hint of sadness behind the telepath's words. *You may have been tempted by a vision of another world, but I suspect you have known all along that it is a world of which you could never be a part. Nor do you need to be. It would be best for all concerned if you did not pursue this matter.*

Ororo was still trying to take all that in, still trying to work out what it meant, when a pair of missiles shot out of the helicopter's backside and streaked towards her. Avoiding them wasn't a problem—but mindful of the overpopulated city below, she also had to manipulate the air currents around them so as to set them down gently on a nearby flat rooftop. She would fetch Wolverine to deactivate the missiles safely later. Shaw's helicopter, in the meantime, had receded into the distance. She could have caught up to it again, but she was beginning to think that perhaps Tessa was right, that she should leave well enough alone.

She thought about Sage, the person that Tessa had become in a now-obsolete future. Perhaps she would become that person again. Only now did Ororo regret that she had not taken the time to question Sage about her ties with the X-Men, and about how far back they went.

For days, she had been asking herself what she might become if she were to join Shaw's Inner Circle, even for the purest of motives. She had wondered if she could live the life of a double agent or if it would consume her; how many compromises she would have to make. Blackheart's dream reality, little as she could remember about it, had failed to answer that question, showing her only what she had wanted to see. But perhaps, she thought now, the answer had been in front of her all along and she just hadn't noticed it.

She took a long detour on her way back to the Hellfire Club building, not wishing to see her fellow X-Men again until she had imposed some order upon her chaotic thoughts.

Shaw had charmed her into believing that he was not beyond redemption. But the White Knight—the Shaw of the future—had lied to her. And the younger Shaw had never told her how he had come to usurp his older self. Ororo had her suspicions, but she hardly liked to think about them. She had been reminded of how ruthless Shaw could be: she certainly could not trust him, and she realized now that she would never have been able to change him. It was far more likely that, given the right circumstances, he would have changed her.

He had not waited for an answer to his proposal. It had probably been this, more than anything, that had prompted her to take to the air and follow him. Unfinished business. She had been looking for a sense of closure. But Tessa had been right about another thing: in her heart, she had known that she could never have become Shaw's White Queen. She had known it ever since she had challenged him in that abandoned office alongside Battery Park, when he had turned up in the White Knight's costume. Perhaps even before that.

She couldn't help but wonder how long he had known it too.

When the Beast awoke, he was lying flat on his back in a bed. A drip was attached to his left hand, and a band around his right arm monitored his blood pressure. He felt empty, like a sack of flesh with no substance, and his head was stuffed with cotton wool—but his overwhelming feeling was one of joy. He was alive.

As his vision cleared, two shapes came into focus. Moira Mac-Taggert and Bobby Drake were sitting by his bedside. He did not recognize the room behind them, but his nose detected the familiar antiseptic scent of hospitals everywhere. "Is it...all over?" he asked weakly.

"You don't have to worry about a thing, Hank," Moira assured him. "The X-Men dealt with Selene, and you're on your way back to being fighting fit."

"Jeannie got you here just in time," chipped in Bobby. "She sat with you until she was sure you were out of the woods."

"We'll transfer you to the infirmary at the school as soon as we can," said Moira. "A few days' rest there and you'll be fine."

"It's a good thing Moira was still in New York," said Bobby. "She took over here and made sure you got the best treatment. She did the operation herself."

Moira shot him a silencing look; obviously, she had not wanted Hank to hear that information just yet. He smiled to show her that he wasn't upset. "I took it as read that you must have performed a transfusion. May I assume that the medical staff of this establishment were less than thrilled at the prospect of exposing themselves to my mutant blood?"

"When they heard you'd had the Legacy Virus..." said Moira apologetically.

"I understand," said Hank. There was no use getting angry about such things; not if he couldn't change them. "And..." He didn't want to ask the question, but he knew he had to. He summoned up his courage and forced the words from his throat. "...the cure?"

Moira laid a gentle hand on his, and shook her head sadly.

Hank didn't know how to feel. Things could have been a lot worse, he knew that—but still, he couldn't quite accept that he had worked so hard, suffered so much, for nothing. He thought about the funeral he had attended in the small town of Newhill, Massachusetts—less than a fortnight ago, although it felt like much longer. A young man had been buried that day: a non-mutant by all accounts, but he had fallen victim to the Legacy Virus nonetheless.

Hank knew that there would be more funerals.

"You should have taken more of my blood!" he insisted as if, in his anguish, he could turn back time and make it happen.

"You had none to spare," said Moira, "and the reaction in your bloodstream had probably run its course anyway."

"You might have been able to salvage the super-cell before it extinguished itself!"

She responded with a firm shake of her head. "A small chance, at the expense of your life. No, Hank. You might be prepared to play those odds, but I'm certainly not."

"We took the cure away from Selene," said Bobby in an optimistic tone, hoping to inject some cheer into the conversation, "that's the main thing."

"He's right, you know," said Moira. "We don't have to make compromises, Hank. You don't have to put your life on the line and you don't have to throw in your lot with the likes of Shaw. You've developed a cure once, you can do it again."

Behind her words was the unspoken implication: *I won't let you feel guilty about being cured while I'm still dying.*

"But the data from the Kree computer...it's..."

"Lost, yes—but we still have our memories, Hank. I learned a lot beneath that island, and I'm sure you did too. I've got a dozen new ideas to try out—and as soon as you're up and about again, I expect you to come out to Muir Island and help me."

Hank grinned and, miraculously, he felt some of the pain and frustration of the past two weeks draining away. "You can count on it, Doctor MacTaggert," he said.

A weary Jean Grey returned home at last, to the building that was presently known as the Xavier Institute for Higher Learning, in the small Westchester town of Salem Center. Even as she stepped into the hallway, however, she heard raised voices coming from the direction of the lounge. Cyclops and Wolverine were at loggerheads, as usual. She hesitated at the lounge door and listened. It had been a long couple of days. She was tired, and she didn't know if she had the spirit to mediate between her husband and her friend again.

"You were taking one hell of a risk!" said Cyclops.

"Depends how much value you place on Selene's life," came Wolverine's curt response. "Me, I wouldn't give you a plugged nickel for it."

"She could have been a valuable hostage against Blackheart."

"Turns out she was more use to us dead, though, doesn't it?" Jean nodded to herself as she understood what the row was about. Wolverine had murdered the future Selene in cold blood. Regardless of how things had turned out, it wasn't in Scott Summers' nature to let such an action pass without comment.

"And what if you'd been wrong? What if killing her hadn't reversed the effects of the spell? What if we'd had to live with the consequences?"

"I *wasn't* wrong—and that's what burns you, isn't it Summers! Your poor liberal conscience can't cope with the fact that taking out Selene was the right thing to do."

"What 'burns me,' Logan, is that you acted against my explicit orders."

"I saw a chance. I took it."

"You should have discussed it with me first."

"Oh yeah, sure. And we'd have been standing in the wreckage of Manhattan right now, still yakking about Selene's human rights with half our team lying dead around us."

"Or we might have found a better way to resolve the situation."

A door opened on the upper floor, and Rogue's voice drifted down the staircase: "Bathroom's free!" Cyclops and Wolverine continued to argue, apparently not having heard her. It didn't take Jean long to convince herself that it would serve them both right if she left them to it and jumped the queue. A hot bath and a long sleep, that was what she needed.

She stifled a deep yawn and fought to keep her eyes open as she climbed the stairs. Cyclops's muffled voice followed her. "You went too far, Logan. You took a gamble. Next time, you might not be so lucky."

"And next time," returned Wolverine, "you might not have someone around to do what has to be done for you. The whole world could suffer for your squeamishness."

Jean found the familiar rhythms of the exchange oddly comforting. She knew that nothing would be resolved today. Scott and Logan would each remain as intractable as the other.

And she smiled to herself as she realized that she would have it no other way.

* * *

The helicopter had transported Shaw and Tessa to an airfield, where they and their pilot had transferred to a private Hellfire Club jet for the long flight back to Hong Kong Island. The plush quarters at the rear of the plane contained a freezer cabinet, into which Shaw had placed the vial of blood. It would have to be analyzed to confirm that the vital super-cell was still present, but he was fairly confident that he had succeeded beyond his own expectations.

He had procured the Legacy Virus cure for himself, and neither the X-Men nor Selene even knew that he had it. Not only that but, during her brief contact with Storm's mind, Tessa had discerned that Shaw's enemies believed the cure lost altogether. It was his and his alone.

For once, however, he could not turn his thoughts to the future. They were mired in the past, and specifically in he cold cemetery where he had come face to face with his destiny.

He couldn't close his eyes, because when he did he found himself back there, standing over Donald Pierce's corpse, the barrel of a gun pointed at his head. He felt his muscles tensing as time seemed to stop. His gaze was riveted upon the finger of his future self as he watched it closing inexorably around the trigger. He acted a microsecond before he heard the retort, his heart hammering against his chest as he leapt beneath the deadly pellet. He broke out in a cold sweat of relief as he realized that, against all odds, he had survived. He pushed his tired and weakened legs as hard as he could to propel himself at his attacker before he could let off another shot. He didn't quite make it, but the second pellet missed too, and Shaw felt the soft brush of the White—or rather, the Black—Knight's jacket against his shoulder.

The momentum of his charge had been sapped, of course, but he had expected as much. He wrapped his arms around his future self's torso, looped a foot around his leg and stole his footing. The two Shaws fell onto the hard ground and rolled over and over, locked together, each fighting to end up atop the other. But the present-day Shaw had exhausted his strength on Pierce and Deathstrike, while his other self was fresh and fully charged.

He ended up on his back, his opponent sitting on his chest and pinning his arms down with his knees. The future Shaw had dropped his gun during the struggle, but his hands were around his younger self's throat, his thumbs pressing down with unbearable force. There was no kinetic energy involved in this type of attack, nothing for Shaw to leech off. In his enervated state, he could only wait for the pressure on his windpipe to suffocate him.

"I don't expect you to believe this," said his future self through gritted teeth, "but I'm doing this for your—for *our*—own good. I'm saving you."

"From...what?" croaked Shaw. He had managed to tear one hand free from beneath his attacker's knee, and he used it in a futile attempt to unfurl the fingers that were choking him.

"Yourself."

"I've told you, I won't...become you!" The very idea that he could have anything in common with this spineless, wretched creature revolted him.

"You will. You won't be able to help yourself. It starts with a small compromise. You can tell yourself you're biding your time, serving the Black Queen only until you see an opportunity to depose her. But the days turn into weeks and the weeks into months and years, and the opportunity never arises. And with each day, you're forced to make another small compromise, to abase yourself further and further until there is nothing you would not do in the name of self-preservation. And then, one day, you'll realize that you are no longer biding your time, no longer playing a part; this has become your life. You are a cowering slave, eking out a pitiful existence in squalor and misery and there is no way back for you."

"I'd...rather...die," spat Shaw with all the venom he could muster.

"I know," said his future self—and the haunted look in his eyes was enough to make Shaw cease his struggles for a moment.

"Do you think," continued the unmasked White Knight, "that every time I look in a mirror, I don't see what you are seeing now? I used to have such dreams. I used to believe the future would be mine. Now, my only dream is to destroy the past. I disgust myself!"

"Not...as much as...you disgust me..." Shaw freed his other hand, and his fingertips brushed against something on the ground beside him. Something heavy and metallic. It had to be the gun. He reached for it, his muscles straining, but he couldn't quite get a grip on it.

"I used to be a successful businessman," his future self lamented. "I used to command respect. That's how I want the world to remember me; not like this. Never like this."

Shaw felt the pressure on his windpipe lessening as his would-be killer's resolve was eroded by self-pity. He seized his chance. He pushed at the elder Shaw's chin with the heels of both hands and forced his head back. He squirmed beneath the weight of his opponent's body, thus unbalanced; he brought up his knees and managed to shift himself a valuable inch to the right before the grip on his throat was reasserted. His future self's face was a mask of insane hatred that must surely have been mirrored in Shaw's own determined expression.

He wasn't prepared to die like this.

He reached for the gun again, and this time he was close enough to pick it up.

The elder Shaw relinquished his hold and blanched as his younger self interposed the weapon between them. The weapon that had been designed to kill him.

Shaw's throat was burning and he couldn't speak, but he didn't need words to convey his intentions. His attacker scrambled to his feet and backed away nervously. Shaw stood too and followed him slowly, his eyes narrowed, his lips set into a grim line and the gun leveled unwaveringly at his future self. The elder Shaw came to a halt as he backed into the wooden marker of his son's grave and almost toppled backwards over it.

"You can't do it," he insisted in a breathless whisper. "If you kill me now, you'll end up here yourself. It *will* happen, one day."

It was the worst thing he could have said.

Shaw opened his eyes with a start. The image of his own death was too stark, too disturbing. But he couldn't so easily dismiss the expression of horror on the face of his distorted reflection as the tiny pellet had exploded at his chest, splaying itself across his soiled white waistcoat. He hadn't even tried to tear it off, knowing that it was already too late, that the deadly nanites were already digging their way into his flesh.

The scream had come a second later, the elder Shaw doubling up as he fell to his knees, his arms clutched around his stomach in agony. Then his head had snapped backwards, his spine arching until it had seemed as if it must break. Tears had leaked from his wild, madly staring eyes and drool from his mouth as he had fallen onto his side and twitched like a swatted insect. The scream had tailed off into a throaty whine, but it had not stopped.

Shaw feared that, in his mind, the scream would never stop.

After he had killed himself, he had staggered away through the headstones and been violently and repeatedly sick. He had sat on the hard ground with his knees up to his chest, staring at nothing. He had lost track of time, but at least an hour had passed before he had been able to return, before he had stooped beside the cold corpse of his future self and begun to strip his white clothes from him with trembling hands.

It had been an arduous and gruesome task, but by now Shaw had rediscovered his resolve. He had known what he had to do. He had sworn to himself that this future would never come to pass, that he would fight it until the last breath in his body. He would take on Fate itself, and he would win.

He had busted open a dilapidated janitor's shed in the corner of the cemetery grounds, and found tools within. He had laid his victim to rest a few feet above his son. But before he had refilled the grave, before he had cast that first shovel full of soil, he had hesitated. He had taken a final look down at the image of his own face, pale and lined but at peace at last. And he had wondered if he had given his future self what he had wanted after all.

Perhaps the elder Shaw had missed with those pellets on purpose. Perhaps he hadn't really wanted to kill his past self, but rather to galvanize him, to renew his sense of purpose. For all his talk of predestination, perhaps he had hoped that the course of his life could be changed after all. Or perhaps that was just what Shaw wanted to believe now.

The aircraft gave a sudden shake as a loud clunk reverberated around its hull. It could just have been turbulence, but it paid to be cautious—and in any case, Shaw was glad of the distraction. He levered himself out of his comfortable seat and made his way forward to the cabin. He never reached it.

The door in front of him was flung open, and a horribly familiar figure barred his path. Standing behind the new arrival, Tessa gave her employer a helpless, apologetic shrug.

The man was taller than Shaw, and his bulky costume made him appear larger and more imposing still. He was dressed in regal colors of red and purple, and a cloak of the latter hue swept down from his shoulders. A red metal helmet encased his head but left his features visible. His face bore the lines of age and the deeper scars of experience, but his eyes burnt with a zealous and dangerous white fire.

This was the man with whom Shaw had forged a reluctant alliance; the man who had raised an island from the seabed for him and helped to finance his research into a Legacy cure; the man with whom he had had no intention of sharing his spoils. He had known that this meeting was inevitable, but he had not expected it to happen so soon. He hadn't expected his so-called partner to board his plane in mid-flight and confront him like this.

"I believe you have something for me," said Magneto.

He didn't wait for an answer. Without taking his eyes off Shaw, he extended a purple-gloved hand to point across the compartment. Magnetic forces crackled around the freezer cabinet in the corner, and its metal lid sprang up with such force that it almost flew off its hinges. The precious vial rose up from within, and sailed through the air into Magneto's grasp. The vial itself was made of glass, and it took Shaw a moment to deduce that the master of magnetism had controlled the iron in the Beast's blood itself to summon it to him.

"Very well done, Shaw." Magneto sounded as if he were congratulating a particularly dim pupil who had finally got a piece of work right. "You have redeemed your mistakes; you have outwitted both Selene and the X-Men." A smile softened his sharp features, but his eyes burnt no less intensely. "I was beginning to wonder if you had it in you."

With each condescending word, Shaw's hatred for his unwanted ally grew deeper. He wanted to hit him, to take the hard-earned cure back from him, to wipe the smile from his face. But he held himself back. Magneto's physical power was too great. It would take cunning and careful planning to outmaneuver him. Fortunately, Shaw knew how to be patient. His time would come.

He forced a polite smile as he showed his guest to a seat—but once Magneto's back was turned to him, the smile fell away and he breathed in deeply to suppress his building anger.

And that was when he made the mistake of closing his eyes again.

Again, he saw the wretched figure that he had once become. He saw the pain, the regret and, worst of all, the weakness in his future self's eyes, and he could hear his voice. It rang in his ears and vibrated around his skull.

"It starts with a small compromise."

When Shaw opened his eyes again, Magneto was filling a chair, his arms and legs spread confidently across the cushions. He had removed his helmet to reveal a head of steely gray hair, and he was directing an equally steely stare at his host. Shaw fixed his smile onto his lips again and said, "Perhaps you would care for a drink?"

Magneto shook his head. "We have much to discuss." He returned the vial to the freezer cabinet with a wave of his hand, and settled back in his seat.

"We have the power to cure the Legacy Virus," he said. "Now, at last, we can put the next stage of my plan into operation."

TO BE CONCLUDED